MILE HIGH BABY

AN AGE GAP, SURPRISE PREGNANCY ROMANCE

AJME WILLIAMS

DESCRIPTION

"Have you joined the Mile High club yet?"
"No..."
"Do you want to?"
I shouldn't have said yes... but I did.

A panicked phone call from my father has me boarding a plane and flying cross-continent. I never expect to meet a brazen, distinguished silver fox on the plane.

Much less the older gentleman initiating me into the Mile High club right then and there...

We agree never to meet again after our spicy encounter.

Until I meet with my father, who's hired a bodyguard for me.

Alex Sterling. My father's best friend... and my mile-high lover.

My father thinks I'm in danger and Alex is the best man to protect me. Maybe we'd both do a better job of staying out of harm's way... if we could keep our hands off each other.

But when our steamy encounters result in a baby bump, I know I have to hide the truth from my father... as well as his enemies who are still out to hurt me.

Except now it's not just me.

PROLOGUE

Victoria Lawrence Banion

I'd gone mad. *What the hell am I doing?*

Two long fingers slid inside my pussy as firm lips tugged on my nipple.

Oh, right, I was letting a complete stranger fuck me in the first-class bathroom on a transatlantic flight from London to New York.

A shimmer of delicious pleasure radiated from my clit to the rest of my body.

Okay, so I knew what I was doing. The question was why? I was no prude. I'd had my share of sexual encounters before, but never with a complete stranger. All I knew was his name. Sterling. I didn't know if it was his first or last name. Hell, maybe it wasn't his name at all. Then there was the fact that I was on a packed commercial flight. One scream of pleasure and the entire plane would know what was going on. And it was quite possible that I'd scream.

His thumb brushed over my clit as his fingers thrust inside me again, and his lips sucked harder on my nipple. He was totally making me rethink my attitude toward older men. Not that I had anything against them, but I'd always heard a man's sexual prime was in his twenties or maybe thirties. This man was definitely pushing fifty, which made him my father's age. I pushed that thought out of my head because, ew.

Sterling was teaching me that with age came experience, and based on the way he had my body humming and my blood coursing like liquid fire, he had honed his skills well over the years.

"Jesus fuck, your pussy is wet. I have to taste you." He tugged me down from where he'd perched me on the edge of the small sink. He scooted backward in the small space, sitting on the toilet lid as he pulled my hips forward. He dipped his head, his tongue lapping through my folds. My hands shot out, bracing against the wall on each side of the restroom as my legs shook. Good God, I was going to disintegrate into a gelatinous puddle. But if I melted into nothing, it would be so totally worth it.

I brought one hand down, threading it through his sexy silver hair. "Yes, yes, don't stop."

He groaned against my pussy, and I felt it reverberate through my body. I hadn't wanted to be on this flight. I hadn't wanted to cut my trip to Europe short. But thank God I'd decided to go home early because every woman deserved to be thoroughly fucked like Sterling was fucking me. Every neuron in my body fired up and shook. I was pretty sure I was going to detonate in a way that would let everybody on this plane know exactly what we were doing. The end result would probably get me banned from the airline for life, but holy hell, it would be worth it.

He pulled his head back, and the loss of contact elicited a desperate mewling sound from me. I looked down, wondering why he'd stopped. My juice covered his nose and mouth, and I had an urge to lick it off his face.

The gentle brush of his thumb over my clit told me he wasn't stopping. "I'm going to make you come. You're going to come so hard you're going to want to scream. As you can imagine, on a crowded plane, that's going to be a problem."

Good point. I didn't trust myself to be quiet or believe that putting my hand over my mouth would work. I reached through the small space to my purse by the sink, pulling a pen out and sticking it in my mouth like a bit. Hopefully, it would work.

His pale blue eyes looked at me with amusement. "All right then, Victoria, hold on."

I hadn't been completely honest with him about my name, either. My name was Victoria, that was true, but most everyone I knew called me Tori. Right now, that didn't seem important.

I nodded at him as I continued to brace one hand against the wall and the other on his shoulder.

Seemingly satisfied, he turned his attention back to my pussy. He used his fingers to pull open my folds as his tongue swirled around my clit, sending a shockwave through me.

"I can't wait to drink your juices." He slid two fingers inside me as his lips wrapped around my clit and sucked. His fingers rubbed over that exquisite spot inside me, and holy hell, every cell inside me exploded with pleasure. I threw my head back, letting out a long, feral moan as my body shook. Wave after wave of orgasmic bliss rushed through my body. It was the type of orgasm your girlfriends bragged about or you read about in romance novels but never quite believed were true. Now I was a believer.

As my orgasm came down, so did my ability to stand on my own two feet. Luckily, Sterling stood, wrapping an arm around me and once again lifting me until I was seated on the edge of the basin.

His hands went to his belt, undoing his pants. He shoved them along with boxer briefs down. His dick sprang free, and I moaned at the thought of feeling the length and girth of him inside me.

"My cock is ready to explode." He rolled a condom over his length, and I was impressed that condoms came in a big enough size to fit him. He was the epitome of well-hung.

He held his dick, rubbing the tip through my folds. "Tell me you want this."

"I do. God, do I want it."

With his free hand, he lifted my thigh, opening me and hooking my leg around his hip. "Tell me specifically what you want."

My brain was on the fritz, but coherent enough to understand what he wanted. "I want you to fuck me with your massive cock, Sterling."

1

Alex Sterling - Two days earlier

I closed my laptop and downed the final finger of whiskey, glad to have the issue of Lorraine Madsen complete. It wasn't unusual for me to work late at night, but this wasn't a usual case. First, as the head of the European office of Saint Security, I rarely did fieldwork anymore. Second, and worst, was that this case wasn't a company case. It was personal. Lorraine betrayed me in the worst way possible, and I wasn't talking about my heart. I knew when I had left the military and joined Saint Security as an operative twenty-three years ago that love and ever after weren't going to be part of my life. And I was okay with that.

I wasn't anti-marriage or family. It was great for people who wanted it, although in my lifetime, I'd seen many people get married and have a family, only to have it totally implode on them. I knew myself well enough to know I couldn't make a woman happy. I had too much wanderlust.

Growing up, I'd done all the things I was supposed to do—play sports, get good grades, and go to college to get a degree. And for the first twenty-one years of my life, I felt like I was dead inside. I wanted adventure, travel, excitement, and nothing that would hold me back. My father wanted me to join the family business, but that wasn't going to happen, so he disowned me. I responded by joining the military.

The military held tight control over the people who worked for them, but it came with travel and excitement. And when it was discovered that I had a unique set of skills, I was recruited by Noel St. Martin, the founder of Saint Security. At that time, he provided mercenaries to the highest bidder, but eventually, he turned the company into a global security business that worked with the most powerful and richest people in the world. And that work suited me just fine as well.

My work had given me plenty of adventure and excitement. There weren't very many places on the globe that I hadn't been to. The only glitch was the injury I sustained three years ago that resulted in my leaving the field to take over the running of the European office. Being a bureaucrat didn't sound fun, but being based in London meant I was a hop, skip, and a jump away from skiing in the Alps, or swimming in the Mediterranean, or any other adventure my mind could think up.

As I rose from my desk to get another glass of whiskey, I had to wonder if all this desk riding had made me soft. How hadn't I seen what sort of woman Lorraine was? Had I been distracted by her made-for-fucking body? She had a round ass and large tits, all fake, but still. She had plump lips and a mouth that could suck off my sizable cock with ease. She also liked adventure and travel, so I had broken my one-and-done rule I adhered to with women. Not that we were an item. Ours wasn't a relationship based on love. It was based on a lust for life and fantastic sex.

And then one morning, she was gone, along with a sizable chunk of my nest egg. I was paid very well for what I did. I didn't have a lot of expenses, minus my adventures, so I'd been able to save up a sizable sum, enough that I planned to retire in two years at the age of fifty and really travel and experience life like I wanted. But Lorraine took enough money that retiring wouldn't be an option, at least not in two years.

Pissed at her and at myself for letting her dupe me, I vowed to make her pay. No one fucked with Alex Sterling and got away with it. I took two weeks off from work, leaving Wally "Cutthroat" Cuthbert in charge. Then I used my skills to hunt her down. Tonight, she was rotting in a jail in Paris, and with Interpol notified, apparently, there were other jurisdictions interested in talking to her. It only took me three days to make it happen. I didn't get my money back, but I got justice.

I downed my whiskey and set my glass in the sink. I went to the only bedroom in my one-room flat and tugged off my T-shirt and my lounge pants, climbing under the sheets buck naked. I still had eleven days off. Maybe I'd head up to Iceland to one of its fantastic outdoor geothermal spas.

On my side table, my phone buzzed. I considered ignoring it because I didn't know anybody who would call me except for work, and I was off. But in case it was an emergency, I picked up the phone and looked at the caller ID.

Henry Banion

My lips twitched up in amusement. I poked the answer button. "Henry Banion, how the hell are you?"

Henry and I had been roommates and fellow womanizers and adventurers in college. Although our lives had gone in separate directions, we'd never completely lost touch. Seven years ago, he'd somehow convinced me to go to our twenty-year college reunion. He had a nineteen-year-old daughter at the time, but she was off traveling or something. So despite the fact that we were forty-one, we lived like we were twenty-one again. I wasn't sure about everything that we did those few days because we'd lived it up that much. There were swathes of time in which I had no memory, which meant we'd had a raucous good time. Maybe I'd go see him for the remainder of my vacation.

"Alex, how are you?"

Something about his voice dampened my enthusiasm. "I'm hanging in there. What's up?"

"I need to hire you to protect my daughter."

My gut clenched. Of all the jobs we could be given at Saint Security, protecting a rich man's daughter was the worst. Those girls were always entitled and bossy. Henry was a good guy, and I'd never met his daughter, but I did know he came from very old money, which meant chances were good that she was a bratty daddy's girl.

"I don't do that sort of thing anymore, but I can hook you up. We've got some really good people in New York—"

"No. I want to hire you. I need someone I know can be lethal if needed, and whom I can trust."

Lethal? "What sort of shit have you gotten yourself into, Henry?"

The guy ran a media conglomerate. How much trouble could news be?

"George Pitney has taken umbrage with a number of things we've been publishing about his business."

"Jesus fuck, Henry. George Pitney? You're going to end up like Jimmy Hoffa, and nobody knows what happened to Jimmy Hoffa." That sounded like an exaggeration, but it wasn't. George's business looked to be on the up and up, but under the hood, it was filled with corruption. Before my boss Noel found his morals, we'd done some work for George. That man had a black heart, and I had no doubt that he'd do whatever, including kill, to protect it.

"I know. But I'm not as worried about me—"

"You should be."

"I'm more concerned about my daughter. I'm willing to take whatever repercussions are coming my way, but I don't want any landing on her. I've been doing some work with law enforcement."

I pinched the bridge of my nose. "Jesus, you do have a death wish."

"The thing is, they're close to indicting him and arresting him. But as you know, the tighter a noose squeezes, the more violent the attempt to save oneself is."

I suppose I didn't need to remind Henry that George had gotten free of every legal noose that had been attempted on him.

"And while I know that Saint Security has a stellar reputation, I can't risk hiring somebody I don't know. Whatever it costs, I'll pay you," Henry finished.

I thought of the crap ton of money that Lorraine had taken from me and for a moment considered naming it as my price. But Henry was my friend. For all intents and purposes, he was my only friend. He sounded scared and desperate, and I couldn't blame him, considering who he was dealing with.

It wasn't Iceland, but going to New York to protect Henry's daughter would definitely be an adventure. I had nothing better to do over the next eleven days, and maybe a real assignment was something I needed to get my head back in the game.

"I'm in London right now, but I can catch a flight tomorrow back to New York. I can only give you ten days for sure. After that—"

"Ten days is fine. Thank you so much, Alex. I owe you."

"You don't owe me anything. And don't worry about fees."

"I can't ask you to work for free. Not with the risk you'll be taking."

I grinned, even though I knew he couldn't see me. "I thought you knew, Henry. I live on risk."

2

Victoria

I sat near the window in my hotel room with a hot cup of coffee, because tea just didn't do it for me. All my meetings were done today, and I was working in my hotel room. I had my laptop open and was checking in on various aspects of my little empire.

I had started my media platform for experts, Masterverse, as part of a college assignment in a business class. But I enjoyed it so much that I continued working on it, expanding the features and growing the platform into a global media resource. It wasn't as big or expansive as the one my father ran. The family media company was started back in the early 1900s, and my father was the fourth generation to be running it. But my little business supported a lifestyle that I enjoyed since I could run it from anywhere.

I probably could have lived a traveling lifestyle without building a business. My father would have wanted me to work in the family business, perhaps even one day taking it over. But even without that, my father had always been very generous in giving me a monthly allowance. He and I were very close, since we were all we had. My mother had run off right after I was born, and while my grandpar-

ents were around up until about five years ago, they were the old
money sort to believe my father should've left me to be raised by
nannies and later boarding school. They were from an era in which if
you had a crap ton of money, you had enough not to have to raise
your kids.

That's not to say I didn't have a nanny, but my father was always
with me at breakfast and dinner. Even when he took over the family
company full-time, he made sure to attend my school events and
dance recitals. And he was one of the biggest supporters of my
business.

Over the last two years, my business had done well enough that
I'd started saving the allowance my father gave me and living on my
earnings. I wasn't sure what I was going to do with the savings. I liked
knowing it was there in case of emergencies, but maybe I'd throw my
father a blow-out party in two years when he turned fifty.

Last year, I hired a few people here in London to help manage the
international aspects of my business. That was why I was here now,
meeting with them. But my meetings were over, and after I finished
today, I planned to take a few days off and make a trip to the Isle of
Skye to see fairy pools. It sounded like a magical place.

It was nearly three when I finished checking in and dealing with
the little fires. I was getting ready to pack and book my trip to Scotland when my phone rang. I checked my caller ID and saw my
father's name flash. My heart rate sped to a full sprint. He knew I was
out of town and wouldn't call unless it was an emergency.

I answered the phone. "Dad? What's wrong?"

"I'm fine, Princess, but I need you to come home."

Those words sounded so ominous to me. Was he dying? "Yes, of
course, but what happened?"

"I don't want to go into it over the phone, but suffice it to say that
you need to come home. I'll feel much better knowing that you're
here."

Didn't he know that being so obtuse only freaked me out? "I'll
catch the next flight that I can." I wondered how soon I could book a
flight. Most airlines booked beyond capacity, and I worried I wouldn't

be able to get a seat until tomorrow or the day after. "But you have to tell me what's going on. You've got me worried sick. Are you ill?"

"I'm fine. Right now, everything is okay. I just really need you to come home."

Anger boiled up. "Dammit, Dad, what's going on?"

"We've just been having a little bit of trouble with some people who aren't happy with what we're printing."

Immediately, my thoughts went to George Pitney. There was no evidence of all the dastardly deeds he was rumored to have done, which was probably why he wasn't in prison. But I doubted there was a person alive who didn't believe he'd done them. I knew Dad's investigative journalism division had been doing some deep dive exposés on George, but would George so blatantly attack my father or any of his writers? If the rumors of his past deeds were true, the answer was yes.

"Are you safe?"

"I'm fine, Tori, but I'd feel much better knowing you were home."

If my father felt this desperate to have me home, I was going to go home. "I'm almost packed, and I'll get the next plane to New York."

I lucked out in that there was one first-class seat available on the six o'clock flight to New York. By the time I'd been able to get to the airport and through TSA, the flight was nearly ready to leave. I had just made it to the gate as they were getting ready to shut the doors. I rushed through to the plane, the last passenger to board.

As someone who enjoyed traveling but not dealing with airports, I'd learned how to pack light on my trips, which meant I carried my luggage, along with a backpack that held my computer and purse items.

"Welcome aboard," the well-groomed, thirty-something steward greeted.

"Thank you." I made my way up the aisle toward my seat assignment.

If the only seat option on the plane had been regular class, I would have taken it, simply because my father was in such distress. But I was very excited to have a first-class seat. I wasn't one of those size-one skinny Minnies. I was what my grandmother had called *big-boned*. Personally, I thought my bones were probably the same size as every other five-foot-five woman. My curves came from loving food. Like many young girls, as a high schooler, my weight bothered me. Cutting carbs, intermittent fasting, and running three miles a day got me down to a size six, but I was miserable. The idea of spending the rest of my life not having San Francisco sourdough bread, or home-made Italian pasta, didn't sit well. I'd since discovered that there were plenty of men who liked women who weren't constantly worried about their weight and had curves. All that to say that I was a bigger girl and liked having the extra space that first-class seats afforded me.

I reached my seat and put my bag overhead.

"We're getting ready to take off, but once we're airborne, is there a drink I can get you?" Free drinks were another perk of first class.

"Cola and vodka?"

He gave me a nod and went back to the steward area.

I looked across the seats to see the gentleman sitting by the window. His profile, with his cropped silver hair and lines around his eyes, was the epitome of the distinguished gentleman. My father was like that. In fact, I had girlfriends who often commented on how they wouldn't mind taking my father for a ride. He gave a whole new meaning to the word filth, or in this case, FILF. Every time they said it, it made me cringe. It was my dad they were talking about fucking.

I suppose I could see the attraction of an older man, other than my dad, but that had never been my type.

The man's head turned as I moved to sit next to him. Wow. For an older man, he was hot. He had pale blue eyes and tanned skin. There was an edge or intensity to him that made me think of James Bond, the Daniel Craig version. Hot but lethal. I wouldn't deny that my girly parts took notice.

His eyes scanned me up and down, and when they returned to my face, he gave a slight smile and then turned his head back out the window.

I guess he wasn't into younger, bigger women. Or maybe it was that I was dressed like a college student during finals week. I had on a pair of old jeans with a rip in the knee and a plain white T-shirt over which I wore an oversized button down shirt that had my company's logo on the pocket. I didn't have on any makeup, and my long, dark hair was pulled up into a messy knot on my head.

I sat and put my belt on and then leaned back, letting out a breath. Whew. I'd made it.

"You nearly missed the flight."

The man's voice was dark yet velvety. How weird that I would notice that.

I opened my eyes and looked at him. "I wasn't planning on flying back to the States today."

"What were you planning on?"

I shrugged. "I was planning on heading up to the Isle of Skye in Scotland. Maybe take a look at the fairy pools."

He arched a brow, intrigued. "Have you been there before?"

I shook my head. "Nope. That's why I was thinking about going there. I've done most of the regular stuff in the UK. Now I'm trying to get to things I've never visited before."

"It's beautiful up there."

This time, I was the one arching a brow in intrigue. "You've been there?"

"There aren't many places in this world that I haven't been."

I studied him, noting that there was an air of money around him despite the raw intensity. I wondered if he was one of those billionaire playboys who was spending family money and making the world his playground. I didn't have anything against that lifestyle, per se. I definitely could live like that. But it seemed like life needed purpose, so I was glad to have started my business that allowed me to do both. Maybe he had a business that allowed it too.

"I'm Victoria," I said, holding out my hand, since it appeared we might be plane buddies.

"Sterling." He shook my hand.

It was hard not to notice how warm his hand was. And his fingers were long and strong. I wondered if he rock climbed. "Are you heading back to the States for fun? More travel adventures?"

He shook his head. "Going back to help a friend. Depending on how long that takes, I might swing back and up to Iceland. If not on this trip, then another."

"Iceland?"

"Some of the most beautiful scenery you'll ever see. Plus, they've got magnificent geothermal spas."

That did sound fun. I pulled out my phone, typing myself a note to research Iceland and geothermal spas. Then I checked to make sure that my phone was on airplane mode as the plane pulled away from the gate.

"If you hadn't intended to be going home, why are you?"

"To help my family," I said.

His eyes narrowed as he scrutinized me again. "Let me guess, your father?"

I studied him back. "Why would you say that?"

He shrugged. "You seem like a daddy's girl."

I suppose technically, I was, but the way he said it made it sound bad. "You have something against daddy's girls?"

He gave me a look of indifference. "They're not so bad, except for their general sense of entitlement and brattiness."

I gaped. "Listen, old man, I have not done a single thing in the few minutes that we've known each other that would be considered entitled or bratty. Second, I'm not a fifty-year-old man pretending I'm twenty, gallivanting around, spending his inheritance in every corner of the world."

His expression was a mixture of offense and amusement. "What makes you think I'm gallivanting around spending Daddy's money?"

I tried to adopt his deep velvety voice. "'There isn't a place in this world that I haven't yet visited.'" I gave him a hard stare. "Only rich people who have no responsibility and an endless amount of money can do something like that."

He had turned back toward the window as if he was done with the conversation. Fine by me, Mr. Prick.

The plane took off, and I reached down to pull out my tablet thinking I might watch a movie or read.

"I'm not quite yet fifty, and I do have responsibilities. I'm just fortunate to have a career that involves travel or allows for it."

I didn't look at him as I tapped the side of my tablet. "Good for you, Mr. Magoo."

"Now you think I'm blind too?"

I shrugged. Mostly, I said it because it rhymed, but Mr. Magoo was old too, wasn't he?

I wanted to continue to ignore him, but the need to set him straight about me was too strong, especially since he'd bothered to tell me about himself.

I turned to look at him. "For your information, I am very close to my father, and I'm not going to apologize for that. He raised me pretty much on his own, so it wouldn't I be a shitty daughter if I wasn't devoted to him? And second, while I *can* gallivant around the world like a spoiled princess, I don't. I've earned my way by building my own company."

"I'm sorry if I offended you."

I harrumphed. "Yeah, well, maybe you should stop being so judgmental. Is it me or do you just hate women in general?"

He turned his body in his seat so that his shoulders were almost facing me. "I've given you the wrong impression. I love women."

It was a smarmy line, and yet, weirdly, my reaction to it wasn't repulsion. "Let me guess, you love women, but because you're so ill-mannered, you don't have any luck with them."

He let out a free, deep-throated laugh that surprised me. "I can see why you would think that. I suppose if a shrink were here, they would say that I was taking my anger at the last woman I was with out on you. Like you, she was beautiful and sexy as fuck with a taste for travel off the beaten path."

I blinked in incomprehension. He thought I was beautiful? And had a body that was sexy as fuck?

Finding my voice, I said, "Did you accuse her of being a spoiled brat too?"

He shook his head. "She ran off with a sizable chunk of my retirement, which has soured me a little bit."

No doubt. "Well, I'm not like that. I don't have to steal, but even if I were hungry, I wouldn't."

His eyes narrowed like he was scrutinizing me. "You know, I think I believe you."

I rolled my eyes. "Gee, thanks." I was going to let it go. The steward arrived with my drink, and I took a moment to sip it. But the cool liquid didn't soothe the burn. I had to know more. "Did you get your money back?"

"Nope. But I did put her in jail."

"I suppose she had it coming."

"She had a thirst for adventure. I'm sure she wasn't counting on the prison type, though."

I shuddered at the idea of being locked away between four closed-end walls.

"Before it was over, we had some pretty amazing adventures." His expression turned into a combination of wistful and lusty, like their adventures didn't involve climbing to the top of Everest but instead having sex on it.

"So, these adventures aren't really about traveling to cool locations. It's about being with a sexy as fuck woman?"

"I like both." He leaned forward slightly, his eyes intense. "What about you? What do you like?"

I liked adventure and sex, but I'd never really had them together. Right now, the thought of it seemed exciting. And weirdly, I wondered what it would be like to go on one with him. But I wasn't going to tell him that.

Instead, I asked, "What is the wildest adventure you've been on?"

He sat back, his eyes tilting up as if he were thinking about it. Finally, he looked at me. "It's hard to just pick one. And the truth is, the next adventure could be the wildest one of all if you found someone who was game enough to join you."

For a moment, I sat like a dolt as something about his words confused me. Was he propositioning me? Was he suggesting that I was his next adventure?

My brain told me that he was a dirty old man, but my hormones were screaming, "Yes, please." For an older man, he was sexy as fuck, and his manner, albeit abrasive at times, added to his allure.

"The nice thing about these types of adventures is that they tend to be one and done. That's what makes them exciting. It's a once-in-a-lifetime thing. You won't ever see the other person again, which is in fact quite freeing, allowing you to explore in ways you might not with anyone else."

Oh. My. God. His words were making me so wet. Was he saying "you" to mean me specifically, or in general?

He stared at me for a long moment and then sat back. "But not everyone has the spirit of adventure like that."

"I do." The words were out of my mouth before I'd even thought them.

He looked at me and his blue eyes revealed sexual interest. "Shall we find out?"

I hesitated because that would be crazy. I didn't know this guy. He was old and rude, even if he was intense and sexy with large hands.

He stood, and I shifted my legs to let him out into the aisle.

"Where are you going?"

He nodded toward the front of the plane. "All this talk has made me hard. I'm going to go take care of it. Or maybe an adventure waits for me."

Holy hell.

He made his way up the aisle and gave me a wink as he disappeared into the bathroom.

Stay in your seat, Tori.

The fact that I had to talk myself into staying in my seat said something because what I really wanted to do was go find out what adventure might await in the restroom with my seatmate Sterling.

My hormones and my head were at war, but ultimately, my hormones won. I stood and made my way up toward the restroom, casually glancing at other passengers, wondering if they had noticed that Sterling had gone to the restroom or would notice when I followed him into it. But most people were either working on their laptop, watching a movie, or sleeping.

I made it to the restroom and tried the doorknob. He hadn't locked it. I pulled the door open and found him leaning against the wall, a smirk on his face.

I stepped into the bathroom, closing the door behind me and locking it.

He stepped up to me, his hands coming to my hips. "I hope your table and chair are in the upright position, because I'm about to take you for a ride."

3

Alex

I was a man who lived fairly frugally. The exception was travel. I didn't care very much about luxury. What I cared about was comfort. My 6'2" frame needed legroom, and I didn't much like having other people's elbows poking into me. Fortunately, I was able to get a first-class ticket on a flight from London to New York.

Although I was technically off, since I'd be leaving the country, I felt compelled to check in with Saint Security here in London to let them know that I would be heading to the United States for a week or so. Then I contacted the New York office to let them know that I would be in town in case there was anything I should check in on. The truth was, if Henry was having troubles with George Pitney, he was going to need more than me protecting his daughter, and I wanted to talk with people I trusted in the company about beefing up Henry's security. I understood that Henry had concerns, and so I would honor his request by protecting his daughter myself. It was unlikely that George Pitney would infiltrate anyone working with Saint Security, so having extra men wouldn't be a problem. Yes, we had done some work for George in the past, but there was no love lost. Once the company dropped its mercenary program, it now only worked with people it deemed were on the up and up. Or at the very least, we only did work that was on the up and up. No more morally questionable ops for us.

I boarded the plane, and a steward brought me a whiskey to enjoy as the rest of the passengers boarded. I used the time to make a quick call to Archer Graves who ran the West Coast operations of Saint Security, but he had also taken over the company when Noel retired. It had been a shock to me when Noel left the business. It'd been a bigger shock when I heard he'd gotten married and had a couple of kids.

Archer, whom Noel had put in charge of the company, had also married and had kids. And hell, not that long ago, Dax Sheppard, the last person in the world I ever thought would get married outside of myself, also got married and had a couple of kids. It made me wonder if there was something in the air or the water on the West Coast. I made a mental note to avoid that area, which was a shame because there were some beautiful outdoor adventures in places like Yosemite or the Pacific Northwest.

After everyone boarded, it appeared that I wasn't going to have a seatmate. I was glad to have the extra space to stretch out during the eight-hour flight. But then, at the last minute, a young woman rushed onto the plane. She dressed like a college student with jeans ripped at the knees, a T-shirt, and an oversized men's shirt over it. Her hair was tied up in a messy bun. But while her clothes weren't much to look at, the woman had curve after curve. I liked curves. And holy hell, her eyes were a color I wasn't sure existed. It reminded me of the color of Lake Pehoé in Chile. I suppose turquoise would be the closest color. Once I was able to tear my gaze away from her eyes, it drifted down to her lips, which were full and lush.

I turned away, looking out the window partly so as not to appear like some old pervert, but also because I couldn't allow my overactive libido to get the best of me. Oh, sure, ten years ago, I would have been intrigued by the idea of a mile-high adventure, but I liked to think I had matured since then. That wasn't to say that I didn't like sexual adventure because I did. But right now, I needed to keep my head in the game, which was figuring out how to keep Henry and his daughter safe from George Pitney.

And yet . . . I couldn't help myself. I had to talk to her. Yes, I was a bit of an asshole. I suppose I was hoping she'd be offended and ignore me because the more I looked at her and talked to her, the more the urge for her grew. And she was offended, but she didn't ignore me. She stood up to me, called me out, and that was it for me. A strong, feisty woman, with curves and lips made for kissing . . . or sucking . . . Good Christ. Thank God she wasn't a college student, as my next move would make me a fucking pervert. As it was, I was the clichéd dirty old man.

"The nice thing about these types of adventures is that they tend to be one and done. That's what makes them exciting. It's a once-in-a-lifetime thing. You won't ever see the other person again, which is in fact quite freeing, allowing you to explore in ways you might not with anyone else." Would she understand what I was suggesting?

I watched her, but she didn't respond. Ah, well. I tried. "But not everyone has the spirit of adventure like that."

"I do."

I was sure she spoke before she'd had time to think. That told me she was interested even if she was hesitant.

"Shall we find out?"

When she didn't respond, I decided to take matters into my own hands. I wasn't going to spend the next eight hours with a hard-on.

I stood, and she moved her legs to let me out to the aisle.

"Where are you going?" she asked.

"All this talk has made me hard. I'm going to go take care of it. Or maybe an adventure waits for me." If I were lucky, she'd join me. If not, I'd take care of business.

It was a little bit unsettling how much this woman turned me on. But there was no way I was going to go through the rest of us flight with a hard-on. One way or the other, my dick was going to be dealt with. The question was, was she going to help me with it?

I made my way to the restroom, opening the door, sending her a wink, and stepping in. I closed the door behind me but didn't lock it. I decided I would wait a few minutes before whipping out my dick and stroking one off.

My sense was that she was a woman who wanted adventure and excitement in her life, but she hadn't indulged in it very much. I was certain that she wanted to join me in the bathroom, but she wasn't sure if she had the courage to do so. That is, until there was a slight knock on the door.

I put my hands on her hips and tugged her close. "I hope your table and chair are in the upright position, because I'm about to take you for a ride."

The first thing I did was push up her shirt and bra to get a look at her tits, and Jesus fuck, they didn't disappoint. They were large and soft and best of all, real. Then I discovered her pussy, and it, too, was like a wonderland. Hot. Wet. Tight.

Sex in a bathroom is no easy feat on a commercial flight these days. But I was determined to make the most of it, including tasting her pussy. That too didn't disappoint. She had a sweet, exotic taste. I worried we'd get caught before I could fuck her, especially if she turned out to be a screamer. Thankfully, she found a workaround and I was able to make her come and drink up her juice. Christ, it was good.

I was practically shaking as I set her back on the sink and freed my dick. "My cock is ready to explode." I rolled a condom over my length, enjoying the way she watched my dick. Most women had a moment of trepidation, but not Victoria. If I wasn't mistaken, she wanted to suck it. I wondered if we'd have time for that, but I had to get inside that hot pussy or die.

I held my dick, rubbing the tip through her folds. "Tell me you want this."

"I do. God, do I want it."

With my free hand, I lifted her thigh, opening her and hooking her leg around my hip. "Tell me specifically what you want."

"I want you to fuck me with your massive cock, Sterling."

"Fuck yeah." I sank into her sweet heat. God damn, like the rest of her, it felt perfect as her pussy swallowed me up. I could feel the heat. Her pussy massaged my cock, making my eyes nearly roll back in my head. I wished I had more time, a bigger space, a dick that wasn't already on the verge of exploding.

I moved, doing my damnedest to keep control. I rubbed my thumb over her clit and sucked a nipple, driving her back up to the brink.

Her fingers gripped my arms. I was sure I'd have marks. Good. I knew I was doing it right when a woman left her mark.

"Oh, God . . ." She buried her head against my neck as her entire body tightened. Her pussy squeezed my cock like it was never going to let go.

"Ah, fuck." I bit my lip to keep from roaring out as pleasure ripped through my body. I pumped and pumped until I couldn't feel my legs.

I had fucked a lot of women in my life. Lorraine, for all her thievery, had been one of the best, until now.

I didn't know if it was Victoria's age that made her seem young and innocent that had my blood boiling at inferno levels, or maybe it was her feisty attitude. Whatever it was, combined with her luscious body, it had just given me the orgasm of a lifetime.

I wanted to stay in the restroom long enough for recovery and do it all over again, but it wouldn't be long before an attendant came looking for us or somebody else in first class wanted to use the bathroom. So reluctantly, I stepped away, even as my dick twitched at seeing just how wet her pussy was. God, I'd have done anything to have seen my cum dripping out of her.

I pulled off the condom, tying it and tossing it into the trash bin. Then I turned my attention to her, still perched on the edge of the basin, looking thoroughly fucked. It made her even more gorgeous.

I held my dick and rubbed it through her pussy lips. The sensation of my bare cock on her sent electric currents through me.

"There are still several hours of the flight left. Perhaps we can meet back here later," I suggested.

She looked at me, her eyes a little stunned. She blinked, but then she smiled, and my next wish was to have those plump lips wrapped around my cock.

She shifted, and as she did, the tip of my dick entered her. I groaned as I fought twin instincts—one to withdraw because I didn't have a condom on, and two, wanting to thrust in and feel all that sweetness around my dick.

She let out a little gasp. "Why wait?"

Her words were like music to my ears, but I still gripped the edge of the basin. "I don't have another condom on me." Jesus, I must be getting old since I wasn't better prepared.

I prayed to God she would tell me she was on the pill. But even if she was, it would be a risk for her to let me, a perfect stranger, fuck her. I needed to back off. I might be a horn dog, but I was a careful one.

"I think you should thrust that thing inside me one more time and then let me suck you off."

Holy hell. My brain actually froze for a moment. I wondered if maybe I was dreaming. I had to be. But I wasn't going to wake up now. I did as she said, thrusting hard and deep just once, and fucking hell, she felt good. I so desperately wanted to do it again. Instead, I withdrew, and she slid off the sink base and sat on the toilet lid. She wrapped her hand around my dick and put it in her mouth. The feeling of her lush, plump lips on my dick was the thing of fantasies. Yep, this had to be a dream. The fucking best dream I'd ever had.

I threaded my fingers through her long tresses, tugging her hair down. She looked up at me, passion in her eyes. It made my insides clench. It was like she could see into me.

I pushed it away and instead focused on fucking her mouth. My balls tightened and my hips rocked.

"Take it," I chanted as I felt the force of my orgasm build. "Drink it. Drink my cock."

Her fingers rubbed right behind my ball sacks as she sucked me to the back of her mouth. My orgasm blasted through me. I emptied into her mouth, pumping again and again. She worked to take it all, but cum dripped at the edges of her mouth. I'd been right. The next adventure could be the best one.

I EXITED THE BATHROOM FIRST, giving her a moment to clean up and fix her hair. If anyone knew what was going on in the bathroom, they didn't give any indication.

When she returned to her seat, we had a drink and dinner and good conversation. I wanted to get her back in the bathroom again, but it didn't happen.

When we landed in New York, it was on the tip of my tongue to ask her full name and her phone number. Or I'd give her my address and tell her to show up at my place. I wasn't done with this woman. The only thing that stopped me was how unsettling it was that I was thinking such things after the memory of Lorraine. I wasn't going to allow my dick to get me in trouble again.

As the plane pulled up to the gate, I turned to her. "Thank you for an exciting flight."

A beautiful blush came to her cheeks. She smiled. "I suppose I should thank you as well." Her eyes studied me, and for a minute, I wondered if she was about to ask for my contact information. I worried that if she did, I wouldn't be strong enough to tell her no, so I turned away, reaching under the seat to grab my backpack and breaking the crazy, erotic tether between us.

When we got off the plane, she exited first, and I gave her a few moments to get ahead of me. It was all I could do not to run after her and ask for a night.

But I remained strong, ordering a car at the airport and having it take me to one of the corporate apartments held by Saint Security. When I arrived, I tossed my bags to the side and headed straight for the small bar that each of the apartments held. I poured several fingers of whiskey and took it to the window, looking over the night view of New York City.

I was still arguing with myself about not getting Victoria's information. Had I done so, she might be here now and we could fuck the night away on the couch or in the bed, anywhere, everywhere. Then tomorrow, we could go our own way. God, how I wished I had done that.

Oh, well. I drank my whiskey and then texted Henry to let him know that I had arrived in New York and that I would be there tomorrow to see him. He texted me back that he was glad that I was here and that he and his daughter would be waiting for me.

I grabbed my carry-on case and headed back to the bedroom. I pulled out my grooming bag and headed to the bathroom, doing a quick brush and floss, then I stripped naked and got into bed.

Immediately, Victoria came to mind, and while it wouldn't be as good as it had been on the plane, I allowed my fantasy to play out. I wrapped my hand around my dick and imagined all the deliciously wicked things I could do to her until I sprayed cum over my chest.

I did a quick return to the bathroom to clean myself up, and then I climbed back into bed. It was time to let my luscious in-flight entertainment, Victoria, go and focus on keeping Henry and his daughter safe.

4

Victoria

I had nearly asked Sterling if he wanted to continue our adventure tonight in New York, but I knew he'd say no. He'd said one of the benefits of an adventure like ours was that it was one and done and we'd never see each other again. Judging by the way he'd turned his attention away from me once the plane pulled up to the gate, I knew that we'd had our fun.

I arrived back at my building, feeling exhausted. It might only be just after ten p.m. in New York, but it was after three in the morning in London.

"Welcome home, Ms. Banion." Jones, the doorman, opened the door for me. He was an older gentleman with a sweet disposition and a twinkle in his eyes.

"Thank you, Jonesy."

His cheeks reddened as they always did at my nickname for him.

I took the elevator up to my cozy apartment space, shutting the door behind me and sighing. Dorothy was right, there was no place like home. Not that I didn't like traveling, but it was nice to be back in my own space. My apartment wasn't as big as some of my affluent peers', but I felt the space was just right. It was housed in a building built in the 19th century, so it had architecture that gave it charm and sophistication. I had everything I needed, from a bedroom and an office to an adequate kitchen. The living area had windows that practically rose to the high ceilings.

I put my bag in my room and went to the kitchen to get a bottle of water. I carried it over to the window and pulled out my phone to call my father and let him know I was home.

"Hey, Princess, where are you?" My father calling me Princess was a sweet term of endearment. I knew he still thought of me as his little girl. God, what would he think if he knew what I'd done with Sterling?

"I'm in New York. I just got back to my apartment."

"You're not coming back here? When I said come home, I didn't just mean to New York. I think you should come stay with me."

My father's home, which had been my grandparents' home and my great-grandparents' home before them, was large and had plenty of space for me not to feel crowded by my father. But I was tired and not interested in making my way across the city.

"I'm exhausted, Dad. I'm safe here for now. I'll come by in the morning."

"Is Jones on the door tonight?"

I rolled my eyes knowing that Jonesy would be getting a call from my father to make sure he was extra diligent. "Yes, Jones was on the door, but I think he's off in a little bit."

"Lock your door and don't open it to anyone. Okay?"

"Tell me what's going on, Dad."

"I will, but I'd rather do it in person. I'll let Knightly and Mrs. Tillis know that you will be here in the morning."

I thought of Knightly, my father's chauffeur, butler, and whatever else he needed. The man had worked for my grandfather and had to be close to eighty. For over fifteen years, my father had tried to get him to retire, but he said he wouldn't have anything to do if he didn't work for the Banion family.

Then there was Mrs. Tillis, who wasn't all that much younger than Knightly and wouldn't retire for mostly the same reason. She basically ran the household, so I'm sure she'd already made up my room and had checked with the cook about making some of my favorite foods. I suppose it was a testament to how my father treated them that they were so loyal.

"I'll be safe. I'll see you tomorrow, Dad. Good night."

"Good night, Princess."

I padded my way back to my bedroom and got ready for bed. I climbed under the sheets and closed my eyes, falling asleep almost instantly.

I woke the next morning to the most delicious dream involving Sterling using his fantastic mouth on my pussy. I took care of the ache between my thighs and then hopped out of bed to take a shower. I'd just finished getting dressed when there was a knock on my door.

For a moment, the silly woman in me hoped that Sterling had hunted me down. I went to the door, looking through the peephole. It was odd that no one in the lobby had called up to let me know I had a guest.

On the other side of the door stood Knightly. Gee, what a surprise. Of course my father would send him over to pick me up. Since everyone in the building knew Knightly, they would have no problem letting him.

I opened the door and grinned at the man who in some ways was like a grandfather to me. My own grandparents had always been a bit aloof, as if they'd never been around children. Knightly and Mrs. Tillis were always the ones who would sneak me little candies when my dad wasn't looking.

He stood looking stoic until I launched myself forward and wrapped my arms around him. "Did you bring me something?" It was an old game between us starting back from the times he would sneak me those pieces of candy.

He gave me a hug and his serious, stoic face morphed into a big smile, his silver eyes twinkling. "Of course, I did. Why would today be any different?" He put his hand in his pocket and pulled out a tiny plastic bag full of mint green colored M&Ms.

I laughed, loving how he spoiled me as badly as my father did. "Is the M&M's store open this early?"

"I picked them up yesterday when your father said he would be asking you to come home." His face turned serious, and all the joy at seeing Knightly fell away.

"What's going on?"

"That's not for me to tell. But I'm here to get you and take you over to your father's place. He'll explain everything."

That had always been the downside to Knightly. His true allegiance was to my father, and he wasn't going to tell me my father's business.

"Well, let me get my purse."

"Have you packed a bag? Because I believe your father would like you to stay with him."

I considered grabbing the bag I hadn't unpacked last night, but I shook my head. "I'm not committing to anything until I hear what Dad has to say. After that, if I need to get some things—"

"Me and Mrs. Tillis will take care of it."

I grabbed my purse and headed out with Knightly. As I stepped out onto the street, the scent of baked goods drifted over to me. I turned to the bakery a few doors down. "Let's stop and get Dad some of those lemon cookies that he likes."

Knightly gave me a firm stare. "Your father's orders are to—"

"I want a doughnut, Knightly. And I want to get Dad some lemon bars."

If Knightly pushed it, he would win this battle, but luckily for me, he liked to spoil me. He hadn't told me my father's secret, so I was pretty sure in his mind, letting me get a donut was my consolation prize.

"I will drive you over."

"It's right over there." I pointed toward the bakery just a few doors down. I started to make my way over.

"I'll be waiting outside."

It was just after eight thirty, which meant I'd missed the early morning rush. There were still some customers there, but the bakery's busiest times were closer to seven thirty and then again around lunch and then later at four thirty.

I got into line behind a blonde woman who was holding the hand of a child who must've been four or five years old.

The child tugged on his mom's hand. "Mama, which cookie do you think Grandma would like best?"

The blonde woman turned her head to look down at her son. "Her favorites are oatmeal raisin cookies."

I let out a small gasp as recognition came to me. "Samantha?"

The woman's head swiveled toward me, and it took her a moment, but then she said, "Tori?" She tugged her child closer to her as if protecting him, which seemed like an odd gesture. Samantha and I had been the best of friends in college. We had lost touch over the last couple of years when she'd moved away after getting her degree. The night before she left, we ate a lot of ice cream and drank a lot of wine and bawled our eyes out, so this reaction seemed a little off.

Undeterred, I opened my arms wide and tugged her in close for a hug. "How are you doing?" I pulled away and looked down at the little boy beside her. "Oh, my God, you're a mother." I put my hand on my hip, tilting my head to give her a look. "No wonder I haven't heard from you in such a long time. You've been busy." I worked to stay positive even as I was realizing that she must've gotten married to have this child and she hadn't notified me of any of it.

She smiled back, but it wasn't until she looked down at her son that the smile felt genuine, not forced. "This is Pax."

I bent over and held out my hand to him. "It's so nice to meet you, Pax. I'm Tori. I'm an old friend of your mom's."

Pax looked up at Samantha, who gave him a nod, and only then did he take my hand and shake it. "My real name is Paxton, but people call me Pax."

"My real name is Victoria, but people call me Tori." My mind flitted back to Sterling and the way he'd called me Victoria. Maybe I'd rethink my name again.

Ahead of us, the customer got her cookies and the line inched forward.

"Are you back in New York for good or are you visiting your parents?" I asked.

Samantha's forced smile faltered. "My mom is ailing, and my father couldn't handle it, and he's run off with his secretary or something."

"That mother f—" I glanced down at little Pax. Then I turned my attention back to Samantha. "I am so sorry. Is there anything I can do to help?"

She shook her head. "No, but thank you, Tori."

An idea struck me. "Why don't you and your mom and Pax come over to the house sometime for dinner? My dad's been rattling around in that old place all by himself since my grandparents died."

"I didn't realize your grandparents died. I'm sorry."

I nodded. "Yes, a few years ago. I'm sure my father would love to see you again."

Samantha again forced a smile, and it made me want to reach across and shake her, wondering what had happened to our friendship that she seemed so aloof. "That's nice, Tori, but my mom is very ill. She doesn't really get out much."

"That's why we're here. We're going to get her some cookies to cheer her up," Pax said.

"That's so sweet of you."

The customer in front of Samantha paid for their items, and the person behind the counter called over to Samantha to let her know she was up.

"It was good seeing you, Tori." She turned away, and with her hand clutching Pax's, they stepped up to the counter to order cookies.

I was still thinking about the exchange as I sat in the back of the car while Knightly drove me over to my father's house on Riverside Drive. I absently ate the chocolate sour cream doughnut and held the bag of lemon bars for my father as I thought about the odd encounter.

"Do you remember my friend Samantha?" I asked Knightly.

"I do."

"She was in the bakery, but she was kinda weird toward me."

Knightly glanced at me through the rearview mirror before turning his eyes back to the busy New York streets. "Rumor has it that Mrs. Layton isn't doing very well, and to make matters worse, Mr. Layton apparently has left her." Knightly made a face like his words had left a sour taste in his mouth.

I couldn't blame him. Who left their wife of nearly thirty years when she was ill? Then again, I never liked Mr. Layton very much.

"Did you know she had a son?" I asked him.

The way Knightly's brows arched upward told me he hadn't. "I didn't. I didn't even hear that she'd gotten married."

The whole thing was very odd. As old as Pax was, she had to have met her husband and gotten pregnant not long after she left New York.

I had to push Samantha and her strange behavior away as Knightly pulled into the underground garage of my father's mansion. Knightly must've had a button in his car to warn staff when he was arriving home because Mrs. Tillis was there waiting as we pulled in next to the elevator entrance.

I didn't wait for Knightly to help me out. Instead, I opened the door and exited, pulling Mrs. Tillis in for a hug.

She squeezed me tight. "Welcome home, dear. It's going to be such a relief to your father that you're home."

"I'm pretty annoyed at all this cloak and dagger stuff. What's going on?"

Mrs. Tillis patted my hand. "Come upstairs and your father will explain everything to you. Have you had breakfast? Cook Caroline has made Belgian waffles."

I just had a donut, but I could've had ten donuts and still, I would want to have Caroline's Belgian waffles.

I smiled like I was ten years old on Christmas day. "Yes, of course."

The three of us entered the elevator, and Mrs. Tillis pressed the button for the main family area of the mansion. This floor housed my father's den, along with a family and a formal living room, the kitchen, and the dining room.

I exited the elevator and went straight to my father's den expecting that's where he would be. As I entered the room, I saw him standing at the window, looking out over the part toward the river. In some ways, my father was like Sterling in that he had the shock of silver hair and was the epitome of a distinguished older gentleman. But he wasn't sexy because that would be gross.

As I neared, I saw that he had gray stubble along his cheeks and chin, which was unusual. He was always so clean shaven.

"I'm here, Dad."

He turned to face me, and my heart stopped in my chest. His cheek was red and swollen, as if someone had punched him. Over his eye, there was a line of stitches.

I ran over to him. "What happened?"

He held his arms out, taking mine in his hands, holding me back slightly. "It's worse than it looks. I'm fine."

It didn't make any sense. Had he fallen? Then I remembered the comment about an unhappy subject of his stories. "This is George Pitney?"

He arched a brow and then winced, clearly in pain. "Why would you think that?"

"Because you said someone was unhappy with what you were publishing, and I knew that you were doing a series of stories on him. He's the only one I could think of who would do something like this."

He let out a long sigh and then took my hand, moving me toward one of the couches where he set me down. It was still early in the day, but he walked over to the bar and poured himself something to drink. I might've chastised him for it, except he looked like he could use a drink.

"It's not just the stories, Tori. None of us have revealed sources, but we have agreed to talk to law enforcement."

"Then why isn't he in jail now if he did this to you?"

My father let out a derisive laugh. "George didn't do this. At least not directly. He's a slippery man, which is why he's been able to get away with so much. But the law is closing in, and that has made him even more dangerous. That's why I want you home. What I'd really like is for you to stay here with me."

I didn't not want to stay with my dad, but I had my own life to live and a business to run. "I'm not involved in any of this. I like my place."

He gave me a curt nod. "You're not involved, but you're connected to me, and really, the best way for somebody to hurt me would be to hurt you."

My stomach clenched at the idea that I could be in danger.

"I know that you have a life to live, and so I've taken it upon myself to hire a bodyguard for you."

I frowned. "A bodyguard? Is that really necessary?"

Once again, my father arched a brow and then winced. "They got to me, and I'm always fairly protected."

He wasn't wrong. "If you're not going to stay here, then I'm going to absolutely insist that you have a bodyguard. But even if you move in here with me for the time being, I want you to have a bodyguard. I don't want to take any chances. Not with you."

The idea of a bodyguard following me around twenty-four, seven felt intrusive, but I could see my father's distress so I nodded my acquiescence. I would do as he asked because I wanted to ease the stress he was feeling.

"Your guest is here, sir," Knightly said from the doorway.

My father perked up a little bit. "Send him in, Knightly." My father looked down at me. "Alex is one of my oldest and best friends. I wish I could see him under different circumstances, but he's going to be the perfect person to look after you until this is all over."

I thought of all my father's friends, and while he'd talked about an Alex, I'd never met him.

I stood and took my father's hand. "I look forward to meeting him."

Knightly stepped aside, and the gentleman entered the room. My father moved toward him, embracing him. "Alex, thank you so much for coming."

I stood rooted to my spot as I looked at my father's oldest best friend. As it turned out, I had met him. I had sex with him on the flight home yesterday.

5

Alex

O*h, fuck.*

I was going to hell. Not that I ever thought I was a candidate for heaven, but now there was no question about it. When my time on this earth was done, I was on the express track to hell. I'd fucked my best friend's kid. My stomach roiled and threatened to come up.

Pull it together, Sterling.

I stepped forward and extended my hand. "Nice to meet you, Tori."

She blinked up at me, and I prayed to God she would hide her surprise. Finally, her brows lowered, and she took my hand to shake. "Nice to meet you too, Alex."

I jerked my hand back because her touch immediately took me back to the cramped bathroom on the airplane and the way those hands had wrapped around my dick. Jesus fucking Christ. This was a nightmare.

Henry patted me on the back, but his face grew concerned as he looked at his daughter. "Are you okay, Princess?"

The bile threatened to come up again at hearing him call his daughter Princess. She was a grown woman. Oh, yes, I knew just how much of a woman she was. And she had consented to our tryst. But that didn't keep me from feeling like a fucking creep.

I watched Victoria, hoping she'd pull it together. *One and done,* I reminded myself. I just needed to cut off all memories of yesterday. Hopefully, she would too.

"Yes, it's just, well . . . with Alex here, it's making this seem so real."

Henry's expression was filled with remorse. "I'm so sorry that you have to go through this. If I'd known—"

She shook her head. "This isn't your fault, Dad. It's George Pitney's. I support whatever you have to do to put him away." She glanced up at me, but I didn't know what her expression meant.

I waited for her to continue her statement, starting with "but", but she didn't. I realized that I wanted her to refuse my services. I couldn't be her bodyguard. And it wasn't just because of what we had done the day before. It wasn't just because of the self-loathing and guilt that threatened to bring me to my knees. It was because I knew without a doubt that I wanted her again. Being a bodyguard meant a lot of time alone with the client. I was a professional, and I knew I could resist. But the growing urge, the way it would build and add pressure, was a torment that I didn't want to have to deal with.

I'd been to Henry's home before. I knew it was its own little fortress. With a few extra men, Henry and Victoria could be safe here.

"You know, if you stayed here with your father, you wouldn't really need a bodyguard."

She looked up at me, her eyes narrowing as if she was taking offense at what I was saying. How the hell did she not see what I was offering was a way out of this intolerable situation?

"You really can't expect me to stay cooped up indoors for however long this is going to take, do you?" she asked.

"Whether she stays here or not, I want you on her twenty-four, seven, Alex."

I winced, and Victoria flinched. Last night, all I wanted was to be on her twenty-four, seven. Now, the thought of it made me sick.

I tore my attention from Victoria to Henry. "Henry, I want to do whatever I can to keep you and your daughter safe. But I haven't been active in the field for a long time now. Put me in charge of security and I'll make sure she has the best guard. And I'll make sure the rest of the house and everyone at your office are safe."

Henry looked at me, and his disappointment tore at my gut. "I need someone I can trust, Alex, and that's you. Now I won't say no to the rest, but you're the one I want protecting my daughter."

Victoria crossed her arms over her chest. "He thinks I'm an entitled brat."

I closed my eyes, praying to God for strength until I remembered God would be sending me to hell.

"Victoria?" Henry's voice held shock. "Why would you say something like that? It's rude. Alex and I have been friends for a long time. Since college."

She shrugged. "I saw Samantha today for the first time in years, and she was different."

Henry drew back, his eyes narrowing. "Samantha?"

Victoria nodded. "People change. They grow apart. And let's face it, Dad. He doesn't want to protect me."

Henry's gaze shot at me, his brow furrowed even more. "Is that true?"

In my missionary days, I'd once been tortured, but I didn't squirm as much then as I was doing now. "It's not that I don't want to, Henry. It's that I don't think I'm the best man for the job."

For the life of me, I couldn't figure out why Victoria was so incensed about this. Unless, of course, she wanted a repeat of yesterday. Even after my experience with Lorraine, I might have gone ahead with a repeat of yesterday, but not now. Not now that I knew she was Henry's kid. If there was a God, he would strike me dead now so I didn't have to deal with this.

"Based on all I see, you look fit to me."

I shot Victoria look asking her to please be quiet. Did she want her father to know what we'd done?

"And I'm not hiring you just for your fitness. I trust you, Alex.

You're smart. You understand people. Please, old friend, don't let me down."

The walls of the large den threatened to swallow me whole. I could barely breathe. "I tell you what. I'd like to talk to the cops on your case. Then I still need to talk with my supervisor at Saint Security. I can't just pick up a case on my own. Once I have the investigation information and the okay from my boss, I'll put something together for you."

"That includes your watching my daughter," Henry insisted.

"Let me make sure I can clear it with my supervisors."

Victoria looked at me like she had yesterday when I thought she was staring straight into my soul. Only this time, she was seeing the lie that I was telling. Sure, I was going to do everything I could to protect them, but I was also going to make sure that my supervisors didn't want me to be Victoria's bodyguard.

Henry gave me a hug. "Thank you. I knew I could count on you."

I patted his back and then extricated myself and got out of there as quickly as I could.

EACH TIME I returned to the States to visit Saint Security, there were always more people I didn't know than those I did. It made sense. We were shipped off to various locations around the world. Several of the men and women I'd worked with before were retired, and new people were hired to replace them.

Walking into the company offices today was no different until I saw Dax Shepperd. He was younger than me by about ten years, but he'd been a great operative right out of the gate, so we'd worked together with Noel and another friend, Bastion. It was such a fucking shock and shame to have learned that Bastion turned against Noel, trying to kill him. Last I heard, Bastion was sitting in a Mexican jail.

"Hey, look what the cat dragged in," Dax said as he came over to me with his hand extended.

I gave his hand a hearty shake. "I could say the same about you. I thought you were out West."

"I am, but I'm back taking care of a little bit of business and visiting my wife's family."

I shook my head. "When I heard you got married, I thought it was a joke."

Dax flashed a grin, which was unusual for the man I had known before. "Love of a good woman. You should try it."

I shuddered at the thought. Especially since I had the worst taste in women. I had one who had stolen from me, and another turned out to be the daughter of my friend. Nope, I was better off being a lone wolf in this world.

"What brings you in?" Dax asked.

"Technically, I'm on vacation, but I have a friend who has run into some trouble with George Pitney."

"That's never a good thing to do," Elliott Watson said, joining me and Dax. Like Dax, Elliott was someone I'd known from the old days and another person who knew firsthand about George's ruthless, sometimes bloodthirsty, ways of doing business.

"Do we have anything else going on right now related to George?" I asked Elliott, who, like me, retired from the field and was now running the New York office of Saint Security.

"As a client?"

I shook my head, knowing that ever since Noel had changed the direction of the business, we no longer did business with unscrupulous people, at least if we could help it. "No, I mean has anybody else hired us for protection or investigation?"

Elliott shook his head. "Not at the moment."

"My buddy has been getting threats and in fact was recently assaulted by one of George's people. He wants to hire me to protect his daughter, but technically, I'm on vacation. And I really don't do that kind of work anymore."

"Old man," Dax quipped with a smirk.

I ignored the comment. "I told him I would come in to see what sorts of arrangements I could help make."

"Just for protection?" Dax asked.

"Definitely some protection, but it's my understanding that law enforcement is involved in an investigation and maybe we could pick up on some of that as well. Anything that we can do to make sure that George finally gets his comeuppance would be good."

Elliott frowned. "Why isn't this friend of yours here, hiring us himself?"

"He's understandably nervous and unsure who he can trust."

"He thinks Pitney's infiltrated St. Security?" Elliott asked dubiously.

I shrugged. "I think he's just trying to be cautious. That's why I told him I'd make all the arrangements."

"If you're off, who are you thinking of to protect him and his daughter?" Elliott asked.

"Ideally, I'd like you or Dax, someone from the old days, but I know that's not likely."

"How about Jorgensen?" Elliott raised his hand and whistled. "Jorgensen."

I turned to see a man in his early thirties who looked like he had just walked out of the surf in Southern California, with towheaded blond hair and a tan, approach us.

"Ian just transferred here out of Archer's office in Los Angeles. Ian Jorgensen, this is Alex Sterling. Alex, this is Ian Jorgensen."

I shook hands with the young man, giving him a full assessment based on the firmness of his handshake and his ability to look me directly in the eye.

"Do I have a say in who is going to be protecting me?"

My head swiveled in disbelief as I saw Victoria striding toward us. Not only was she here, but apparently, she was here alone. Not a very smart thing to do with George Pitney on her tail.

"You're supposed to be home with your father," I said gruffly.

"Yeah, well, I had a few things I needed to say to you."

She turned her attention from me to Ian. She thrust out her hand toward him. "Hello, my name is Victoria Banion."

Ian shook her hand, and while I could tell he was doing his best to show no reaction, his eyes gave away his attraction to her. My jaw tightened.

"It's nice to meet you, Miss Banion. I'd be happy to offer you protection."

I bet he would.

She smiled, and her blue eyes took in Ian. A red mist began to form in my brain.

"Well, then—"

I took her upper arm and tugged her away. "Excuse me, I need to talk to Miss Banion." I pulled her into one of the offices and shut the door. "What are you doing here?"

"I told you I had a few things I needed to say to you. You were very rude not just to me, but to my father as well. He trusts you—"

"I know. And what did I do? I fucked his kid." God, I thought I was going to puke.

She flinched. "First of all, I'm not a kid. And second of all, I know it was awkward, but for somebody who makes his living as a spy, you did a very poor job of hiding your thoughts and feelings. My father trusts you, and although I don't know you very well, it would've been nice to have a bodyguard I knew." She gave me a smirk as she shrugged. "But I've changed my mind. Ian will do."

"The hell he will." I didn't know why I said that. She was giving me the out I needed, and yet the idea of Ian spending all that alone time with her made me go fucking nuts. "As you said, your father hired me. Like it or not, sweetheart, I'm your bodyguard."

6

Victoria

I wouldn't lie. Discovering that the man I'd had sex with in an airplane bathroom was my father's friend and the man he hired to be my bodyguard was awkward. Seriously? What were the odds that we'd end up on the same plane and decide to have a little adventure in the restroom?

Okay, so it was beyond awkward. Maybe I should have given Sterling, or Alex, some slack regarding his reaction. When he realized that I was his friend's daughter, the man turned downright pale, and there were a couple of times I thought he was turning green. And then there was how he turned himself into a pretzel trying to get out of the job that my father was so clearly desperate for him to do. Truth be told, it might have been interesting if Alex were my bodyguard, but once he started acting repulsed by me, that intrigue vanished.

Alex was very noncommittal as he left my father's house, but I could tell that he was going to try and get out of being my bodyguard. And while at that point, I was okay with it, I could tell that my father wasn't. So not long after Alex and my father went to his home office, I snuck out of the house. I know it wasn't smart, considering everything that was going on, but I was sure that Knightly wouldn't drive me. I ordered a car and checked the driver's credentials twice and had him drive me to Saint Security's offices.

I arrived just in time to overhear Alex talking about my father's situation to three other men. And when the men introduced Ian Jorgensen, I was all for having somebody else besides Alex be my bodyguard. It was petty since I hoped that Alex would be jealous. God, how stupid was I? He wouldn't be jealous. He'd be relieved.

So it made absolutely no sense when Alex told me that Ian couldn't be my bodyguard because he was.

I gave my head a shake. "You're giving me whiplash. You all but begged my father to let you find somebody else to be my bodyguard, and now that you have, you're not going to make the swap?"

He made a frustrating growl. "I don't know Jorgensen."

"If he works for Saint Security, he must be trained. Vetted."

"But I don't know him. I can't pawn you off to just anybody. Your father is adamant that someone he can trust be your bodyguard."

My hackles rose at his use of pawning me off. Like I was a chore. "You know, my first impression of you was correct. You're a jerk."

"You didn't seem to think so in the bathroom yesterday."

My eyes narrowed. "That comment just proves my point even more. Only an asshole douchebag would make a comment like that."

To his credit, he looked chagrined.

"Your behavior today has totally eliminated any pleasure I had from our encounter yesterday. Now I'm just totally embarrassed and repulsed."

"That makes two of us," he quipped.

"What do you have to complain about?" Why was I still here, taking his abuse?

"I fucked my best friend's kid."

"Once again, I'm not a kid. I'm a grown woman, as you fully discovered."

He started to turn that pale shade of green again. "The point is, you're Henry's daughter."

"And because of that, you don't want to be around me. So let Ian do it."

His lips curled into a snarl in a way that had me wondering if this was just about finding somebody my father trusted. It was like he didn't like Ian, but he admitted he didn't know him. Was it that he just didn't like the idea of Ian being my bodyguard? While that didn't seem possible, I decided to test the theory.

With a shrug, I said, "Ian is good looking and is closer to my age, so it would make sense that I'd be hanging around him."

Alex stepped toward me, another one of those growls emanating from him. "You're stuck with me."

Just to mess with him, I said, "That's fine, but you'd better not get in my way. There's definitely not going to be any more adventures. Like you said, one and done."

His nostrils flared, but he gave a quick nod. "Good, then we understand each other."

As long as I could stay angry at him, it wasn't going to be a problem for him to be my bodyguard. "Good. I'm going home now." I started to turn away, but once again, he took my arm and stopped me at the door.

He stepped close, pinning me in. His heat and scent enveloped me, and I had a flashback to our adventure in the bathroom. My traitorous hormones reacted, making my breath hitch.

He sucked in a breath, and his eyes drifted down to my lips.

Push him away, Tori.

His gaze drifted back up to my eyes, and he cleared his throat as he stepped back. "You stay here with me until I've put a security plan in place. What you can do is call your father and let them know where you are."

I looked up at him defiantly. "How do you know he doesn't know that I'm here?"

He shook his head. "Because nobody is with you. That tells me you snuck out."

Dammit.

"Stay here. Call your dad. I'll be back." He jerked the door open and left like he'd done at my father's house. Like he couldn't get away fast enough. Jerk.

I didn't want to talk to my dad and explain how I'd gotten here, so I texted him, letting him know I was at Saint Security with Alex. I didn't like taking orders from Alex, but he was right. My father would worry when he realized I was gone.

With that out of the way, I scrolled through my email until Alex returned with one of the other men he'd been talking to before.

"Victoria, Dax Sheppard. Dax, Victoria Banion," Alex introduced us without interest. We'd barely said hello when Alex jumped into business. "Henry's house is fairly secure, but I'd like a team to go through the place to find potential weaknesses."

Dax sat at the table and nodded. "You said he was jumped. Where was that at?"

Alex shook his head. "I don't know. I'll talk to Henry, and I'm going to get in touch with the investigation. I think—"

"What about you?" Dax said to me. "Do you know where your father was jumped?"

The fact that Dax had to ask me showed that Alex was acting like I wasn't there. Or I didn't have anything to share. Which, in terms of Dax's question, I didn't. "I don't know. He'd be most vulnerable on the street leaving the house or office."

Dax nodded. "He doesn't have anyone with him normally?"

"Knightly is usually with him."

Alex scoffed. "He's a million years old. Henry should retire him."

I scowled. "Knightly isn't a horse, Mr. Sterling," I said, feeling worse and worse about my decision to enter the bathroom with him on the flight home. "If my father is going to get rid of dead weight around him, I have other suggestions."

"Sentiment has no place with safety," Alex snapped back.

Dax's eyes narrowed as he looked between me and Henry. "Is Knightly a chauffeur?"

"Yes. More like my father's right-hand man." I glared at Alex. "My father contacted you for help in providing safety. Surely, you can do that without getting rid of my father's most loyal friend."

Alex flinched. I wasn't sure it was from calling Knightly my father's friend or loyal. Both suggested I didn't think Alex was either.

"We work to keep your lives as normal as possible," Dax said, looking at Alex like he'd grown a third eye. "We'll do an assessment of the home, his office, as well as all movements he makes outside of both. What about your place?"

"She's staying with her father," Alex said.

I shook my head in disgust at his gall. "I have my own place."

"We'll—"

"She's staying with her father." Alex's hard stare was on me. "It's what your father wants."

"How would you know? You didn't question him about what happened the other day. You didn't ask him his expectations of your services. You couldn't get out of his house fast enough."

Alex's jaw tightened. "If you were my—"

"I'm nothing to you, Mr. Sterling." I turned back to Dax and gave him my address.

He jotted it down, but not before looking over at Alex as if for permission. Then he rose. "I'll take this to Elliott and begin putting together a team and a plan."

Alex nodded. "Thanks. I'd like to be a part of it." He looked at me. "Can I trust you to wait here while we put together this plan?"

I turned away, looking at my phone.

Dax and Alex left the room. I imagined Dax noticed the animosity between me and Alex. Would he ask about it? Would Alex tell him the truth? Probably not. He was disgusted at himself, and I might have taken pity on him if he wasn't being such a jerk.

I stood and went to the window, looking out over the city, wondering how I'd gotten myself into this mess.

My phone pinged with a text. Thinking it was a response from my father, I checked it.

DADDY's *little girl*

.   .   .

THE TEXT WAS FOLLOWED by a picture of me on the street outside the bakery. A chill ran down my spine. Were Pitney's people following me already? Were they following me from London or just when I arrived home?

The door opened and Alex entered. I pushed my fear away.

His eyes narrowed. "What's wrong?"

"In general or now?"

"Don't fuck with me, Victoria. I know fear when I see it." He nodded toward the phone in my hand.

I sighed. I wanted to be obstinate, but my father hired him to protect us and I shouldn't make it harder for Alex to do his job. "I think it's from Pitney." I held the phone out for him to see the text.

He made that growling sound again. "I'm taking you to your father's."

"You can take me there and explain to us what you're going to do to protect us. But I'm not staying there."

"Don't be an idiot."

Was I being an idiot for insisting on going to my own place? Probably. But I didn't like feeling like my life wasn't my own anymore. I needed some normalcy. I needed to be in my own space. "Don't be an asshole."

"This isn't a personality contest. Pitney isn't playing a game." He looked at me like I was a petulant child, which only made me angrier.

"I see. So in the bodyguard business you have to be rude, condescending, and insensitive? Something tells me that's just you. I think I want Ian after all."

His eyes narrowed. "Because he's younger and handsome? Do you think he'll fuck you?"

I laughed, and Alex didn't like that. He stepped closer to me. Intensity radiated off him. It was heady and exciting. I liked poking his buttons even if I hated it when he poked mine.

"You have a tendency to think you're saying something to get to me, but you only prove what a misogynistic jerk you are."

"You knew that yesterday."

"I did. But yesterday, I thought I'd never have to see or talk to you again. You'd said that, actually. But here you are."

"Are you being difficult just to fuck with me or are you always like this?"

"I can see now why you have bad luck with women. I'm beginning to think the last woman took your money as payment for having to put up with you."

"She's in jail." His eyes were intense as they once again drifted to my lips. "I could lock you away too."

There was a shift in the energy between us. The snap of irritation still whipped between us, but instead of repulsing, there was a pull.

"You like to bully women?"

"I'm trying to keep you safe."

"How can you do that when you don't like or respect me?"

"I've worked for many people I didn't like or respect." His words broke the hypnotic pull I felt at the banter.

I stepped away from him. "The sooner this is done, the better."

"We're in agreement about that."

7

Alex

I was being an asshole. It was my last line of defense to stop me from pulling Victoria into my arms and kissing those delicious, plump, pink lips. Desire coursed hard through my veins, followed by the revulsion of wanting my friend's daughter. It made me surly, and I took it out on the source of my frustration, Victoria.

I hated the way she looked at me as she stepped back when I insinuated that I didn't respect her. I hated it even though that was what I'd wanted to happen. I needed her to put up the wall that I was having a very difficult time keeping between us.

It was time to focus on the task at hand, keeping her and Henry safe from George Pitney. "You need to give me your phone. We need to see if we can figure out where that text came from."

She clutched her phone to her chest. "I'm not going to let you paw your dirty hands through my phone."

"What are you afraid I'll see? Nude selfies?" The words made me just as repulsed as having slept with Henry's daughter. But her hating me was the best way to keep our dirty little secret, and more importantly, to make sure it never happened again.

"Dirty old man."

I flinched, hating the description even as I knew that in her eyes, I was dirty and old.

There was a knock on the door, and it popped open. Ian poked his head in. "We got some of that information you wanted on the current investigation into George Pitney. I thought you might want to take a look."

I nodded. "I do. Can you take Ms. Banion's phone? She just got a text from George or one of his goons. See if you can figure out where it originated from."

Ian entered the room, and Victoria met him halfway, extending the phone out to him. "How long do you need to keep it? I run my own business and this phone is everything to me."

My jaw tightened at how easily she moved toward Ian and handed over her phone. Fucking hell, she even smiled at him.

"It shouldn't be that long. Are you hungry? We can order food. There's a great deli on the corner," Ian said affably.

He was behaving how I would have normally if the situation were different. Victoria had called me a misogynist, and while I absolutely was being one, that wasn't my normal type of behavior. I respected women. In my career, some of the smartest and bravest people I had worked with were women. In some ways, Victoria reminded me of them.

"I am a little hungry," she admitted.

"What kind of sandwich would you like? Turkey?"

Ian must've believed what I think most men thought, which was that women gravitated toward turkey because it was lean. But my sense of Victoria was that she liked food. I didn't think that because of her ample curves. Victoria was a woman who was trying to savor life, and while a turkey sandwich could be good, there were so many other sandwiches one could eat in life.

"Do they happen to have cheesesteaks? I've been craving a good cheesesteak. But if not, then roast beef."

Ian grinned. "They have a great cheesesteak." He turned to me. "What about you? Can I get you something?"

"Pastrami. But first, I want to see the information you've got."

Ian nodded and headed to the door. I followed him, looking over my shoulder at Victoria as I crossed the threshold. "We'll check your phone, and I'm going to look over this information, and then we'll head out."

An uninvited thrill ran through me at the idea of taking her to her apartment. It was just the type of sensation that I needed to avoid. I'd come so precariously close to kissing her in the middle of our battle of wits. I was at my job, for fuck's sake. If I was so tempted here, the possibilities of what could happen while alone in her apartment were too numerous to list. For a start, it included kissing and touching and fucking on any flat surface in her place.

I'd always seen myself as strong. I was a man who could resist temptation and endure physical challenges. But there was no doubt in my mind that when it came to Victoria, my power to resist was nonexistent.

I followed Ian out of the room and over to his desk. Saint Security has a few individual offices, but for the most part, everyone worked in a large open room. It made it easier to directly share information or work collaboratively, as Ian and I were doing as I grabbed a chair and pulled it up next to his in front of his computer.

"This is what I've been able to access on Pitney over the last five years. I wasn't able to pull up anything on the current investigation. Open cases are usually closed to anyone without permission."

I glanced at him. "Can you get permission?"

Ian shrugged and opened another file. "We're working on it. These are the notes I took talking with Eliasson. He's one of the investigators we've worked with quite a bit. And then these notes here." Ian opened another document. "I got these from the District Attorney's office."

I let out a low whistle, impressed at how much Ian was able to get from his contacts. "They're talking to you?"

"Your friend, Henry, told them to give anything and everything to Saint Security. I will add that they were reluctant, so we do need to be careful with this information. We don't want to do anything that might mess up their case."

I nodded in understanding. The best thing for Henry and Victoria's protection was if George Pitney dropped dead, but short of that was putting him in prison for a very long time.

I studied the notes and frowned. "Most of this looks like fraud. What about all the people who have gone missing from Pitney's orbit?"

"In those cases, they need a witness, and all of them seem to have disappeared."

This wasn't good.

"And I will point out that some of them disappeared while George was incarcerated, and since they couldn't testify, he went free. Nobody's been able to pin the disappearances, or more likely murders, on him."

My gut felt like I had drunk battery acid. "Mother fucker."

Ian turned his head toward me, and in his eyes, I saw he was thinking the same thing. "No matter where he is, George Pitney has tentacles to reach anyone, anywhere. I was told that he's been offered witness protection, him and his daughter, but—"

"He's got a conglomerate to run." I knew Henry well enough to know he wouldn't abandon the family business. But I wondered if maybe Victoria would be open to witness protection. The minute I thought it, I dismissed it. She and her father were clearly close, and it wasn't likely she would want to commit to never speaking to him again by going into hiding.

"Can you send this all to me? I'll go through it more thoroughly. Do we have really good investigators here?"

"We all are—"

"I mean in the field. Like undercover. We need to put Pitney away on something more serious than fraud. We need to make it impossible for him to manage his corrupt empire from prison."

"We have a few here, but you'll need to talk to Elliott."

I nodded. "Thanks, Ian." I stood, giving him a pat on the shoulder.

I still didn't like him very much, but he appeared to be solid in his work.

Ian stood and picked up Victoria's phone. "I'll take this over to the tech guys and see what they can figure out about that text."

"Thanks. I'm going to see Elliott."

Elliott had a private office because he was the manager. I knocked on his door, and when I heard the gruff "Enter," I opened it. He waved me in, and I sat in the chair in front of his desk.

Technically, since we both managed offices, we were peers, but I was in New York, his territory, so I needed to defer to him. I laid out the situation, adding information about the text and an overview of what Ian had found.

Elliott shook his head. "You know, the safest bet for your friend is to walk away from all this."

"I know. And believe me, I'm going to make a very convincing argument that he does just that. But I know Henry. He's not going to back down."

"Even if it costs him his life?"

That thought landed in my belly like a lead weight. "Even if." Henry was playing a dangerous game. He wasn't just risking his life, but Victoria's as well, which he knew. He was putting his trust in me to keep her safe. So along with trying to keep my hands off her, I had the weight of keeping her alive. I wasn't sure how I would live with myself if I fucked up either of those things.

8

Victoria

Alex wasn't the first jerk I'd ever been with, but he was definitely the worst. He was the king of assholes. I wished I'd never allowed myself to be lured by him on the airplane. If I'd ignored him, I wouldn't feel like such a monumental fool right now.

Alone in the conference room, I realized I had bigger problems than Alex Sterling. The way the men here at Saint Security were acting about George Pitney made me realize that my father was in some serious trouble. And the text I received today suggested that I was in it now as well.

I wondered if my father was texting or calling me. In some ways, I was glad that Ian had taken my phone so I didn't have to know how upset my father was that I snuck out of the house. Hopefully, he would feel reassured to know that I was at Saint Security with Alex. I scoffed. If my father knew what I'd done with Alex, he wouldn't feel reassured. How in the heck had my father become friends with such a misogynistic jerk douchewad like Alex Sterling?

The door opened, and Ian walked in carrying a bag. "Sandwiches have arrived." He set the bag on the table and emptied the contents.

I moved from the window I'd been staring mindlessly out of and sat down, taking the sandwich he passed to me.

"Do you mind if I join you for a few minutes?"

"Sure. Go ahead." Better him than Alex.

He sat across from me, pulling out a bag of chips and sliding it across the table. "I wasn't sure what kind of chips you wanted, so I just got the regular."

"Regular's fine."

"I got you water too." He pushed a bottle of water toward me. He opened his chips and began putting them on his sandwich. "I know it's childish, but I love it."

I smiled as I lifted my sandwich to take a bite. "The enjoyment of food is never childish."

He flashed me a grin around a mouthful of chip-laden sandwich. It occurred to me that if I wanted information about Alex, Ian might be a good person to ask.

I took a sip from the bottle of water and then asked, "So, do you think I'll be safe with Alex as my bodyguard?"

Ian arched a brow as he popped a loose chip into his mouth. "I doubt there's very many people you'd be safer with. Alex is old school. One of the legends."

"Legends?"

Ian swallowed his food, washing it down with water. "Yes, one of the OG here at Saint Security. It was started by Noel St. Martin, who is now retired. In fact, many of the people in that original crew are gone. Dax, who you met, is still around. And then there's Alex. And there was one guy who broke bad. Bastion something. They should have known by his name, eh?"

I nodded. "But if they're the original group, and most are retired, don't you think Alex is a little old?"

I wasn't really an ageist. Everything I knew about Alex, including everything I had discovered on the airplane, suggested that he was sharp of mind and fit of body. But I was looking for any excuse to find somebody else, and age seemed like my best option.

"In this case, his job is going to make sure that you don't need to be protected from anything. He'll anticipate all the possibilities and make sure that you're completely safe. So, unless you go off script, it's unlikely he'll allow you to be in a dangerous situation. Of course, your outings are probably going to be limited, but that's the price you have to pay when you're dealing with a man like George Pitney."

Ugh. I didn't want my world to be smaller. "My dad says there's some sort of investigation going on and that an arrest might be coming soon. Do you think that will make us safer? And how long do you think it will be?"

Ian smiled, but I could see behind his eyes that he was about to tell me something that wasn't completely the truth. "Once George is off the streets, you should be able to go back to your normal life." What wasn't he telling me?

I'd seen enough Mafia movies to know that the bad guys could often still get to their victims even when they were incarcerated. George had avoided prison all these years. If the rumors were true, part of that was because anyone against him went missing. For a moment, I wondered if I was going to be in danger for the rest of my life, whether George was in jail or not.

"Were you able to get anything on my phone?"

"Oh, yeah." He reached into his pocket and pulled out my phone, handing it to me across the table. "I don't have any details, but our tech people believe they got all the information they need to figure out what's going on. But George Pitney and his people are clever, so it may be some time before we can track down who sent the message."

The door opened, and Alex strode in. His pale blue eyes took in me and Ian eating lunch. "You two look cozy."

Ian straightened and began to pull his sandwich together, shoving it into the bag. "Just keeping her company."

I wasn't sure if it was fear of Alex or reverence for him that had Ian acting the way he was, but as soon as his food was packed up, he excused himself and left. I wasn't feeling particularly hungry anyway, so I wrapped up the rest of my sandwich and put it in the bag along with the chips.

"If you're ready, I can take you home."

I nodded and stood. "Good."

For all the flirting and banter that had gone on between us on the plane, the elevator down to the street and the ride in the car that Alex had arranged were silent.

That is until Alex said, "I know that if we had known who each other was on the plane yesterday, our hookup would never have happened. And because of that, I think we need to avoid telling your father."

I completely agreed with him but still found myself irked by his comment. "No worries, Sterling. I got it. One and done. Like it never happened."

His eyes were intense as they stared at me. "Good."

His gaze drifted down to my lips, and my hormones took notice, fluttering in anticipation. Inwardly, I told them to knock it off.

I turned my head to look out the window. How was it that my libido had a mind of its own? This man was rude and obnoxious, and any of the sexual chemistry I had felt before should have died out. So it made no sense that just a look, or his nearness, could make the desire flare up again. I realized that having him stay in my home to protect me could become a problem. He would be a constant source of irritation, and while my place was nice, it was difficult to find an area of it where I could be completely alone without knowing he was there. I needed a change of plan.

When we arrived at my apartment, I waved to Jonesy as he said hello but didn't stop to chat. Alex and I rode up the elevator and entered my apartment. I left Alex in the living room and went directly to my bedroom, taking out the bag I'd taken to Europe and dumping it out to repack it. Ten minutes later, I carried my bag out to the living room, finding Alex looking out the window.

"I've changed my mind. I want to go stay at my father's house."

He turned around, his body seemingly relaxed as he put his

hands in his pockets and looked at me. "Finally seeing reason, are you?"

My jaw tightened. Why did everything he said sound like he was talking to a petulant teenager?

"It'll be a whole hell of a lot easier to avoid you at my father's house."

His eyes narrowed as he studied me. "Worried about what might happen between us?"

Now why would he say something like that when in the car he was clear that nothing would happen and that what had happened was to never be mentioned again?

"You're not that appealing. You know, for an old man, you sure act like a teenage boy."

Triumph filled me as the smirk on his face faltered. "Now can we go, please?"

He gave me a curt nod then escorted me out of my apartment and back down to the street. On the way in the elevator, he was on his phone, presumably ordering another car. Within moments, one pulled up front, and he opened the door to let me in. My father didn't live too far, but with New York traffic, it was a good twenty minutes before Knightly let us in.

"Your father will be very pleased to hear that you've decided to stay here," Knightly said as he took my bag. "I will take this up to your room."

"I want to be up on the third floor."

Knightly stopped and looked at me. "That was your grandparents' place."

I nodded. "Yes, but they're not here anymore. Being on the third floor will be like having my own space. Plus, I can set up an office there for me to work." I slanted a gaze at Alex. Being on the third floor meant it would be easier to stay away from him as well, but I didn't say that. The quick flare of heat in his eyes told me he knew what I was thinking.

My father entered the foyer from his office. "Is it true you decided to stay here?"

Sometimes, I wondered if the house was wired for sound. But I imagine that Mrs. Tillis had overheard and had told my father I was planning to stay.

"Yes. But I want to stay on the third floor. I'll have my own space and a place to work."

Without hesitation, my father nodded and looked at Knightly. "Can you and Mrs. Tillis set that up?"

Knightly nodded. "Right away, sir." Knightly made his way up the stairs, where I imagined he'd run into Mrs. Tillis already making her way to the third floor.

My father looked at me like he used to when I was a kid and about to get into trouble. "I'm not happy to hear that you left here all alone. Especially right after it was made clear how much danger you could be in."

"Not could be. Is." Alex's voice was gruff.

My father looked at him, concern growing on his face. "What do you mean? What happened?" My father stepped up toward me, his eyes scanning me as if he was looking for a sign of injury.

I held my hand up. "I'm fine. I just got an ominous text message. But Mr. Sterling and his team have already examined my phone." Maybe by acting formal and distant, Alex's tendency to irritate me with his attitude and his sex appeal would lessen. "And I had Mr. Sterling take me to my apartment to pack. I plan to abide by whatever rules need to be set up to keep us safe."

The tension in my father's face lessened, but I wouldn't say there was relief. He looked at Alex. "I can't tell you how much it means to me that you are going to help us with this. And I know without a doubt that I can trust my daughter to your protection."

I rolled my eyes. "Yeah, he's quite a saint."

My father looked at me quizzically. I mustered a smile. "I'm going upstairs to get settled."

My father nodded. "I'll have Caroline make your favorite dinner." He looked at Alex. "You will join us, won't you? You're staying here, aren't you?"

Alex had an expression that looked like he had indigestion. "I'll stay here, but I'm not a guest, Henry. In order for me to do my job, I need to treat it like a job. I need to focus."

My father didn't like that answer. "You have to eat. Surely, you can have dinner with us."

I wanted to tell my father to let it go, but instead I made my way up the stairs to the third floor. We had an elevator, but if I was going to be stuck at my father's house for the time being, taking the stairs would give me exercise. My father had a small gym and even a lap pool, but I wasn't a gym or swim kind of girl. I would've much rather gone to the park and walked or ridden my bike. But that wasn't going to be an option, so the stairs would be it.

I entered the bedroom on the third floor as Mrs. Tillis was just finishing airing it out. "The room hasn't been used since . . . well . . . you know, since your grandparents died, so it's a little stuffy. But anything that you need to make this room feel more like yours, let me know."

"I will. Thank you, Mrs. Tillis."

She left, and I sank down onto the small bench at the end of the bed.

"You might be able to avoid me in the house, but don't get in your mind that you're going to sneak out of here and not have a problem."

Annoyed, I looked up to see Alex leaning against the door jamb with his arms folded across his chest. "You look like my dad."

It was petty, and to be honest, a little pervy, but it worked. Alex had that sick look on his face again.

"Why are you following me around? You're like a bad penny."

"That's right, I am. And I will be until the situation with Pitney is dealt with."

I stood and walked over to the door. His eyes stayed on mine. As I drew near, he inhaled a breath as if guarding himself from me. Interesting.

"I get it, Alex." I shut the door in his face.

9

Alex

She was a spoiled brat. This was exactly why I didn't like being a bodyguard for rich men's daughters.

You're such a fucking liar.

But lying to myself was easier than the truth. I was the one being the asshole because I knew it pissed her off and if I did that, she'd stay away. And the plan was working. I was relieved when she said she wanted to stay at her father's house, partly because I knew it would be easier to protect her there and partly because when I walked into her place and saw her everywhere in it, I knew it would be impossible for me to keep my hands to myself.

Of course, I couldn't just nod and agree to take her to her father's place. Instead, I made a dumbass retort. She was right, I was acting like a teenager. Did she catch on that I was a horny teenager?

When she retreated to her room, I told Henry that I wanted to get a layout of the house as part of my job. But the truth was that I wanted to see where she was going to be. I wanted to see her. God, I was totally fucked.

I prayed to God that with being in Henry's house and focusing on my job, I'd be distracted from the woman who was haunting my every fantasy. But I'd have to stop going up to see her on the third floor. And it absolutely meant no socializing. No dinners with the family.

The truth of the matter was that both Henry and Victoria were in serious trouble, and I needed to focus to keep them both safe.

WALLOWING in my own self-loathing and I suppose embarrassment at Victoria's calling me out and slamming the door in my face, I walked away from her room and set out to check the rest of the house. I grew up in an affluent family, but Henry's wealth dwarfed mine. Henry was the one percent of the one percent. The home was seven stories, including a garage basement located on Riverside Drive. It was on the corner, which meant it had three exposed sides. Front, side, and back. Then there were the shit-ton of windows. It could be a security nightmare, but over the years Henry and his family before him had taken measures to install state-of-the-art alarms, cameras, and other security measures.

I made my way through every nook and cranny on all floors and then returned to Henry's office. I liked adventure, and even danger, which was why I took the job I had. But neither Henry nor Victoria wanted the sort of danger that George Pitney was bringing to them. To be honest, I didn't want it either. Not for them or for me. It was time that I tried to talk sense into Henry.

"Do you have some time for us to talk about what's going on here?" I entered Henry's office and plopped myself down in the chair in front of his desk without waiting for an invitation.

He sat back in his chair, cocking his head to the side. "Something's got you upset."

I shrugged. "I've been through all the information we were able to get about the case against George and the threats against you, and now, today, Victoria."

Henry's eyes narrowed and his body tensed. "I'm glad I brought you in when I did."

"Henry, you're on a fool's errand here. One that will likely get you killed, and possibly Victoria too."

He gave me an annoyed glare. "I don't have much choice—"

"You do. You can let all this go. You told me that you believe there would be an arrest made within the week, but the only thing that they have on him that may, and I emphasize may, stick are fraud charges. I don't have to tell you that even if George is in prison, he can still get to you. Is that what you want? You want to die? For what?"

Henry bristled. "Someone has to stop him, and if someone with my resources can't do it, then no one will. This man cannot continue to get away with everything he does. I know that I am risking my life, but I also know that it needs to be done."

"And you're willing to risk Victoria's life?"

He turned away, his jaw tight. "I will do everything to keep Tori safe. That's why I brought you here." He turned his attention back to me. "You can do that, can't you?"

"For how long, Henry? This thing is not going to be over in a week. In fact, even if you put George in prison, this is never going to go away. You will always be unsafe, as well as Victoria. Is that what you want? To live the rest of your life having bodyguards and looking over your shoulder? Is that what you want for her?"

For a moment, I thought I'd reached him. But then he shook his head and looked at me intently. "I can't back down on this, Alex."

I stood, letting out a sigh. "I figured as much." I pulled out my phone as I turned to leave the room.

"Where are you going?"

"First, I'm going to ask my boss for more time. And then I'm going to get to work to figure out a way to get rid of George Pitney once and for all. If he doesn't get charged with something more serious like kidnapping or murder, you're never going to be free of him. And even then, I'm not sure you'll be free of him."

I reached the door and turned back. "You should really seriously think about the witness protection that you were offered."

He shook his head. "I can't abandon my company and all the people who work for me."

"What about Victoria?" For a man who was clearly devoted to his daughter, he was giving very little thought to how his mission to put Pitney away would impact her.

Pain filled his face. "If it is necessary for her to go in witness protection to guarantee her safety, I will support that." It was clear that he understood that if Victoria did that, he would never see her again.

"Do you think she'd do it?" I asked.

He shrugged but at the same time, shook his head. "I doubt it, but I don't know that she's ever been in a situation like this. She's smart and pragmatic, so maybe."

I headed out the back, onto the small terrace as I called Archer Graves in Los Angeles. Once Noel retired, Archer became my boss, and if I was going to be able to see this through for Henry and Victoria, I would need his permission. At least if I wanted to keep my job.

"Alex, how are you?"

"Can't complain."

"I understand you're in New York and have something going on with the George Pitney case."

I had to hand it to him, he kept his finger on the pulse of Saint Security. "That's why I'm calling. An old friend of mine has decided to take him on."

"Surely, you told him how dangerous that can be."

"I have, but he's adamant that he needs to follow through. And he's not wrong. He has the resources to take George on, but I've told him that chances are he's going to lose. I was hoping that I could get more time here to put things in place to keep him and his daughter safe."

"How much more time?"

"Six to eight weeks. Cuthbert is solid, and I think he can handle running the London office for that length of time."

There was a pause at the end of the line that made me uneasy. "I have concerns with the increase in work that has been coming into the London office. In fact, I was consulting with Noel about the possibility of expanding it."

"Like I said, Cuthbert can handle it." I knew Archer was a man with a wife and kids. Like Noel and Dax, Archer was bitten by the love bug, something I didn't understand and was thankful hadn't happened to me.

But I understood that family was important to these men, and I decided to take advantage of it. "Henry is the closest thing I have to a brother." It wasn't a lie. Henry had been there with me when I made the decision not to go into the family business and was disowned. And I didn't mean by offering a handout. I meant by encouraging me to pursue my dream. It made the fact that I had slept with his daughter so much worse. And the fact that I wanted to do it again, even knowing that who she was, made me a fucking pervert. "The point is, he's important to me, and I need to make sure that he and his daughter are safe."

"I doubt six to eight weeks are going to be enough. Chances are they're going to be in danger as long as George Pitney is living."

"I'm aware of that, but maybe by that time, we'll have a plan in place. Or maybe I can convince him and his daughter to go into witness protection."

There was another pause. "Okay. Six weeks. I'm assuming you're not doing this alone. You're building a team there in New York to help you, right?" Like a true businessman, Archer was thinking of the bottom line. I couldn't fault him for that. The work Saint Security did was expensive. Keeping up on technology, hiring the best of the best in all areas . . . it couldn't be done on a dime.

"Absolutely."

"Good. If there's anything you need on my end, let me know."

"The time is what I need now. Thanks."

When I hung up, I went back inside and found my way to the kitchen. It looked the same as I remembered back when Henry and I were in college and had gotten high on the rooftop terrace and then come down and eaten an entire pie.

As I entered, I saw their cook busy at the stove. At the table sat Knightly, Henry's Butler, and Mrs. Tillis, the housekeeper.

As I entered, Knightly stood. "Is there something I can help you with, Mr. Sterling?"

"I was checking on the guestroom."

Mrs. Tillis stood. "We set you up on the second floor, but we can move you up to the third—"

I shook my head. "I would like to be on the main floor."

The home was the most vulnerable on the main floor, but it had the added security of being two floors way from Victoria's bedroom.

Knightly and Mrs. Tillis looked at each other for a moment. "I'm sure that Mr. Banion would prefer that—"

"I'm not here as Henry's guest. I'm here to work. To keep him and his daughter and the rest of you safe. The best way for me to do that would be to have a room on the main floor. Can that be arranged?"

They both nodded.

"Of course," Mrs. Tillis said.

"You will be able to keep them safe, won't you?" Knightly asked. The guy looked too old to be working, but I knew the loyalty he had to Henry. It was the same loyalty I felt, except when I considered what I had done to his daughter.

"I'm going to do everything in my power to make sure that they're safe." If we survived this, it would be a fucking miracle.

Victoria

When I came down to dinner, I prepared myself to deal with Alex. There wasn't an extra place setting at the table, which told me my father hadn't been able to change Alex's mind and have him join us for dinner. I was relieved because I couldn't look at Alex and not be snippy with him. His attitude was maddening, even as I recognized that it had to be awkward for him. I mean, I got it. Alex had sex with his friend's daughter. I understood how creepy that might seem.

But I wasn't a child. I was a grown woman. And Alex was right in that had we known the connection between us, we probably wouldn't have had sex. We couldn't change the past. We had to simply move forward. It seemed to me we could do that without Alex being a jerk. Then again, for all I knew, that was his regular MO. In fact, it probably was as I recalled how he called me a brat before he even knew me on the airplane. Which once again begged the question. How had my father and Alex become friends?

"It's wonderful to have you home again, Tori," my father said, sitting at the head of the table while I sat along the side. "I wish it were under different circumstances, but—"

"Are you sure you know what you're doing, Dad? When I was at Saint Security today, I got the impression that taking on George Pitney was even more dangerous than I had originally thought."

My father extended his hand, putting it over mine and giving it a squeeze. "I'm very sorry to have brought you in on this. And I promise you, I'm going to do everything I can to keep you safe."

"What about you?"

My father's face turned determined. "Someone needs to stop him."

"And what if he stops you first? Then what? He'll still be doing all the things that he's doing, only you'll be gone and I'll be alone. You're the only family I have."

My father's expression filled with regret. "I know that, sweetheart, but I have to pursue this. Besides, you're not totally alone. You've got Knightly and Mrs. Tillis and Caroline."

I rolled my eyes. "I love them all, but they're not my family." I had never met my mother, and even now, I didn't know who she was or whether she was still alive. My father had said she didn't want to be a mother. He said he wanted me, but I suspected that was because he didn't want me to know that he'd been unsure. After all, he was only twenty-two, not in love with my mother, and from a family that would most likely feel shamed by the situation.

My grandparents' version was slightly different and clearly held a bias against my mother. They didn't think she was good enough for my father, and I suspected they paid her to continue the pregnancy and then to go away. I was fortunate that the love from my father was such that the idea of my mother abandoning me for freedom and money didn't impact my self-esteem. But it didn't mean that I wasn't, on occasion, curious about her. Right then wasn't that time. And even if I learned about her or met her, she wouldn't replace my father.

"My plan is to survive. And whether I do or I don't, you're going to live a productive life. Someday, you'll meet somebody and fall in love and have kids of your own."

I shook my head. "You know I don't believe in fairytales, Dad."

He laughed. "I'm not talking about fairytales. I'm talking about finding somebody you can build a life with."

"You didn't." I wasn't totally against marriage and family. It just wasn't part of my plans now.

My father's smile faltered and he looked down at his plate. "Are you settled on the third floor?"

I guess we were changing the subject. "Settled enough. It still smells like Grandmother's rose-scented lotion."

"We can have Mrs. Tillis make any changes that you like."

I shrugged as I mashed copious amounts of butter into my baked potato. "I don't mind it. Kind of makes me think of her."

My father arched eyebrow at me. "In a good or a bad way?" I understood where his question was coming from. My grandmother hadn't been the plump, cookie baking, spoil the grandchildren type. She'd been cool, aloof, elegant, and more concerned about appearance. But she was dedicated to her family, and when it was important, she had been there for me. She'd been the closest thing I'd had to a mother. Granted, many of the important aspects of maternal care were pawned off to Mrs. Tillis, like buying my first bra or teaching me how to use menstrual cycle products.

"Not bad, but hopefully, I won't have to stay too long."

My father feigned a pained expression.

"It's not that I don't like being here with you, Dad, but—"

He waved his hand as he swallowed his food. "I get it. You've got your own life. And I'm truly sorry to have inconvenienced you like this. But now that Alex and Saint Security are involved, I'm feeling more confident that George will be dealt with."

I took a sip of my water and studied my father. I wondered if he really believed what he was saying or if he was just trying to prevent me from worrying. "I hope you're right."

Knightly appeared, refilling our water glasses, and then disappeared into the kitchen again.

"How did you and Alex get to be friends, anyway?" I hoped my question sounded very nonchalant. It wasn't unreasonable for me to want to know about my father's friend, particularly since he was charged with protecting me, right? My question didn't reveal the dirty deeds I'd done on the airplane.

My father had a wistful smile as he held his wine glass, swirling the red liquid inside it. "Alex was my roommate in college." He didn't say more, but there was something in his expression that told me that he was going through a flood of memories of him as a young man with Alex.

My father had always seemed happy and he'd given me a good life, but sometimes, I wondered if he regretted becoming a father at such a young age. He was so young when I was born. He missed many years of sowing his oats. Not that my father never dated, because he did, but he was never in a long-term relationship with a woman. He never spoke ill of my mother to me, but I always wondered if whatever had happened between them was why he'd never married again. I couldn't imagine what that was since it seemed pretty clear I'd been the result of a short-term hookup.

Thinking of my father as a young man with Alex made me curious. "Did Alex know my mom?"

My father's brows rose in surprise. "No. Why would you ask that?"

I shrugged. "He knew you back when you were in college, and I figured that was when you met Mom."

"By the time I met your mom, Alex had left to join the military. Had he been there, things might've been . . . Well . . ."

I frowned, wondering what he wasn't telling me. "What?"

My father sipped his wine and then let out a sigh. "Had Alex been there, I probably wouldn't have been with your mother. But had I not met your mother, I wouldn't have you." He reached his hand out again, putting it over mine. "I know I sound like an old fuddy-duddy father, but you're the treasure of my life."

I smiled, turning my hand over to embrace his. "I love you too, Dad. But don't you ever wish you met someone else? You could have gotten married, maybe even had more kids. In fact, it's not too late. You're not too old."

He laughed. "Not too old. Thank you for that." He shook his head, his eyes casting downward to his plate, and for a moment, I thought I saw sadness cross his expression. "I just never met anyone with which that could happen."

I frowned because it seemed such an odd way to say he hadn't met a woman he felt he could marry. Had there been a woman, but for some reason they couldn't be together? I hoped that wasn't true because I wanted my father to be happy.

"Has Alex ever been married?" I held my breath for the answer and then chastised myself for caring.

My father laughed. "No. But Alex hasn't lived a life that's conducive to marriage and family." My father cocked his head and his eyes narrowed slightly. "I get the feeling you don't like Alex very much. Is everything all right?"

This time, I was the one who broke eye contact and looked down into my dinner. "Yeah, sure. He's just ... gruff, I guess."

"Yes, Alex is a little rough around the edges. You'd think he grew up on the mean streets of New York, but in fact, he's Tate Sterling's kid."

I looked up at him in surprise, although maybe I should've put two and two together. Sterling wasn't that common a name. "But he's not doing the family business?"

My father shook his head. "Alex has too much need for adventure and excitement to lead a corporate life. Tate disowned him when he decided to pursue his dream."

As much as I was irritated at Alex, I was sad to hear that his father had disowned him simply for following his dream.

"You're not going to disown me for not taking over the family business, are you?" I asked jokingly.

"There's nothing you could do that would make me stop loving you or want to disown you. Am I disappointed that you won't be following my footsteps? Maybe. But I am so proud of what you've done on your own, Tori. You've achieved much more than I ever did. I stepped into an already successful business. You've built yours from scratch."

I smiled with pride, loving that my father recognized my achievements.

Still, I sometimes felt guilty that I wasn't working with my father and planning to take over the company as I knew that was what would have made him the happiest.

"I know we've had a bit of an unconventional life, Tori, but I hope that you're happy."

"I am, Dad. I've had a wonderful life, unconventional or not." I thought of Samantha, who grew up in the traditional two-parent family, but I knew it had always been a contentious one. And now her mother was sick and her father had run off. "I told you I saw Samantha this morning, didn't I?"

My father blinked. I guess the change of subject caught him off guard. He gave a curt nod and went back to cutting his steak. "You did. How is she doing?"

"I don't really know, actually. Probably not very well. It sounds like her mom is really sick."

My father nodded.

"Did you hear her father ran off? Who does that?"

My father's eyes remained downcast. "We don't really know what goes on in people's homes. Sometimes, people have to make tough decisions that others don't understand."

Thank goodness there wasn't food in my mouth because my jaw dropped. "You think that there could be a good reason that Samantha's father would leave her mother after her being diagnosed with an illness?"

My father's head jerked up and he blinked. It was such a strange reaction. Not just that he would think there was any situation in which a man leaving his deathly ill wife could be justified, but also because since college, when Samantha and I became friends, my father had been very helpful to her. Not only had she done her senior internship in his office, but he'd also helped her get a good paying job when she graduated. I wasn't too thrilled that the job was all the way across the country in Washington state, but still, he'd been very good to her. So why was he acting like this?

Finally, my father pulled it together. "Of course not. But we all know that Carl Layton was an A-1 asshole. Why Gwen married him, I have no clue. But again, that just goes to show you don't know what's going on with people and the decisions they make."

I wasn't sure what to make of my father's response. I was beginning to think I had walked into an alternative world, one in which I gave in to a sexy older man on an airplane, ended up mixed up with a corrupt businessman with a penchant for making people go missing, and my best friend and father were acting weird.

After dinner, I headed back up to my room expecting Alex to be lurking about. I tried to ignore the disappointment when I discovered that he wasn't.

Once in my room, I changed into yoga pants and an oversized T-shirt, then I padded across the hall to what had been my grandfather's room to use as an office.

I'd come to the realization that the situation with George was probably going to last a whole lot longer than the week my father was expecting. I loved my father to bits, but I didn't want to move home permanently. Especially since it was clear that I couldn't go anywhere. Anything I did, I'd have to have Alex in tow, and the man was too infuriating to hang around.

I opened my laptop and began doing searches on George Pitney. I wanted to get a better idea of what my father was dealing with. Interestingly enough, the information that revealed just how serious a danger my father was in came from articles published in his media outlets. No wonder George felt threatened.

I scraped my hands over my face as my worst fears came true. Whatever was going on with George Pitney wasn't going to be resolved in a week. And worse, as things went on, my father was likely going to be in more danger. I wanted to march downstairs and tell him to back off, but I knew he wouldn't. My father had dedicated his life to business, and in particular, the news side with a mission to disseminate truth, no matter how difficult it was. He'd see it as his duty to expose George and help put him away.

I closed my laptop and made my way out of the room.

"I was beginning to think you tried to escape again."

I startled, letting out a small yelp. Then I turned a harsh glare onto Alex. I wanted to say something rude to him, but what was the point?

Instead, I focused on what I felt was really important. I marched up to him, jabbing him in the chest with my forefinger, ignoring the zap of electricity that shot through my hand. "You need to talk my dad out of this thing with George Pitney."

Alex's hand wrapped around mine but didn't push it away. Instead, he held onto it, resting it against his chest. It made my insides go soft.

"I already have. You know your father. He's going to see this thing through."

Tears welled in my eyes because I knew that my father's mission would likely get him killed. But I didn't want Alex to see them. He'd use them against me. So I did my best to hold them back. "You need to try harder."

"He's more likely to listen to you than to me."

The truth was, my father wouldn't listen to either of us.

"He's the one who needs your protection," I said, trying to avoid the lure of sinking into Alex's strength.

He gave his usual curt nod. "He has extra protection. But that text you received today says you need it too. I can see that you now understand how serious this is."

I don't know if it was because Alex was still holding my hand or because for a moment he seemed to be normal, even sympathetic. Whatever it was, I leaned forward, resting my forehead against his chest. "He's all I have."

Alex's hand cradled my cheek, tilting me to look up at him. "I'm going to do everything I can to make sure that doesn't change."

Our gazes caught, and it reminded me of those military movies when the fighter jets track and then lock onto an object to shoot it down. Our eyes locked just like that. I don't know why, but the moment made me think of our interlude on the airplane. He hadn't been tender on the flight like he was now. But standing this close, our eyes unyielding as they stared at each other, I felt that similar pull toward him that I'd felt on the plane.

Down the hall, the sound of the elevator arriving at the floor broke the trance.

"Fuck." Alex released my hand and stepped away.

His reaction to the elevator's arrival brought me embarrassment and pain. "You sure know how to talk to a girl." I turned to head into my room just as the elevator doors opened and Mrs. Tillis made an appearance.

She looked between the two of us. "Is everything all right?"

I nodded. "My babysitter was just checking in on me."

Alex let out a low growl and then turned and headed toward the stairs.

"He's much different from how I remember him," Mrs. Tillis said as she approached me carrying a set of towels.

"Oh? Did he used to have a personality?"

Mrs. Tillis looked at me quizzically as if she was surprised by the terseness of my voice.

"Alex was always outgoing, looking for the next adventure. But maybe in his line of work, he's learned that not all adventures are exciting. Or maybe he's just worried about your father."

I entered my room with Mrs. Tillis following. "What were they like?"

Mrs. Tillis laughed and shook her head. "About what you would expect two young men from extremely wealthy families to be."

"Womanizers?"

She nodded. "Yes, and parties and extravagant excursions that usually involved some sort of danger."

It was hard to see my father doing anything dangerous. He was always practical and level-headed. But maybe that was because he had to be as he took over a multibillion-dollar company and raised a daughter. Was that why he was going after George? For the element of danger?

"I brought you some more towels. Tomorrow, if you like, we can talk about the rooms and setting them up for your comfort."

Normally, I would have told her that we didn't need to do that since I didn't plan to be here very long. But now that I had a better understanding of the situation, I knew that my stay was going to be longer than planned.

"That would be nice, Mrs. Tillis. Thank you."

"Is there anything else you need?" she asked after she put the towels into my bathroom.

I shook my head. "No. I think I'm just going to read and go to bed."

"Well, good night, then."

"Good night."

When she left, I went into the bathroom, washing up, and then I put on my pajamas and climbed into bed. I didn't want to fall asleep worrying about my father. But as I pushed him out of my head, Alex occupied the space. I tried to push him aside as well, but it was no use. He showed up in my dreams. He was tender like he'd been in the hall tonight, but we were back on the plane. It wasn't long before the dam broke and lust flooded, and he was doing delicious, sinful things to me.

11

Alex

I wish I knew what it was about Victoria that had me precariously close to kissing her while her father worked just a few floors away. Was it the taboo situation of my best friend's daughter? No, because that was the part that made my stomach roil. It made me feel like a fucking pervert. Added to that was the ultimate betrayal of my friend. And yet there I was in the hallway, trying to comfort her as she realized just how much danger she and her father were in. She looked up at me with her large almond-shaped eyes, and I felt myself tumble into them. Why? What was it about her? I thanked the god who was clearly punishing me that Mrs. Tillis arrived when she did. A second later, I would've had my tongue in Victoria's mouth and my body pressed against hers, lost in a desire that I didn't want to have and yet desperately wanted to quench.

As I trotted downstairs, I wondered if perhaps jet lag was the source of my weakness around Victoria. After all, it was after midnight in London now.

I headed to a small nook off the kitchen that I'd taken over as my command center and contacted members of the team to see where things were on Project Keep-Henry-From-Getting-Killed. All the reports back were as they should be. The exterior of the home was secure, and we had two men in place watching twenty-four, seven. We even had eyes on George, although that wouldn't do us much good because George always had somebody else do his dirty work.

I learned the source of the text to Victoria came from a burner phone that was no doubt sitting at the bottom of the Hudson River now. The latest report on the fraud case against Pitney was that the district attorney was vacillating on whether to move forward with an indictment. On the one hand, I didn't blame him for questioning whether to proceed. In my experience, prosecuting attorneys didn't like to indict if they weren't sure it would result in a conviction. Pitney was a slimy, slippery fuck who over the last two decades had been able to escape a myriad of potential charges.

On the other hand, with Henry and Victoria's lives on the line, I didn't want a weak-dicked prosecutor to back off when they should have the same determination to put Pitney away as Henry had.

I made a final loop through the house going top to bottom, avoiding the urge to check in on Victoria when I hit the third floor. With everything looking solidly secure, I headed back to my room. A century ago, the room was where the butler or housekeeper would stay, but today, Knightly and Mrs. Tillis had rooms several floors above.

The room had a bed, dresser, and sink, although the bathroom was outside the room, off the kitchen. I stripped down and put on a pair of running shorts, not sleeping naked as I'd like, just in case I had to get up in the middle of the night. I didn't need Knightly or Mrs. Tillis or Henry to see me running around buck naked. And of course, if I saw Victoria, there was a real chance that I would get a boner, which also wouldn't be good. That was my last thought as I drifted to sleep.

For three days, the routine was much the same. Wake up early and check the house, and then check in with the team. Luckily, Victoria had no interest in going anywhere, and a part of me wondered if that was because she didn't want to have me escort her everywhere she went. Whatever the reason, I was relieved. It gave me more time to work with the team on finding a way to get rid of George Pitney.

After a full day of working and feeling like I wasn't making any headway, I would check the house once again and then head to bed where Victoria would enter my dreams. It was fucking embarrassing to have wet dreams like I was a horny teenager. Two nights, I woke up before the final climax, in which case I headed to the shower and took care of business. But yesterday, I woke up ejaculating in my shorts. The woman was driving me mad.

This morning, I woke with a hard-on and dealt with it in the shower, fantasizing about Victoria's luscious lips around my dick. I did the morning check of the house, contacted everyone on the team, and then headed back to the kitchen where Henry's cook served me the most delicious scrambled eggs I'd ever had, along with toast made from sourdough bread and a dark brew of fancy coffee. I was thinking about the possibility of hiring a cook for myself when Knightly stepped into the kitchen.

"Ms. Banion would like to talk with you."

"About what?" My tone was harsher than it should have been, but I was finally beginning to think I'd manage this case if Victoria stayed away from me. For the first time in three days, she was summoning me.

Knightly arched a brow. "I'm sure I don't know. She's in the dining room with her father."

It was safe for me to see her with Henry around unless there was something about the way I looked at her that gave away all the dirty dreams I was having about her.

I rose from my chair and began to pick up my plate.

"I'll take care of that, Mr. Sterling." Carolyn rushed over and picked up my plate and cup.

"Thank you." I headed out of the kitchen and into the dining room. I entered, keeping my eyes on Henry. "You needed me?"

"Not me. Tori. I've tried to talk her out of it, but she's insistent."

And so now it began. Now that she'd been homebound for three days and was going stir crazy, she was going to become the difficult spoiled child I'd worried about.

"I want to go visit my friend Samantha. And on the way, I would like to get some flowers, maybe some take-out that can be frozen for dinners, and a toy for her little boy."

I wanted to say no and leave it at that, but if Victoria was anything like Henry, it would be a waste of my breath. "Give me a list with the flowers, food, and toy that you want, and I'll have somebody pick them up and—"

"It's not a very good gift if I don't pick it myself."

"It's also not a very good gift if your blood is all over it because Pitney's guy got to you," I snapped. Both Henry and Victoria flinched.

Henry frowned. "It's a little rough, don't you think?"

I turned my attention to Henry. "You're paying me to keep her safe. I have assessed the situation and determined that the two of you are neck-deep in trouble. You're asking me and my men to put their necks on the line for you. If we're going to do it, we're going to do it in a way that minimizes the risk, not just to you, but to us as well."

The expression on both their faces told me that they had never considered the risk to me and my men.

Henry turned to Victoria. "Do it his way, Tori. I'm sorry it has to be like this, and I will find a way to make it up to you, but for now, we should abide by what Alex tells us."

She didn't like it, but she nodded. "I'll make a list and have Knightly deliver it to you. I'd like to leave by ten." I checked my watch. It gave me just under two hours to collect all the items she wanted. The fact that we were in New York, and Henry was a prominent man, meant that we could probably arrange to get everything we needed, ordered and delivered to us within the timeframe.

Two hours later, I escorted Victoria down the elevator to the basement garage and into the car I'd arranged through Saint Security.

Victoria sat beside me, her hands in her lap and her eyes facing forward. She was beautiful and stoic, and I had this urge to break through the cool aloofness she was showing by kissing her. But of course, that would be stupid.

"What time is your friend expecting us?" I asked.

Victoria shrugged.

I arched a brow. "She is expecting us, isn't she?"

Victoria looked at me. "I think your only job is to make sure I get there safely. You don't need to know all the little details."

This oppositional, defiant attitude of hers shouldn't have been such a turn-on. I turned my upper body to face her. "Except it is. I sent men down to her place right after you told me where we were going to check the location because it is my job to know the details. How can I keep you safe if I don't know the details?"

She attempted to glare at me, but I could see that she recognized that she'd been wrong.

I settled back in the seat, clasping my hands together in my lap. "Luckily for you, no one knowing that we're coming is a good thing. "

"How's that?"

"They won't have told anybody that you're coming. You only told me and your father and the house staff, and unless they are in cahoots with George, they're not going to tell him we're going."

"So I did good."

I shrugged. "For you and me, yeah. I'm not so sure your friend will feel the same."

Samantha Layton's family was like mine. Wealthy, but not stratospheric rich like Henry. I would've been surprised that Gwen Layton stayed in her home after her husband left her for a younger woman. But the information I received said she was gravely ill, and moving was a bitch under the best of times. My report also told me that Samantha had been working out in Washington state until her mother became ill, at which time she returned to New York. She had a son, but no one was listed as the father on his birth certificate. I was sure Victoria would think my knowing that was too invasive, but it was my job to make sure there wasn't any sort of crazy conspiracy working against her and Henry. For all I know, George could have been the kid's father.

"How well do you know Samantha?" I asked because my research also told me that they'd been out of touch for a few years. Not that it necessarily meant anything. Henry and I were frequently out of touch, but our friendship was always intact.

She slanted her gaze at me. "Is this something that you have to know to do your job?"

"Maybe."

"We met in college. We roomed together for a while. And if you're worried about her being a danger, I think she's all right. She interned at Dad's company for a while. He even helped her get her job. And now she's home taking care of her sick mom. I think I'm going to be safe."

She was probably right. The fact that Henry knew her, and helped her, went a long way toward making me feel more secure about this visit. I didn't know Victoria well enough to know how well she picked her friends. All I knew was she was Henry's daughter and was willing to fuck a stranger on an airplane.

We arrived at the house and her driver pulled to the curb. We all exited the car. The driver pulled all our items out of the trunk. We bought enough stuff that the three of us were needed to carry it all to the door.

As we walked up the steps, I scanned the area, noting the two Saint Security cars I'd arranged to have on site.

Victoria knocked on the door, and we waited several minutes before a middle-aged woman answered. She showed no recognition of Victoria, which to my mind was a good sign since she'd been hired only eight months ago. Had she recognized Victoria, I'd have been suspicious.

"Can I help you?" she asked.

Victoria flashed a stellar smile, and I had a moment to feel jealous of this woman getting this blast of sunshine. Even in the moments when Victoria and I were getting along, she hadn't smiled at me like that.

Jesus fuck. Why did I care?

"I'm Tori Banion, a friend of Samantha's. I wanted to stop by to say hello and bring some things for them." She motioned to me and the driver holding the bulk of the items we were bringing. I noted how she'd referred to herself as Tori. I called her Victoria, but maybe I should call her by her nickname. No. In my mind, she was Victoria. Beautiful, regal, and mother fucker, I needed to stop thinking of her like that.

"Did you have an appointment?" the woman asked.

"No, I know I'm being rude just dropping in like this."

"Who's at the door, Marie?" A woman with long blonde hair and large green eyes that almost looked like they belonged on a manga character stepped up next to Maria.

Recognition came to her eyes, but her reaction wasn't happiness at seeing her friend on the doorstep. I couldn't quite decide whether she was annoyed or nervous. It had to be annoyed because why would she be nervous unless she knew the danger Victoria and Henry were in?

"Tori?" Samantha's eyes moved from her to me and the driver, and then back to Tori. "What are you doing here?"

"I come bearing friendship and some gifts. I wanted to see you and to help if I can."

All of a sudden, a child's head pressed between Samantha and Maria. Victoria squatted down and leaned forward toward the boy. "Hi, Pax. How are you?"

"Did you bring me something too?"

"Paxton!" Samantha put her arm around the boy. "I'm sorry. He doesn't understand that's bad manners."

Victoria kept her eyes on the boy. "Of course, I brought you something. I brought all of you something." Victoria lifted her gaze to her friend, and I could see concern and maybe confusion on her face.

"I will make some tea. I think it would be nice for Ms. Samantha and Pax to have a friend over." Maria stepped away from the door. Samantha watched her, and I got the feeling she felt betrayed by the act. I was pretty certain Samantha didn't want to visit. But there was no easy way of getting out of it, and clearly, she knew it as she stepped back, holding the door open.

We all stepped forward. I set the gifts in the foyer and took the bags of food from the driver, letting him go. Another woman arrived and took the food from me.

Samantha looked at me.

"This is my dad's friend, Alex Sterling."

She didn't explain why I was there. The fact that she didn't introduce me as her bodyguard indicated she didn't want her friend to know.

Normally, I might've hung around the perimeter while they visited, but in order to make it look less weird and less like I was protecting her, I stayed with Victoria like we were friends hanging out. But that was still creepy, wasn't it? Henry's friend hanging out with his daughter?

If Samantha thought it was strange, she didn't say anything and instead led us to the formal living room and offered us a seat. A few moments later, Maria arrived with tea, serving us as Victoria and Samantha engaged in small talk. It was a reminder of why I had chosen a different life path. It looked excruciatingly painful to pretend to be polite when you didn't want to be. I felt bad for Victoria who clearly wanted to reconnect with her friend, but so far, Samantha didn't seem to want the same.

12

_____

Victoria

Alex was right in that it was rude for me to show up at Samantha's house without calling first. And it had been rude for me not to take the hint that she didn't want visitors.

I hadn't called because I wanted to help her and had the feeling that she would've refused. My not taking the hint to leave was selfish. After seeing her in the bakery the other day, I realized how much I missed our friendship. I justified my selfishness by telling myself that she needed a friend too, and I wanted to be there for her.

What I hadn't considered was how to explain Alex being with me. Saying he was my father's friend didn't make a lot of sense. Why would I be hanging out with my dad's friend? But she didn't question it. Instead, we sat in the living room while I gave Paxton his gift, a large dump truck, and the flowers to Samantha and a bouquet for her mother too.

For a short time, as our conversation was little more than small talk, I wondered if I had forgotten an argument between us. I couldn't figure out why she seemed so distant. She was like a different person.

Was it me or had something else caused her change? It made me wonder what happened to her in Washington. Had she been in an abusive relationship? Maybe her job sucked? I knew that a life filled with negativity day after day could wear a person down. Had that happened to her?

I reminded her of the fun things that we'd done in college, and by the end of our visit, while she wasn't the woman I'd remembered, she was smiling. When it was time for me to leave, I let her know that I understood the challenge she was facing now, but anything she needed, I would help her with. She initiated the hug as I left, and it alleviated the concern I had for showing up so rudely.

During the visit, it had almost been like Alex wasn't there. He remained standing near a window but was quiet. But because he was behind Samantha, I was pretty sure she forgot that he was there until we left.

Alex escorted me to the car and helped me in before sliding in next to me. The driver pulled away from the curb and headed back toward my father's house.

"Do you think people can change?" I asked Alex.

"You mean like going to therapy?"

"I mean, can life change people? I know that extreme situations like trauma can change people, but what about everyday living?"

Alex thought for a moment. "I imagine daily life could create a bigger change than therapy."

I looked at him. "What do you mean?"

"Well, daily life is insidious, isn't it? Challenges or difficulties don't seem like a big deal, but day after day, they can have an impact. The change happens without noticing. Therapy involves a person wanting to change, but most people have difficulty changing on purpose."

I nodded in agreement.

"I take it Samantha isn't the same person you used to know."

"She's not. She used to be outgoing and vivacious. It makes me wonder what her life was like in Washington. And now, she's having to raise her child on her own and deal with her sick mother and the fact that her father abandoned them."

"It can't be easy. But I think she got the message that you are here for her."

I looked at him as hope filled my chest. "You think so? I really hope so."

Alex's hand covered mine and gave it a squeeze. I looked at our touching hands and then up at him, surprised.

He looked at me and then down at his hand, releasing it almost as if he hadn't known he did it. He cleared his throat. "I think your visit meant a lot to her."

I was still wondering about Alex's gesture when we arrived home. He immediately went to see my father, and I headed back to the kitchen because I smelled the scent of chocolate chip cookies. I'd just snagged one that had come out of the oven while Caroline was in the pantry when Knightly appeared.

"Your father would like to meet with you."

I broke my cookie in half and handed Knightly half. "You always sound so serious, Knightly. I think you need a cookie."

He held his hands up in surrender, refusing the cookie. "When Caroline discovers a cookie is gone, I do not want chocolate on my breath to incriminate me."

I laughed and popped the other half of the cookie in my mouth. "Your loss."

I headed out of the kitchen and to my father's office. He was sitting at his desk while Alex was standing over by the window, his arms crossed and a scowl on his face. This couldn't be good.

"You wanted to see me?"

My father let out a long sigh and stood, coming around his desk. His hand gestured toward the couch, indicating I should sit. He sat next to me, taking my hand.

"I need to go out of town for a few days. I'll be leaving tonight."

My brows drew together, and I looked over at Alex to get some idea of what that meant. I turned my attention back to my father. "Are you going into hiding?"

"He should," Alex grumbled.

My father interrupted him. "No. I need to go for business. The Los Angeles office needs me to deal with a few issues."

"Is that safe?" This time when I looked at Alex, I was hoping that he would intervene and tell my father that he needed to stay put until George Pitney was dealt with. From Alex's expression, I figured he had tried, but my father was being obstinate.

I squeezed my father's hand. "If you're going to deal with Pitney, you have to focus. This isn't something you can compartmentalize."

"I know that, Tori. But I have a business to run. We've got thousands of employees who are dependent on my keeping the company running. I'll be safe. I've arranged for extra security while I travel and while I'm in Los Angeles."

"You'll be safer if you stay here. Victoria would be safer if you stayed here as well."

"What does that mean?" I asked Alex.

"The best way to get to your father is through you. But George isn't an idiot. He knows that as long as you two are together, he can't get to you without bringing suspicion on himself."

I swallowed the fear that rose from my gut.

"He's going to look suspicious either way," my father snapped.

"I'm not sure if you've noticed, Henry, but several people have gone missing when they've taken on Pitney. And while suspicion is on him, they haven't been able to prove anything. New York is a big, dangerous city, and there could be all sorts of reasons Tori might go missing."

"That's why I need you to stay put while I'm gone," my father said to me. His eyes held mine with an intensity I'd never seen before. I wanted to ask him to stay for me. Not just for my safety, but for his as well. But I knew my father. He had a duty to the company and to me, and he was doing his best to live up to both.

"You've been doing a great job abiding by the security measures, Tori, and I know it's a huge inconvenience, but while I'm gone, I need you to stay in the house. Anything you need, Knightly or Mrs. Tillis can get for you. Or Alex can arrange to have it delivered."

I didn't like the idea of staying cooped up in the house. That was part of the reason I went to see Samantha today.

I nodded because I didn't want to add extra stress to my father's concerns.

"You know you're not the center of the universe, Henry."

Both our heads whipped around to look at Alex. The scowl was etched deep in his face.

My father bristled. "I never said I was."

"You didn't say it, but you act like it. You're not the only man who can bring George Pitney down."

"But I'm the only one who seems willing to do it," my father charged back.

"Right, at the risk of your daughter's life. Seriously, Henry, it's almost like it's more important for you to put Pitney away than to protect your daughter."

Ah . . . I wasn't sure what to do as my father and Alex's argument escalated.

"I'm doing this to protect my daughter and all the other daughters. Plus, you know, at this point, no matter what I do, Victoria is going to be a target. I have to end him."

"Then hire a fucking hitman."

My brows shot up to my hairline, and I looked at Alex, wondering if that was the sort of thing he and Saint Security did.

Then I looked at my father, wondering if that was the sort of thing that he would do. Would he hire someone to kill George Pitney? I didn't like George and he scared me to death, but hire someone to murder him?

My father's face reddened in anger. He shot up from the couch. "I'm not like you, Alex."

"Maybe you should be because you're putting everyone in danger. You're sitting here asking your daughter to be a good little girl and not leave the house when that is the same directive that I and everyone at Saint Security have given you now that the DA isn't so sure he's going to charge Pitney. But for some reason—"

"I have a business to run. I have people who count on me."

"That's right, and one of them is sitting right next to you. You're going to toss her under the bus so you can go to Los Angeles?"

I stood on wobbly legs, feeling like I was witnessing something I shouldn't be. I almost wondered if there was something deeper going on than the surface level argument about whether or not my father was being unreasonable.

"I'm just going to give you two space to work this out."

My father reached out and took my arm. "I'm sorry for this, Tori. Tell me that you understand what I'm doing."

I nodded because I did understand. I didn't agree with him, but I understood. "I know you'll do what you feel you need to do. I'm going to go upstairs now because I have my own business to run." I cocked my head to the side. "You'll let me know when you leave?"

My father pulled me into a hug. "Of course I will, sweetheart." He kissed me on the side of the cheek. "Thank you for understanding."

I gave him another nod, and as I turned to leave his office, I glanced over at Alex. He was watching me intently, but I couldn't decide if he was upset that I wasn't pushing back against my father, like he did, or just angry in general. It didn't matter. Nothing was going to change the situation. My father was going to take this trip, and I was going to be here, home alone with Alex.

At least I knew I was safe. One thing that I learned from this discussion was that Alex was willing to kill to keep me safe.

13

Alex

I knew why Victoria didn't stand up to her father. She knew he was hard-headed and determined. So did I, but that wasn't going to stop me from trying to pound some sense into him.

Henry knew a little bit of my work between the time I left the military and Noel changed the business from mercenary work to security. But he never asked me about it and I assumed that was because he didn't want to hear the unsavory things that I had done. Had I killed anybody? Yes. But the only one who was caught by surprise by their demise was a bigger asshole than George Pitney. The others died because they were trying to kill me. Luckily for me, I won. And if someone tried to get into Henry's place and get to Victoria, I would kill them too.

But until this moment, my work in my past had never come between us. Henry had hired me because of my work, but his comment about his not being like me made it clear that he held judgment about it. I decided to call him on that.

"You may not like the work I've done, Henry, but don't pretend like that's not the exact reason you brought me in."

He turned his attention back to me, running fingers through his hair. He looked at me with an expression of defeat. "You're right, Alex. But my only request is that you keep Victoria safe. Whatever is involved to do that, I'm one hundred percent in on it."

I interpreted that to mean he was okay with my murdering anybody who got too close to Victoria.

"But I won't beat George by becoming like him."

I nodded that I understood what he was saying. And the truth was, I wasn't advocating for his hiring a hitman, although now that I had thought about it, it wasn't such a bad idea. My goal in saying he should hire a hitman had been to point out that from now on, Henry and Victoria would always be living with George's shadow behind them. It didn't matter if he was in prison.

"If you will excuse me, I need to pack," Henry said, clearly done with the conversation.

I didn't believe him. I was pretty sure Knightly or Mrs. Tillis had already packed his bags, but I nodded again and then exited his office. I headed straight to the nook in the kitchen where I got in touch with my team to review Henry's latest plans.

For a moment, I considered going with Henry to protect him, but when I figured out that Ian would be the one to come over and watch Victoria, I nixed that idea. Truthfully, it was probably better for Ian to go with Henry. He was young and had come from the California office, which meant he knew the landscape and the other people at Saint Security in Los Angeles. At least that was the excuse I told myself. I also had noted in Ian's profile that while he had done good security work, he'd never been in a life or death scrape. I couldn't trust that if shit went down with Victoria, he would be able to respond by taking a life or giving his life if necessary.

While all those reasons were true, I couldn't deny that I didn't like the idea of Victoria being cooped up here with Ian. It was stupid. It was the exact reason I should be the one to leave with Henry. That woman was going to be the death of me.

"If Banion really wants to Stop Pitney, this could be a good time," Dax said as we discussed the new situation.

"How's that?" I asked even though I was pretty sure Dax was thinking that with Henry around, Victoria would be vulnerable, something Pitney might take advantage of.

"Knowing Pitney, the way to stop him is through Henry's daughter—"

"No. I'm not using Victoria as bait."

Dax was silent for a moment. "I know you're friends, but you know as well as I do that they'll always be targets as long as Pitney is a free man."

Or dead.

"It's sounding more and more like the D. A. isn't going to indict," Dax finished.

"Has he been bought?"

"More likely threatened. We're looking to see if either is in play. Until then, we need something more significant to get him on."

"It won't be from a move on Victoria." I was a man willing to risk a lot, but not that. Not her. Henry wouldn't forgive me if I fucked up and something happened to her. The burn in my gut said the guilt would ruin me.

"We need something. Elliott will pull the team out. You know he will."

"Not protection." As long as Henry paid, he could retain our security services. I wondered how Henry would feel about bodyguards for the rest of life. He was lucky he had the money to afford it. For Victoria too, although I couldn't see her living a small life.

"No, but—"

"Keep men on George and his men. They'll fuck up."

Dax was quiet. "Okay. But this is a tenuous situation."

"I know. Thanks for helping me out. Is your family upset about your working during your visit? "

"This was a working visit, so no. But I leave next week, and Elliott is already vacillating on the scope of this case."

I ended the call with Dax as Knightly entered my work area.

"Mr. Banion is leaving. He'd like a word with you."

I wanted to be petty and tell him I was too busy trying to keep him and Victoria safe, but I mustered enough maturity to meet with Henry.

I found him down in the garage. Ian was there, looking attentive, his eyes scanning the private garage. Knightly put Henry's suitcase in the trunk of the car my team arranged to drive Henry to a private airport. Who I didn't see was Victoria.

Henry turned to me, letting out a long sigh. "I said some harsh things. I'm sorry."

I nodded. "I said them too, and I meant them."

"Yes, I know. You're doing what I asked you to do and I'm making your job harder. "

I decided not to remind him of the danger he'd brought on all of us, including Victoria and my team. Instead, I needed him to understand the gravity of the situation. "Henry, this thing with Pitney isn't going to happen like you want."

"We'll talk about it when I get back in a week."

"A week? I thought you said a few days?" I gave the man an inch and he took a mile.

"I need that much time to make plans that will allow me to work more from home. This will keep the business going and allow us to focus on putting Pitney away."

"And if Pitney doesn't go away? I won't be here forever, Henry."

"I appreciate that you're here now."

He shook my hand and climbed into the car.

"Ian," I called before he got into the vehicle.

"Sir."

"Do your best to rein him in, okay? Don't let him do something stupid. "

"I'll do my best."

"Are you in touch with Archer?" I knew all the plans were in place to protect Henry, but I wanted to make sure Ian was on top of it all.

"Yes. We've got men ready there as well."

I nodded. "Good. Safe travels." I watched as a Saint Securely driver, Ian, and Henry drove out of the garage.

"You should have made him stay," Knightly said.

I glowered at him. "I made an effort. How about you?"

He sniffed. "It's not my place."

"Did you tell Victoria to stop him? Because she didn't."

"That's not my place either."

My irritation at Knightly was partly because he was right. I should have made Henry stay. But short of tying Henry up, there was little I could do to stop him.

Back upstairs, I did a quick tour of the house, making sure everything was secure. Entering the kitchen, I found Mrs. Tillis preparing a tray as Caroline cooked.

"Tori is going to eat in her office," she said.

"Is she okay?"

"She's worried about her father, but she's strong."

I nodded. "I can take that up. I need to check in with her, anyway."

"Are you sure?"

"Yes." I smiled in case I was still glowering and that was why she was uncertain.

"And how about you, Mr. Sterling? Why don't you eat with us?"

"You don't have to—"

"I want to. Please." Mrs. Tillis looked at me with hopeful eyes. How could I say no to that?

"Alright, then. Thank you. Just let me bring this to Victoria." I picked up the tray and carried it to the elevator, worried I'd spill something if I took the stairs.

I exited on the third floor and started toward Victoria's room before remembering she was in her office. Shifting direction across the hall, I leaned into the door. "Victoria? I've got your dinner."

A few moments later, the door opened. "Roped into more duties?" She held the door open.

"I volunteered. I needed to check in with you, anyway." I set the tray on a small table in the sitting area of the bedroom. It had been Henry's father's, I think. The large, four-poster bed filled much of the room. There was also an armoire and a dresser. In the window seat sat Victoria's computer, suggesting she wasn't using the table to work . . . at least not today.

"Worried I was going to take off like my father?"

"Not at the moment." I watched her for a moment as she picked up a cooked carrot, wrapping her lips around it as she bit it in half. The images that came to my mind were dirty and forbidden.

I shifted, telling my dick to settle down. "You didn't see your dad off."

She shrugged. "He came by and said his goodbye. I got the feeling he didn't want me there when he left. Like maybe he wanted to talk to you alone."

I nodded.

"Things were heated between you two before. Were you able to kiss and make up?"

The word kiss had me looking at her lush lips. *Fuck! Knock it off, Sterling.* "We sorted things."

"Oh?"

"He said he was sorry for what he's said and I told him I wasn't."

She arched a brow as she took another bite of her carrot.

"I don't mince words. Everything I said was the truth."

She sighed. "He can be stubborn. Was he so hard-headed when you were younger?"

I hated being reminded that I was so much older than her. "I don't know that I'd say hard-headed, but he always had a strong sense of right and wrong."

"And you don't?"

I studied her, wondering what she thought of my less than stellar character. "Right and wrong is usually a matter of perspective."

"He thinks he's right to take this trip and you don't because of the danger."

"Life isn't so black and white. It's filled with gray."

She took another bite of carrot and my dick was about ready to pop his head out from the waistband of my pants.

"I should go. Your food is getting cold." I'd just made it to the door. "Alex?"

I turned, surprised to see she'd come after me, meeting me at the door.

"Yeah?"

Her eyes were wide. Her scent wrapped around me. My mind told me to step away, but I stayed put.

"Do you really think my father should have Pitney killed?"

"I was just pointing out that the problem with Pitney isn't going away even if he is arrested."

Her teeth sank into her bottom lip. Jesus fuck, how much I wanted taste her mouth.

"Would you kill someone if asked?"

Unable to stop myself, I hooked my finger under her chin and then rubbed my thumb over her lip. "Are you asking?"

Her breath hitched, but I wasn't sure if it was from my question or my touch.

Her phone rang, breaking the spell holding us. Shit. I stepped back, wondering how I kept forgetting she was off limits.

"I'll leave you to get that. Enjoy your dinner." I strode out of her room and down the stairs, willing the exertion to dampen my desire for a woman I couldn't have.

I entered the kitchen heading to the bathroom, intending to take a cold shower.

"You made it. I have a plate warming for you."

I stopped short at Mrs. Tillis's words. She sat with Knightly and Caroline at the table in the middle of the kitchen. I'd been so consumed by Victoria, I hadn't noticed them.

I cleared my throat and searched for polite words to tell her that I changed my mind.

Mrs. Tillis rose from the table and pulled a covered plate from the oven. She removed the foil, setting the plate on the table and smiling up at me expectantly.

"I'm sure Mr. Sterling doesn't want to join us," Knightly said. "No doubt Mr. Banion would think us impertinent to ask. "

"Why?" I asked.

Knightly's jaw tightened. "You're Mr. Banion's friend . . ."

I moved to the table. "Right now, I work for Henry just like you."

Caroline remained silent, watching the situation play out.

"I'm sure Mr. Banion wouldn't agree."

"Yeah, well, Henry isn't here." I inhaled the scent of my food. "It smells delicious, Mrs. Tillis."

"Thank you."

We ate in silence for a moment, then Knightly asked, "Was Miss Victoria okay when you took her food to her?"

I nodded. "To be honest, I think she understands the depth of danger she and Henry are in more than he does, or at least more than he's willing to admit."

"She was always a smart girl," Mrs. Tillis said. Her colleagues nodded in agreement.

"I HOPE she'll do okay with Henry gone, " Caroline said, earning a warning glance from Knightly. I guess she wasn't supposed to talk about Victoria's private business in front of me. Well, too bad. If there was something I needed to know to keep her safe, I was damn sure going to hear it.

"Why wouldn't she?"

"She's not one to be kept cooped up," Mrs. Tillis said. "She has a bit of wanderlust, I'm afraid."

"She'll be stir crazy in two days," Caroline added. "Maybe three."

Knightly arched a brow at me "You'll have your work cut out for you then."

Mrs. Tillis laughed. "Remember when she snuck out to follow that boy to Costa Rica?"

What boy? Irritation flared.

"What was his name? Tommy? Johnny?" Mrs. Tillis's brow furrowed as she tried to remember.

"What happened?" I asked, trying to act curious, not jealous.

"I caught up to her at the airport," Knightly said, apparently deciding it was okay for me to learn the family history.

"You, not Henry?"

Knightly shrugged like it was no big thing. "Henry was out of town. Tori had just turned eighteen and wanted to experience life.

Henry promised her a trip, but it was postponed when a business issue popped up. She was okay for a day or so then met some young man in the park who filled her head with adventure and saving the world."

"You say that like it's a bad thing," I said.

"Adventure and saving the world aren't bad," Mrs. Tillis said. "Running off with a man you don't know to the jungles of Costa Rica isn't smart."

I thought of Victoria on the plane and how she'd accepted my call for adventure. At the time, I could tell she craved excitement, but I'd believed she'd never acted on it. Now I knew she had. Or at least had tried.

"After that, she channeled her energy into college and building her business," Knightly said with a hint of pride.

"Hopefully, she'll do that this week while Mr. Banion is gone," Caroline said.

"She'd better," I growled, causing everyone to look at me. "And you should help make sure of it too. I'm not a babysitter, and I don't want to put my men in more danger because Victoria is bored."

Knightly glared at me but nodded. He knew I was right.

LATER IN BED, I reflected on what I'd learned about Victoria. She had a thirst for adventure. She'd also opted out of joining the family business, just like I had. But in her case, she wasn't disowned. I had to admire her ingenuity in starting a business that allowed her freedom to work practically anywhere.

I thought of all the places in the world she could go. I could show her the fairy pools she'd missed in Scotland. Then I could take her on safari in Africa and later explore the Amazon.

Fuck! No, I couldn't. Good Christ. I needed to stop thinking of her.

I punched my pillow and prayed for Henry to finish his business and return quickly. I needed to finish this job and return to my life.

14

Victoria

I did my best. I really did. I tried to keep myself busy. But by the third day cooped up at home, I was at my wit's end. The problem I had was that I knew Alex wouldn't take me anywhere and I couldn't sneak out because Saint Security men were guarding the house.

I sat in my office window seat, looking longingly out the window at the world passing by. Perhaps that was my problem. I couldn't distract myself from all that I was missing by staring at all I was missing.

With my laptop in tow, I moved to the table and focused on work. writing, editing, and checking all the data that told me how my business was doing. An hour later, I had a conference with my staff, and after that, I worked on marketing. When that was done, I continued to distract my irritation by brainstorming ideas to expand services and scale up.

When the lure of life outside won out, I called Samantha, hating that I couldn't tell her the real deal of what was going on. I worried she'd avoid me if she knew I was entangled with George Pitney. So, we mostly talked about her son and some of my travels and work. I told her Dad was still a workaholic.

"The guy is always on," I said. "I wish he'd get a life."

"He's never met anyone outside of work?"

"Nope. My dad is a confirmed bachelor. I think he envies his friend Alex." Alex. He could have been a distraction, but he'd made his position clear. So now I had to distract myself from him too. It wasn't too hard. He was my bodyguard, but I rarely saw him.

"The man who was with you the other day?" she asked.

"Yeah, him."

She was probably waiting for an explanation about why Alex was with me, but I couldn't tell the truth and I didn't want to lie.

"Why would your dad envy him?"

"Alex is the love 'em and leave 'em type. He's all about excitement and adventure in the moment." He was sexy as hell, although I wasn't going to admit that. Samantha would probably think it was weird that I had the hots for my father's friend.

"So your dad never met anyone he could love?"

I remembered dinner with him in which I had an inkling that maybe there had been a woman, but for some reason, it couldn't become anything.

"I don't know, actually. Maybe. He was sort of cryptic about it."

"When?"

"What?"

There was a pause. "I just wondered if it was recent. Maybe he's seeing her in California or something."

I thought about that and realized she could be right. With George Pitney trying to get at Dad, that was something that could get in the way of a relationship. There were just too many problems. One was that he wouldn't be visiting her in California if there was no future with them, and two, the feeling I got from Dad was that the relationship took place a while ago.

"Maybe, but I think it was in the past."

"It's too bad things didn't work out for him." Samantha had a surprising attitude considering her father's abandonment of her mother. Plus, being a single mom suggested she hadn't been lucky in love either. I wanted to ask her about it, but I got the feeling she didn't want to talk about it.

We chatted a little longer and then said our goodbyes. The minute the call ended, the stirring of discontent came again.

Reaching my limit, I marched downstairs to the area off the kitchen where Alex worked. He was staring intently at something on the computer.

"I have to get out of here."

"No" He didn't even bother looking up from his computer screen at me.

"Yes."

This time, his gaze lifted, and he looked at me like I was a petulant teenager. "No."

"Come on, Alex. I need fresh air. Fusion food truck food. Room to move."

"This house has seven levels. You have plenty of room."

"Please. Surely, there is a safe place we could go." A thought came to me. "How about the Hampton house?"

His expression didn't change. "You'll be a sitting duck there." He let out a long sigh. "Think of this as a new adventure."

I smirked at him. "Yeah, right. How come you're not going stir crazy? You're cooped up too."

"I'm not, though. First, I'm working and second, I can walk out of here any time I want. "

"Rub it in, jerk." I turned and left, knowing my effort had been futile.

"Don't think you'll be able to escape," he called after me.

I gave him the finger.

Once again, I tried to occupy my time. I went down to the gym but lasted only five minutes on the treadmill even with the video set to have me walking in the Alps.

I gave up and went back upstairs to the kitchen to get a snack. As I approached, I heard Caroline upset about something.

"It's not good."

"It's just one meal, Caroline," Mrs. Tillis said.

Not wanting to interrupt, I went to my father's bar and poured a large glass of wine. I brought it up to my bathroom and filled my tub with water and my grandmother's lavender bath salts. Undressing, I got into the tub with my wine and tried to let go of all my frustrations. My dad's hard-headedness. Alex's infuriating attitude.

"I hate him," I said to my wine. *But you want him.* That was the most annoying. Even when he was a jerk, he was sexy. Looking at him, my body remembered all the erotic things he'd done, and it wanted him to do it again. That made me hate him more.

My fingers were well pruned when Mrs. Tillis found me. She knocked on the door, and not feeling modest since she'd given me baths as a child, I told her to come in.

She smiled. "What a nice way to spend your afternoon."

"I'm out of wine."

"Why don't you get out and get dressed? Dinner is about ready." She held up a towel.

I stood and exited the tub. She wrapped me up and then walked over to get my robe hanging behind the door.

"What's for dinner?" I asked as I dried myself off.

"I'm not sure."

I frowned as I took the robe Mrs. Tillis held out for me. "What was Caroline upset about earlier?"

Mrs. Tillis's eyes stared at me like the proverbial deer with its eyes caught in headlights. What was going on?

"Oh, you know her . . ." Mrs. Tillis waved a hand. "Get dressed." She left the bathroom and my room.

With a shrug, I made my way to my room. I opened the dresser holding the few clothes I had. Maybe that was how I could get out. I could tell Alex I needed to pick up more things at my place.

I tugged on a casual denim skirt and a loose, flowery top. I let my hair down. I had nowhere to go, so there was no reason not to be comfortable.

I opened the door of my bedroom and stepped out into a wall of man.

"What?" Was there a problem that had brought Alex to my door? Or maybe he was just making sure I hadn't snuck out. Like that could happen.

"I'm here to escort you to dinner."

My brow furrowed. "Why? Have George's men infiltrated and will grab me on the stairs?"

He shifted, looking uncomfortable. "Dinner is up on the roof terrace."

"Oh." Why hadn't I thought about going up there sooner? Are there snipers or something? Why did Alex need to be by my side to go to the terrace?

"Do you want fresh air or not?" Irritation laced his tone.

"Yes."

He held his hand out toward the elevator. I followed his directive and stepped inside. He joined me, hitting the button for the terrace. He stood next to me, his hands clasped in front of him, his eyes facing forward. He looked like a government G-man or, I supposed more accurately, a bodyguard.

I leaned forward and blew on his ear. I don't know why except he looked so serious.

He turned his head, his pale blue eyes a mixture of annoyance and something else. "What are you doing?

"Trying to rattle you," I said with a grin.

"I don't rattle."

"I don't rattle," I mocked in his tone.

His brows drew together. "What has gotten into you?"

"This is what happens when you keep me caged up. If you don't like it, you can let me out of this house."

"That's not happening."

The elevator reached the terrace. The door slid open, and Alex again gestured for me to proceed.

I stepped out and my breath caught. Fairy lights glinted on the potted trees and pergola. Knightly and Mrs. Tillis were setting a variety of items on the set table. Items that looked suspiciously like food truck food containers. Then she went to the small bar and picked up a bucket with a wine bottle poking out.

"You did this for me?" I asked them both. It wasn't what I truly wanted, but it was a sweet gesture.

"Not me." Knightly's lips were pursed in disdain. He nodded toward Alex.

I turned around to Alex standing behind me. "You arranged this?"

He shrugged and looked off into the city skyline as if uncomfortable. "I figured if you couldn't go to the city, the city could come to you."

"Well, you are full of surprises," I said to Alex.

A pink hue came to his cheeks. I found it incredibly adorable and sexy.

"Well . . . enjoy your meal." He turned to leave.

"Wait. You're not joining me?"

His eyes flared in warning as he glanced at Knightly and Mrs. Tillis.

"I'm not your guest."

"If you don't need anything else, we'll leave you to your evening," Knightly said.

"There's more wine in the wine cooler, and the music system is on if you'd like music," Mrs. Tillis said, following Knightly to the elevator.

I nodded as my joy at this surprise was replaced with disappointment. I was getting fresh air, food truck food, and space to move, but I had to enjoy it on my own. Be careful what you ask for.

"Thank you," I managed to say as Knightly and Mrs. Tillis entered the elevator, the door shutting them in.

I turned back to Alex. "This is really sweet, but—"

"You're not acting like you think it's sweet."

"You're going to leave me up here all alone."

"I gave you what you wanted and you're still whining." His tone was like a parent to a child.

His words were like a punch to the gut. Despite what happened on the plane, he saw me as a spoiled little rich girl. If I were sixteen and had a crush on him, it would make sense. But I was a grown woman, so his attitude made me feel like a fool.

Fueled by hurt and anger, I asked, "Why did you bother?"

"I was trying to make a difficult situation more tolerable. I should have known it wouldn't be enough."

I glared up at him. "It would be enough if you'd join me."

Again, heat flared in his eyes. "I can't do that."

"Right. Because you're not a guest." I shook my head, hating my stupid hormones for finding him so sexy. Maybe that was why I started acting petty. "I bet Ian would have joined me."

Alex's jaw tightened. "You like Ian, huh? Is that what's really agitating you? You need to get laid?"

His words shocked me. I gaped and then turned away. How was it that every word out of his mouth felt like a smack to my ego?

"You can go." I hoped my voice sounded dismissive. I walked over to the terrace wall, looking out over the park toward the river.

"Fuck. Victoria, I'm sorry."

"I doubt it. Just go. You gave me this nice evening. Let me enjoy it."

He didn't say anything, and I thought he'd left. I hated how disappointed that made me feel. What was wrong with me?

My first inclination that he hadn't left was when his scent wafted up around me. He stepped up next to me, his gaze looking outward as mine had been.

"This isn't smart," he said.

"Which is it, Alex? I'm horny or stupid?"

He looked at me, and I saw genuine regret in his eyes. "I always say the wrong thing." He shook his head. "That's not true. Sometimes, I'm an asshole on purpose."

"You're good at it. Is it just for me or are you like this to everyone?"

"It's you."

I rolled my eyes even as the hurt from his words assaulted me again. "Why don't you go hide in that hole of yours in the kitchen?"

"I am hiding there." His voice was terse with an edge like it was my fault.

"Maybe you should have gone with Dad. Then you wouldn't have to hide." Hide from what I wasn't sure, but I figured it was from the revulsion he felt at having fucked me, his old buddy's daughter.

"I thought about it."

"So why didn't you?"

He was quiet for a moment. "Because the idea of Ian being here with you wasn't something I could bear."

Huh? I turned to look at him, wondering what he was getting at.

"Being around you is hard, Victoria. You're Henry's daughter."

I thought I was beginning to understand. "So, you're the one who wants to get laid."

"I don't know that I'd put it like that."

"How would you put it, then?"

He gave a small laugh. "You make me crazy with need."

My breath hitched. I turned my body to face him. He did the same. "Need for what?"

I could see the struggle in his eyes. He wanted me, but he was friends with my father. I didn't want to come between him and my dad's friendship, and yet I hoped I won.

"The need to touch you. To taste you. To bury myself inside you."

In an instant, the tingle of titillation shot to full-on wet arousal. "And that's why you hide and act like a dick?"

His lips twitched upward. "Yes."

"Just to be clear. We're talking about sexual frustration, right?"

"Yes, Victoria."

"I know it well."

"Do you?" He reached out and pushed a tendril of my hair blowing in the breeze behind my ear. The agitated intensity in him was gone. It was as if he'd resigned himself to the inevitable.

I nodded, hoping I was right. "I feel it too."

"Do you?" he repeated.

"Yes, but not for Ian. Not for anyone else, actually."

A low growl emanated from him as he stepped closer to me. "Who, Victoria? Tell me who has you sexually frustrated?"

"You know who."

His hand banded around my back, and I knew then that he was giving in to this crazy desire between us. I knew it was a mistake, but I was giving in too.

"I need to hear it," he said.

"You." The word was barely out of my mouth before his lips crashed down on mine. I moaned as electric pleasure rocketed through my body. I gripped his shirt as I felt the world fall away.

"Have you been dreaming of me?" he asked as his lips cascaded along my neck and his hands slid up, cupping my aching breasts.

"Yes."

"Good, because you've been fucking haunting my dreams." His fingers pinched my nipples, making me gasp as another surge of erotic energy bolted through me.

He turned me, facing me away from him. I gripped the terrace wall as I waited for whatever he was going to do. His lips dragged along the back of my neck as his hands slid up my thighs, pulling my skirt up.

"Are you wet for me?" His hand slid between my thighs.

"Yes."

"Mmm," he murmured against my neck as his fingers slid inside my panties. "So wet." With a quick move, he tore my panties away, shocking me. Then his fingers were sliding along my pussy lips. My knees went weak and I gripped the wall harder.

"We're not in an airplane now, Victoria. Don't hold back. I want to hear you come."

I wondered for a moment if my cries of pleasure would reach Knightly, Mrs. Tillis, or Caroline. Or the rest of the Upper West Side. His other hand pinched my nipple as he rubbed my clit, and I didn't care who heard.

"Alex." God, how he could make me ache.

"That's right. It's me making you feel good. Remember that, Victoria." His hands were like magic, rubbing, pinching, probing until the pressure built.

"Oh, God . . ."

"Are you there? Are you going to come?" His voice was raspy in my ear. "Let it out, Victoria."

My hips moved in time with his fingers as my orgasm built steam until the pressure burst. I cried out, my hips gyrating as they sought more of Alex's magnificent touch.

"So fucking beautiful," he growled in my ear. "I need to be inside your sweet, wet pussy." His hands left my body, and I nearly crumpled to the terrace.

I heard his zipper, and I eagerly awaited the feel of him inside me.

"Fuck." His tone was agitated.

"What?" God, if he didn't get inside me soon, I might implode.

"I don't have a condom."

"I'm on the pill." Deep inside, I knew it was wrong to make such a decision in the throes of passion. After all, I didn't know him that well except that he was a man who fucked many women . . . many he didn't know, just as he had me on the plane. Then again, he was my father's friend. He appeared healthy and responsible.

"Are you sure?"

"Sure that I'm on the pill—"

"Sure that you're okay with this. I'm healthy, but—"

"Fuck me already, Alex."

In a single, hard thrust, he filled me. It felt like what I imagined drugs did for the person in need of a hit. A moment of complete bliss and relief, followed by greater need.

"Say it again," he growled in my ear. "Tell me what you want . . . what you need."

"Fuck me, Alex."

15

Alex

This was wrong. So, so wrong. Yet it felt too fucking right to stop.

Her pussy wrapped around my dick like it was made for it. Hot. Snug. Pulsing. My dick had never had it so good. Any thoughts of how wise it was to fuck my friend's daughter on the terrace of his house while its staff could show up any moment to check on her left my brain. All there was were Victoria and the sweetest sensations coursing from my dick to every neuron of my body.

"Do you feel me fucking you?" I said into her ear as I withdrew and plunged in again.

"Yes ... more ..."

She was like a wet dream come to life. A luscious ass to grip as I drove into her. A pussy that sucked me in deep. Words and moans that told me she was feeling it too.

"Alex ..."

"What do you need, baby?" I was doing my best to hold out until she came again, but I could feel the edges of my orgasm encroaching.

"Do you feel me fucking you?"

God, this woman. Whatever I dished out, she gave back. It could be irritating, and yet I so fucking loved it. "Your pussy is fucking the hell out of me." I drove in again. "Fuck . . . I'm almost there. Touch yourself, baby. Make yourself come. My dick wants to feel you come on him."

"Oh, God." She kept one hand on the terrace wall as the other slid between her legs. Each time I thrust in, I could feel her fingers touching herself, and it was driving me to the edge of madness. Her body jerked, her head threw back, and her pussy tightened around my cock like a fucking vise.

I roared as my orgasm took me by surprise with its speed and intensity. "Fuck . . . yes . . . fuck . . ." I pistoned in and out of her, drawing out the pleasure, emptying myself into her.

Jesus fuck. I felt like my world was tilting. I rocked in and out until finally, my dick was limp. That was when the guilt flooded like a tsunami.

"Fuck." There was no doubt that she heard the shame in my voice.

"Don't. If you regret this before you even leave my body, I swear to God, I'll make your life miserable."

"I'm sorry."

She gave me a shove and pushed her skirt down. "I now understand why you're a bachelor. It's not by choice."

I redid my pants. "It is by choice." Her comment had me wondering if she thought there was something more between us besides insatiable chemistry.

"I suppose since you admitted to being a dick as a way to repel women, maybe you're right. You're good at it, by the way. You could at least wait until your dick is out of me, but whatever." She pushed around me, and I felt a desperate need not to let her walk away.

It made no sense because her anger was what would save us both. But it unsettled me that she thought I was so heartless, so careless with women. She wasn't necessarily wrong, but I didn't want that for her.

"Victoria." I reached out and took her arm to stop her.

She glared up at me. "Why do you call me that?"

Her question threw me for a loop. "It's your name."

"Everyone calls me Tori. You don't. Why?"

"I . . . ah . . . I know you as Victoria." My heart clenched tight in my chest because the truth was, everyone called her Tori. Only I called her Victoria. Like it was my special name for her. Like she was mine.

"So should I call you Sterling?"

"You can call me whatever you want."

"How about bast—"

I pressed my fingers over her mouth. "I get it. You're pissed at me. I'm sorry for that, but—"

"I get it too. You can't deal with wanting to fuck your friend's daughter."

I winced, not liking hearing what I'd done. Jesus. I thought I was stronger than that. At least stronger than my dick. Victoria had a pull on me that I didn't understand. It was unsettling to be so helpless.

"I'm sorry."

She let out a frustrated "Ugh" and pulled away from me. She went to the table, sitting down in a huff, and began opening the food containers. I wanted to say something to change this situation, but there was nothing to say. There was no changing the reality that Victoria was Henry's daughter. God. Imagining how he'd react if he knew what I'd done to Victoria made me sick.

I picked up her torn underwear and like a fucking pervert tucked them into my pocket. I told myself it was to hide the evidence of what I'd done, not a souvenir.

Then I strode to the elevator. "Have a rice meal, Victoria," I said as I passed her.

She didn't respond.

I stepped into the elevator, too much of a coward to look at her and see the evidence of my using and then hurting her.

I arrived at the kitchen level and made my way toward my room, needing a moment to get my shit together.

"Did you join her for dinner?" Knightly's voice was tinged with disapproval.

Shit. I hadn't noticed that Knightly and Mrs. Tillis were at the table. Caroline was doing dishes.

"You were up there a long time, Mrs. Tillis said."

"I was checking the area and upper floors."

Knightly's brows furrowed as he watched me. My stomach clenched as I worried that he knew I was lying. God, if he knew what I'd really been doing, Henry would be on the next flight home to kick my ass. I'd be out of a job for sure for fucking a client. Interesting how my biggest concern was how wrong it was to fuck my friend's daughter and only now did I consider I'd be fired too. Except hadn't Dax's wife been a client?

So what, Sterling? Jesus. Victoria was just a woman I was hopelessly attracted to. It wasn't anything more than lust.

"I do hope she's okay. It's too bad we couldn't invite a friend over. I heard Samantha Layton was back home," Mrs. Tillis said.

"She's got her hands full with Mrs. Layton," Knightly said.

"Yes, of course. Poor thing. Both of them."

"I'm heading to my room. I'll be checking the house later." Hopefully by that time, Victoria would be done with her terrace outing and Knightly, Mrs. Tillis, and Caroline would be in for the night as well.

"I'll go up and see if she needs anything," Mrs. Tillis said more to Knightly than to me.

Once in my room, I collapsed on the bed, letting my self-loathing consume me. Some was from betraying Henry, but mostly, it was from hurting Victoria. I wondered how Mrs. Tillis would find Victoria. Would she reveal what I'd done to the woman who appeared more motherly than servant? That should have caused fear, but mostly, it caused anguish.

I wallowed long enough that when I returned to the kitchen, it was empty. I went to my work nook and started the evening check-ins with the team, starting with Ian.

"All is well here. Banion is abiding by our rules. Archer made a visit here, which I think impressed the importance of keeping to the plan onto Banion."

"Good. Any sign of Pitney's goons?"

"If they're here, they're laying low."

I was glad that Ian understood that simply not seeing signs of danger didn't mean it wasn't lurking. "Let me know if anything comes up."

"Will do."

I disconnected from Ian and contacted Dax, who was in charge of keeping tabs on Pitney's court case. It occurred to me that I might have to do it when Dax returned home to Las Vegas. That is if Elliott didn't pull the plug on that part of the investigation.

"Hey, Alex. Nothing new to report. Pitney is making PR rounds looking like a fucking hero. He's made a donation to a homeless shelter to provide education to the kids residing there."

"What a motherfucker."

"Yeah, considering many in this shelter are homeless because he evicted them from a new property he bought. I'm not sure if he's going to raze the building or convert it to high end condos, but—"

"What about the D.A.'s case?" What Pitney did with his new building didn't concern me as much as what he planned for Henry.

"Yeah, well, Pitney's uptake in popularity has the D.A. even more uncertain about pursuing prosecution on what little evidence of fraud that they have."

"Fuck." I pinched the bridge of my nose with my thumb and forefinger.

"We did learn that a news piece about the evictions is about to be published on all of Banion's media properties. That could push Pitney to do something."

It likely would, but Pitney wasn't stupid. "Maybe, but my guess it would be like all the other cases. We wouldn't be able to link him to anything he did to Henry."

"We could still set him up. With him out of town, the daughter could be—"

"No!" I probably said that with more emotion than I should. "She's already had her life upended by Henry. Besides, Henry wouldn't go for that."

"Alright. It's your call."

After speaking to Dax, I checked in with the team on duty outside the house. They indicated all was clear. I checked my watch. It was nearly nine p.m. My stomach growled, and I realized I hadn't eaten since that afternoon. I left the nook to find something to eat. I searched the fridge, finding lunch meat and cheese. I prepared a sandwich thinking that I would have liked to have had some of Victoria's food truck meal. I sighed at the reminder of how spectacularly I'd fucked up with her.

I ate my meal in the quiet dark of the kitchen. I liked solitude. I liked the quiet and ability to live my life without a thought or care.

I shook my head wondering why I was having to remind myself of that. Victoria, of course. Fucking hell. Just my luck that the one woman who could have me rethink my life as a bachelor was the one woman I couldn't have.

Frustrated, I finished my sandwich and set out to do the final house check of the night.

I started from the garage level and worked up. I skipped the third floor, telling myself Victoria was fine, but really, I just wanted to be sure she was asleep before I checked her area. What a fucking coward I was. A better man would own up to his bullshit.

Once I completed all floors but the third, I made my way down from the seventh floor to Victoria's rooms. Which should I try first? Hoping she was in her bedroom asleep, I went to her office. The door was ajar and the light was off. I gently pushed open the door, poking my head in. She sat on the window seat in the dark except for the light the moon shone in.

She turned her head toward me and pursed her lips in disgust as she realized it was me invading her quiet. "Seriously. I just wanted fresh air. I wasn't trying to escape."

It took me a moment to realize she was referring to her open window. I was about to nod and leave her alone, but somehow, I ended up in her room.

She arched a brow. "Are you really going to close my window? I'll close it when I'm done."

I stopped short, wondering what the hell I was doing in her room.

She watched me, and the irritation morphed into something that looked like panic. She jumped up and rushed to me, taking my forearms in her hands. "Something happened. Is my dad okay?"

Holy hell. Even without trying, I was causing her pain. "Henry is fine."

Her eyes searched my face as if she wanted to verify my words.

"Everything is fine." I swallowed, because that wasn't totally true. With her standing so close, her warm hands gripping my arms, everything inside me shifted, putting me off kilter. "Well, that's not true."

"What's wrong?"

"I can't stop."

She continued to look at me in confusion. "Stop what?"

"I can't stop thinking of you. Of wanting you."

16

Victoria

I *am grateful.*

I said the words over and over again as I ate delicious Asian tacos, Indian naan-wiches, and several sweet treats. It was nice of Alex to arrange this and for Knightly and Mrs. Tillis to help.

I am grateful.

I poured another glass of wine. I really was thankful, but this was nearly worse than spending all my time cooped up in the house. Yes, it was a lovely warm evening on the terrace with delicious food, fine wine, and music I'd turned on to drown out the fact that I was here by myself. As nice as this was, it was miserable to experience it alone.

I knew there were people who'd kill to have the love of a good parent, great supportive people around, and of course, money, so I was being a brat complaining about being in a gilded cage.

When the elevator opened, my heartbeat kicked up a notch thinking Alex had changed his mind.

Mrs. Tillis exited, and my disappointment turned to self-chastising. That damned man was making me crazy.

"How are you doing? Enjoying the food?"

I put on a smile. "Yes. Thank you for helping with this."

"Of course. We could all see you needed a change of scenery, so when Alex mentioned it we all jumped in. Well, Caroline balked, but she came around. She was the one who suggested the dessert."

I smiled. See? I had so much to be grateful for. I stood and picked up my wine glass. "Thank you again. I'm going to head down to my office now." I picked up the bottle of wine too. There was no sense in letting it go to waste.

She frowned. "Not working, I hope. It's late."

"I just have a few things to deal with."

She tsked. "When you decided not to follow your father's footsteps, I was glad because it meant you could have a life, but you work as much as he does."

"I enjoy my work." That wasn't a lie. I realized that all this business with my father and distraction from Alex had in some ways pulled my attention away from my ambitions. Yes, I'd been working, but danger and Alex had been hanging around the fringe of my focus. I needed to stop that, at least where Alex was concerned.

"Hopefully, all this terrible business with your father will end and you can resume your travel."

"Let's hope." But I wasn't going to hold my breath. I understood this problem with Pitney wasn't going away anytime soon.

When I got to my office, I carried my wine bottle and glass to the window seat. I didn't bother turning the light on. The moon was bright, giving the room just enough light.

I had no intention of working. Instead, I sat and wallowed in the difficulty of my current situation.

Wanting fresh air, I opened the window. Maybe I should have stayed on the terrace.

I'd been sitting for a while when the door creaked open and Alex entered. I wanted to jump up and punch him for bringing so much frustration into my life. Here he was, after all the things said on the roof and all we'd done, and now he was going to chastise me for opening the window like I was a child.

But he didn't say anything. I realized that the way he was looking at me was different from his usual irritation. That was when I panicked. Something happened to my father. That had to be why he was here.

I rushed to him, needing to know what happened. He said nothing was wrong, but there had to be based on his demeanor.

"I can't stop."

What was he talking about? "Stop what?"

"I can't stop thinking of you. Of wanting you."

My heart beat against my ribs in a mix of excitement and warning. "You also can't stop regretting or feeling repulsed by me." For once, the warning beat out desire and I started to pull away.

But he took my hands in his. "Henry is like a brother to me."

"That would make me your niece, so yeah, I see how gross that would be." I tugged my hands away.

He flinched at my niece comment. Then he sighed. "He'd see it as a betrayal. Hell, he'd see it as inappropriate. He'd think I was a sick bastard. I defiled his daughter."

I laughed humorlessly. "No you didn't. Lance Dawson did that."

He let out an exasperated breath. "Do you really not understand?"

I glared at him. "I understand that you're hot for your friend's daughter and when dick wins over your conscience, you regret it."

He gave me a helpless stare.

"Do you really not understand what that's like for me? I let you touch me and then you act repulsed. It's humiliating."

His expression was stricken. "I'm sorry."

"Yeah, yeah, you keep saying that. Maybe you should go back to hiding and treating me like Henry's spoiled brat."

"Is that what you want?"

I laughed derisively. "Since when has what I wanted factored into this?"

He scowled. "I never touched you without your consent. "

"Yes, the sex was mutual. The whiplash from your wanting me one minute and being repulsed by me the next is not."

"I'm not repulsed by you, Victoria. It's me not wanting to betray Henry, and yet I have."

I watched him, wondering why he was saying all this. He got his rocks off. Now he could move on.

I can't stop thinking of you. Of wanting you.

"What if I wasn't Henry's daughter? Would it be different?"

He moved closer, and while I should have retreated, I didn't.

"Yes. Absolutely. "

"How?"

He gave me a pained look. "You know how."

"You and I could have our wicked way with each other."

"I guess you could put it like that."

"How would you put it?" Where did he see this going if my father wasn't in the way?

"We're two consenting adults enjoying each other's company."

Okay, so he wasn't feeling more than a powerful physical attraction. "What about one-and-done?"

"Sometimes, one time isn't enough."

"Well now you've had two."

"Two isn't enough either." His eyes were dark, filled with desperation, but I couldn't be sure whether it was desire for me or frustration at his desire.

"Is that why you're here? To get your fill?"

He sighed. "I'm here to tell you I'm sorry for—"

I help up my hand. "Yes, I know, Alex. I'm tired of hearing your apologies. I understand your situation and I appreciate how difficult it is for you."

"I don't think you do."

"Do what?"

"Understand how difficult this is for me." His hand cupped my cheek. "You're smart, feisty, funny, brave and adventurous." His thumb brushed over my bottom lip, and it took all my will to not moan or give in to his touch. "I wanted to have dinner with you and learn about all your goals and dreams. I want to let you out of here and then follow you on whatever adventure you go on next."

His words chipped away at the hate I tried to have for him. "That would be stalking."

"You like different."

"I do. Very much."

I stepped back because I was precariously close to jumping him. "Well, you can't have me. Not anymore. Not if each time your guilt has you acting like an asshole."

"I can't fight it, Victoria."

"Unless you can resolve your hang-up—"

"I'm here, aren't I?" he snapped and then let out a frustrated breath.

"I'm still your friend's daughter."

He studied me for a moment. "Do you feel it? This . . . pull? If I wasn't an asshole, wouldn't you want to indulge it?"

"I think you know the answer to that."

"What if we did that? We indulged it . . . burned it out, but made sure that Henry never, ever found out. No one can find out."

"I'll be your dirty little secret?" I supposed I should have been offended by that, and yet there was some titillation. Perhaps it was that adventurousness in me that he'd mentioned.

"It's not like that, Victoria. I don't see this as sordid. It's more than that."

"More?"

He shifted uncomfortably in what I assumed was concern about my thinking more meant way more. But it couldn't. Not if no one, especially my father, couldn't know. Truth be told, I wouldn't want my father to know. First, I wouldn't want to come between him and Alex, and second, I was sure he'd see me differently if he knew, and I didn't want that either.

"I respect you, Victoria. I don't want to hurt you but—"

"I get it. I don't want my father to know either."

We stared at each other for a long moment.

Finally, I shrugged. "We have about three more days until my dad is home."

Like on the terrace, Alex's lips and hands were on me so fast. I gave in to it, knowing I was as helpless to this attraction as he seemed to be.

"This time, we have a bed," I said.

His pale blue eyes shone with wickedness that made my blood flow molten hot. "Let's take advantage of that. Get naked, Victoria. I'm going to discover every inch of your luscious body."

Luscious body. I loved that. I stripped and stood before him, for the first time feeling self-conscious.

"Fucking Christ, you're beautiful." His expression, his eyes, the way they shone with admiration and awe, did more for my ego than his words. "Lie down and let me make you feel so good."

Was it weird that I was going to have sex in my grandfather's old room? Yep. That was until Alex's hands and lips were on me again. He wasn't joking when he said he was going to discover every inch. From my neck to my breasts, down to my belly, skipping my pussy as he sucked on my inner thigh, likely leaving a mark, and down to my ankles. I never knew I had an erotic spot there. By the time he was back up to my pussy, I was a quivering mess. With one flick of his tongue over my clit, I was flying.

"You taste delicious, Victoria," he said as he lapped up my essence. "More." He feasted on my pussy until I was coming again, and again.

"Alex . . ." I needed a moment to catch my breath.

"Ready for my cock?"

Okay, so maybe I didn't need a breather because I absolutely needed his cock. I pushed him back.

"My turn." I straddled his thighs and dragged my hands down his chest. He was hard, the lines of his chest and abs making me drool. I licked a nipple, loving how he hissed. I moved lower, lower.

"I won't last long," he warned as I eyed his dick, hard, thick, standing up as if it was presenting itself to me.

"Long or short, I don't care." I licked a pearl of precum off his tip. His dick twitched. I took it in hand and sucked it hard.

"Fuck," he growled, his hips bucking up.

I decided to give as good as I got. I licked, sucked and stroked until he was chanting obscenities. Just before I thought he might come, I stopped.

"Jesus, fuck . . . I'm there."

I maneuvered over him, resting my hands on his chest. "Come inside me." I swear his eyes rolled back into his head.

I slid down over him, savoring how thick and hard he was. How deeply he filled me.

His hands gripped my hips, urging me on. "Make me come, Victoria. Fuck . . . blow my mind."

I started to ride him. I watched all the nuances of expression on his face—need, torment, anticipation. Soon, my own need took precedence over watching him. I gave in to it, rocking and riding him, reaching for the ultimate pleasure.

"Fuck . . . I can't wait." His hips bucked underneath me, his essence filling me. The idea of him filling me was all it took to push me that last bit, and I cried out as my orgasm flooded through me.

I rode him until my bones were jelly. I collapsed on him. As I caught my breath, I wondered what he was going to do now. I held my breath as I waited to find out if he meant what he said, or would guilt and regret have him fleeing again?

His hand slapped my ass. "Jesus fuck, woman."

I smiled as that had to be a good sign. "You alright there, Slick?"

"My dick has never had it so good."

His words might have been dirty, but they filled me with happiness. Maybe he said that to all his women, but I pretended it was true.

"I confess my pussy is feeling pretty lucky."

He rolled me over, his eyes intense as he looked down on me. "One more rule."

"Oh?" I held my breath, unsure whether I'd like a new rule.

"My dick is the only one in your pussy while we're indulging this thing between us."

"That goes for your dick. No other pussies."

"You got it."

I laughed. "Should we shake on it?"

He shook his head. "We should fuck on it."

17

Alex

It was wrong, but heaven help me, I was going to squeeze every last moment of joy out of my time with Victoria. I rationalized it by telling myself I'd already betrayed Henry. It wasn't like if I said, "We only fucked once," he'd be okay. Once or a dozen times, it didn't matter. The potential damage was done.

Then there was the excuse that it would only be until Henry arrived home. As long as the staff didn't get a whiff of what we were doing, there wouldn't be an issue. I knew deep down that I was lying to myself and playing with fire. But each time I saw Victoria's smile, received one of her sharp barbs or teasing comments, or when I sank into her luscious body, it was worth it.

That first night, we fucked like rabbits and the only problem was that I had to leave her room before I was finished to get back to my room so no one would be the wiser. I had a moment to worry that I would never get enough, but that was crazy, right? At some point, the attraction would wane. Hopefully, before Henry got home.

The next day, she showed up where I was working in my kitchen nook. It was after lunch so all the staff were off doing whatever they did between lunch and the time to prepare for dinner.

"I'm bored," she pouted.

My dick went full-tilt when I saw her. She was wearing a robe. Was she naked underneath? Panic slid up my spine at what Knightly or Mrs. Tillis would think of finding Victoria nearly naked in the kitchen and me with a woody the size of a redwood.

"Poor little rich girl," I responded.

"I'm going swimming." She opened her robe just briefly, and good Christ, she was naked.

"Good idea." Or I think I said it. My brain was fritzing out.

She sighed as she closed her robe. "Some distractions work better than others, though."

"Oh?" If I didn't fuck her soon, I'd have to excuse myself and rub one out.

"The terrace dinner was nice, but later that night . . . wow." She made a gesture to indicate her mind was blown. The man in me felt pretty good about that. "Swimming will be nice, but—"

"Looks to me like you're skinny dipping."

She nodded. "Maybe something mind-blowing will happen. You know what they say . . ."

"What do they say?" My eyes were riveted to the V-line of her robe where I could see the swells of her ample tits. Tits that my mouth watered to suck.

"Luck is what happens when preparation meets opportunity." She dragged her hand over her chest down to her cleavage. "I'm prepared for the opportunity to get lucky."

Jesus fuck. I swallowed as need all but consumed me. It was possible I'd come right there. That would be a first. Except for nocturnal dream state ejaculations, I'd never come without actually fucking or stroking my dick.

But I had work to do.

"What about you, Alex? Are you feeling lucky?"

"I'm hotter than fuck."

She smiled, and it was like the sun. I was in fucking trouble.

"Well, you know where I'll be." She turned and sauntered out of the kitchen, my eyes riveted to her ass. Yep, I was fucked.

I turned my attention to the computer. I could take a break, right?

I made it to the pool area just as she dove in. My heart did weird things in my chest as I saw her naked form glide through the water. She came up on the other side and gave me a sexy smile.

"Opportunity has arrived." I dove in, gliding straight to her pussy, which I licked before coming up for air. Then I fucked her like my life depended on it.

The next night, she showed up late in the kitchen. I'd already fucked her in her bed and was now in my work area finishing up a few things. She entered, her hair mussed and her lips swollen from the kisses I'd given her just a few hours ago. She was wearing her robe again, and my dick was already rising.

"Going swimming?" I asked.

She shook her head. "No. I'm hungry." She opened the fridge. Because of the angle of my nook and the refrigerator, I couldn't see what it was. All I knew was that I was disappointed she hadn't shown up to seduce me.

"Oh, damn," she said.

"Something wrong?" I asked.

She appeared at my nook. Her robe was open, revealing that delectable skin of hers. Dripping between her tits was something that looked suspiciously like chocolate syrup. "I spilled," she complained with a pout.

Warning bells clanged in my head. We were too exposed. There was too much risk of getting caught. My adrenaline kicked up the same way it did when I was jumping from a plane or skiing unplowed territory of a mountain.

"Let me help you." My hands slid behind her, gripping her ass as I tugged her close. I ran my tongue over the chocolate, moaning at the taste of the cold, sugary syrup on her hot, exotic skin.

When I finished, I looked up at her. Her smile was sweet and sexy as she held up the bottle of syrup. "Would you like more?"

"Fuck yeah." I took it from her and moved her into the kitchen. I lifted her onto the island and then squeezed the chocolate all over her. She'd come four times before she took the bottle from me and demanded a turn.

I've had a lot of diverse sexual experiences, but never chocolate on my dick. The chocolate was erotic, but the way Victoria devoured my cock . . . I'd never come that hard, that long, in my life.

Later that night, as I lay alone in my bed, I realized that Henry would be home the day after tomorrow and I was nowhere near burning out this fire for Victoria. In fact, it seemed to be burning hotter.

TWO NIGHTS LATER, I understood what "going cold turkey" meant. I enjoyed seeing Henry and Victoria's reunion. I was glad he was home safe and had been able to make preparations for the business that would make it easier to protect him. But Jesus fuck, my balls were turning blue from lack of contact with Victoria.

I sat in his office reviewing everything I knew at this point with him and Victoria. I wasn't a man who was easily spooked, but I was terrified that some look or gesture I'd make toward Victoria would reveal what I'd been doing. What I wanted to keep doing. Even when we weren't fucking, the woman ensnared me with her strength, her humor, her openness. I felt bewitched. I was well and truly fucked. I understood now that when this ended, and it would—it had to—I'd feel like shit. There would be a hole left by her absence. I wasn't looking forward to that.

"What happens if the D.A. doesn't move forward?" Henry asked, drawing me from my dirty thoughts of Victoria and my fear of getting caught.

"It'll be more of the same if you continue to write shit about Pitney. If you're lucky, he'll resort to non-lethal tactics."

Victoria frowned at me. "Like what?"

I shrugged. "Like finding ways to fuck with the news. Filing a lawsuit for harassment. Questioning your sanity. The truth is, these business types get rid of the thorns in their sides more by discrediting or ruining them than by killing them."

"Then why the threats? Why have me assaulted?" Henry asked.

"Because he was facing prison and you were the person feeding the world with his misdeeds. He knows this current investigation started from a story your media ran. Now that the D.A. is backing off, he can use all this to make you look nuts."

"That's better than dead," Victoria said.

My lips twitched but I quickly worked to hide it.

"Are you running the story about the homeless?" I asked.

"You bet we are. We're not only exposing the evictions and the hypocrisy of his donation to the shelter, but also the connection between him and the judge that allowed him to evict everyone with bogus complaints. He even turned off the heat and air, which is against the law. There is so much wrong with this. This is only the tip of the iceberg."

"Jesus, Henry."

"What? It's wrong."

"It is, but a judge is going to want to squash this."

"By squash, what does that mean? An order not to print the story?"

I shrugged. "Could be, or it could be something more permanent."

"You mean dangerous?"

I nodded.

She looked from me to her father, but I knew her worried expression wouldn't hold any weight with his duty to help those being fucked over by George Pitney. For a moment, I considered offering to take Victoria out of the country to keep her safe. It was selfish, I knew, but not necessarily wrong. If Henry was going to continue this mission, Victoria would continue to be a potential target or collateral damage.

She turned back to me. "Is George really that dangerous that he'd go after someone prominent like my father? He's well-liked in the city. That could backfire."

I thought back to years ago when I still worked out of New York and I and several other Saint Security operatives provided security to Pitney. He was more subtle back then than he was now, although he was still pretty subtle. But bodyguards were like furniture, there but not really seen. I'd overheard Pitney order his men to make lives hard for people Pitney didn't like and to pay off officials. I'd reported it to Noel, who terminated our business with Pitney. In those years, Pitney's success had only emboldened him. Too many people went missing in his orbit for it not to be on purpose.

"We have to assume it's a risk he's willing to take," I said.

Victoria looked back at her father. "Can't someone else take up this mantle?"

"Who?" Henry looked tired as he sat behind his desk. "If the D.A. isn't going to do anything, who else will?"

She sighed, knowing as I did that it was fruitless to talk him out of it. "I have work to do." She rose from the couch she'd been sitting on.

"You do understand, don't you, sweetheart?" Henry asked her.

She nodded. "I know you feel the need to do this. I don't agree, but I understand." She left the room.

Anger bloomed deep. I wanted to throttle Henry for putting her through this. "Has work always been more important than her?"

Henry's eyes were dark as they looked at me. "That's a fucked up thing to say."

"Maybe."

"She understands. She said so."

"She said she understood that you felt the need to do it."

"Right."

"Clearly, you don't understand or care about the impact it has on her. And because you don't, the message you give her is that she's not as important as your righteous mission to end Pitney."

"You don't know anything about being a father. She's my daughter, not yours." His words were a reminder of how fucked up my behavior was. I was old enough to be her father.

"I don't need to be a father to see how this hurts her. Worries her. And Jesus, fuck, Henry, you're committing her to living in hiding. For a man who wants his daughter to live her life, run her own business, and travel the world, you've made sure that can't happen."

"I don't need this from you." Henry stood and went to the bar.

"You know I'm right. This shit is going to bite you in the ass, Henry. I just hope Victoria isn't the one they'll target to get at you." I was precariously close to revealing too much, if not by my words than by my emotional outburst. I strode out of the room and went directly to the third floor.

I found Victoria in her bedroom, staring out the window.

"I won't let anything he does hurt you," I said, shutting her door and going to her. Warning bells clanged, but I didn't give a fuck. I pulled her to me, wanting—no, needing—to reassure her.

She leaned into me, letting me hold her. "Do you mean my father or Pitney?"

"Both."

She looked up at me with a wan smile. "My hero."

I wanted to be that, I realized. The truth of it hit me like a two-by-four. I was falling for this woman. I was falling for my dumb-ass friend's daughter.

"I don't know how much longer I can tolerate staying here."

"I know." I kissed her head.

"This is going to sound like rich girls' problems, but I miss my stuff. My home."

"So let's go there."

Her eyes rounded as she looked up at me in surprise. Truth be told, I was surprised I said it. I probably did because she wanted that and to get at Henry for being such a hardhead.

I quickly calculated what it would involve to let her return to her place and keep her safe trying to keep my own bias out of it. Yeah, right.

"You'd still need protection."

Her eyebrows waggled. "I've got my handy dandy bodyguard."

I swallowed hard as emotion swept through me. She didn't know just how much she had me. "You'd still need to be sequestered."

"But I'd be in my own space. And you are always good for entertainment."

I should say no. Tell her I was wrong. "Let me make the arrangements. I imagine Henry won't like it, but—"

"I'll be the one to talk to him. I can be hard headed too. I'll tell him I'm going. That's it. No discussion. I'm sure he'll pay for whatever needs to happen, and if not, I have some savings."

Henry would fucking pay to keep her safe. I'd make sure of that. "Okay. Pack your stuff and talk to your dad. I'll send men over to check out your building."

"Not Ian, though," she said with a cheeky smile.

"Oh?"

"He makes you grumpy when he's around me."

I laughed. "You know how to un-grump me." I kissed her even though I shouldn't. Then I strode out of her room feeling like I was walking a tightrope. On both sides sat doom, and yet I was going to walk that motherfucker.

18

Victoria

Wow. Shocking! Alex was not only going to take me home, but he was taking me to stay. I didn't even have to beg. I wondered if it was because he was pissed at my father. Not that he was solely motivated by that. I think he was worried about me. Maybe he even cared for me.

I won't let anything he does hurt you.

It wasn't his words so much as the intensity behind them that made my heart crack open. Something inside me heard *I love you.* My head knew it was stupid to think he felt that. My heart didn't seem to care. It wanted his protection. His strength. Whatever he could give, I wanted.

I packed my bag, nervous and excited by the adventure about to happen. I carried my bag down and set it by the door.

"What's this?" Knightly said. "Don't let Mr. Sterling see this. He'll drag you back kicking and screaming."

"He's taking me home."

"This is your home," Knightly said sternly.

"I'm sorry, but I need to go to my place."

He nodded. "You're all grown up. But we sure loved having you around." He reached into his pocket. "I meant to give this to you earlier." He handed me a bag of chocolate covered peanuts.

"My favorites."

"There's more where that came from if you stay."

I gave him a hug. "You're the best, Knightly."

"We'll miss you."

"Thank you for understanding. Now let's hope Dad does."

Knightly nodded, and I headed off to my father's office. I rapped on the door and opened it a pinch, enough to peek in. "Knock, knock."

"Come in, Tori." He waved me in, standing. He came around his desk. "You're not angry with me, are you?"

"Not angry. A little irritated, but that may be from being cooped up."

He sighed. "I'm sorry." I knew he was, but not enough to change his plans.

"Listen, Dad, I can't stay here indefinitely. I'm going home."

He frowned. "It's not safe. I doubt Alex will be okay with that."

I sucked in a breath, hoping he couldn't tell that I was falling for his friend. "He's taking me. He's making plans now."

My father recoiled. "What? He didn't say anything to me. I'm the one who needs to approve—"

I took my father's hands. "I told him I'd talk to you. If you trust him like you say you do, then you have to trust him now."

"Is this because I won't back down?"

"It is only that this situation is going to draw out and I can't live like this. I need to go, and if you don't want to continue to pay Saint Security for the extra—"

"Of course, I'll pay." He looked at me like I'd grown a horn. "Just because I need to follow this through doesn't mean I won't do everything to protect you." His hand cupped my cheek. "You're my world, Tori."

"I know, Dad. You need to do you and I need to do me. Do you understand?"

He sighed. "I guess I have no choice."

I hugged him.

"Sometimes, I forget you're your own woman. I'm not sure how or when that happened. I'm so proud of you."

When he pulled away, his kind expression toward me morphed into annoyance as he looked over my shoulder. "Alex."

I turned to see Alex in the doorway with several bags. Next to him stood Ian. "We're here to report on the change of protection for Victoria."

My father nodded. "Yes, fine. Come in."

Fifteen minutes later, with all the reporting and planning done, I kissed my father goodbye and headed down to the garage where Alex had arranged a car. As I slipped inside it, I had an unsettling feeling in my gut.

"Are you alright?" Alex asked as the car pulled out of the garage.

"I'm worried I won't see my father again."

"Why?"

"I don't know. Maybe I'm feeling guilty. Like I'm abandoning him."

Alex took my hand, surprising me with the gesture since we weren't in private. What if the driver saw? "You're not abandoning him. He's put you in this situation, and I imagine he's relieved that you're doing your thing. He might be selfish with this mission of his, but he doesn't want it to impact you."

"I guess you're right."

"Do you want me to tell you about the time your dad got caught with his pants down?"

I looked at him, wondering what the heck he was talking about.

Alex had a grin on his face. "It involved honey and a girl."

I laughed. "You're joking."

He held his right hand up. "I swear it's the truth."

As Alex regaled me with stories of my father in his younger years, we wove through the city to my apartment. The last time I'd been there with Alex, I'd been annoyed at him. This time, I was half in love with him. It was dangerous to my heart, but what could I do?

My only choice was to enjoy the time we had together until it ended.

Jonesy wasn't on duty when we arrived. I waved to the doorperson there as I led Alex to the elevator. Once I stepped into my apartment, I stood for a moment, taking it all in.

"I'm home." A feeling of freedom and peace washed over me.

"This place suits you," Alex said, coming to stand next to me.

"You think so?"

He nodded.

"How so?"

His eyes turned wicked. "It's clearly a place a sexy-ass woman lives."

I smirked. "You see that without even seeing my bedroom?"

He dropped our bags he'd been carrying. "I see your sexy ass. That's all I need." In an instant, he scooped me up. "Where is the bedroom? Or we can do this here."

I pointed toward the door of my room. "It's there, or we can do this here."

"By the time we're done, we'll have done it everywhere."

My heart did that flutter thing even as my brain told me not to read anything into it. This was just sex. Hadn't he said he wanted to burn off this thing between us?

But for me it was more. In only a short time, my annoyance had turned to affection. Not because of all the sex, of which there was a lot. In the moments after sex, or simply alone in our own bubble, we talked. Today was the first time he'd told me stories about my dad. Normally, he shared his adventures like his treks through the Amazon or scuba diving in the Mediterranean. Except for the woman who'd taken his money, he'd done most of his traveling alone. He didn't say so, but I knew it was by choice. Back on the plane when we first met, it was clear that he didn't want emotional entanglements. When he needed sex, he'd find a willing woman who, like him, only needed the physical release without the emotional connection. But now there was both the physical and emotional, at least for me. It would hurt when he left.

I pushed that away as he tossed me on my bed.

"I'm going to make you scream my name," he said as he undressed. "Now that there's no one to hear."

My pussy tingled with excitement. It was hard to believe he could make me more aroused or cause bigger orgasms than he already had.

"Maybe you'll scream my name," I said, also getting undressed.

"Let's find out." Once naked, he laid his body over mine, taking my hands and holding them over my head. "How adventurous are you?"

I was going to spontaneously combust. "What do you have in mind?" We'd had sex in all sorts of ways already.

"I want to fuck those fantastic tits of yours."

I looked down at my breasts. "Really?"

He laughed. "Do you think it's weird?"

I shook my head. "No. I just wonder if there's enough friction for you."

"I'm going to come all over your tits, but first." He rolled us until he was on his back and I was over him. "Come sit on my face so I can make you scream."

This wouldn't be the first time he'd used his mouth to make me come, but it would be the first time in this position. I'll admit, I worried a little bit that I might suffocate him. I followed his urging and straddled him.

"You're wet, Victoria. I can't wait to drink you up." He dragged his tongue through my slit.

I gripped the headboard as electric pleasure shot through me. "Oh, God."

"Mmm . . . so fucking good." His tongue flicked over my clit, and I rocked in response. Soon, his tongue was fucking me, sliding in and out of me. Fire rushed through my veins. My body trembled as need coiled tighter and tighter.

"Alex . . ." I teetered on the edge.

"Come, Victoria." His mouth was on me again, demanding, relentless.

"Alex!" I cried out as my orgasm slammed into me. My hips

rocked as I rode the delicious sensations until boneless, I collapsed, sitting on his chest.

He maneuvered us until I was on my back, still panting. "See how sweet you taste?" He kissed me with my essence still on his lips. He trailed his kisses down until he reached my breasts. "These are magnificent tits. Round. Soft." He sucked on one breast. "Your nipples are pink and hard." He flicked his tongue over one. "I have to fuck them, Victoria."

I nodded because I still couldn't find the breath to speak.

He rose, straddling me until his dick rested over my diaphragm. "It's going to be so fucking hot to see my cock swallowed by your tits."

His words made my pussy clench with excitement.

He pressed my breasts together and slid his dick between them. "Oh, yeah . . . so fucking hot. Can you hold them?"

I replaced his hands, holding my breasts as closely together as I could.

His pale blue eyes were filled with wild heat as he watched his dick move in and out my breasts. I could feel it lengthen, thicken with each stroke.

I adjusted my hand so I could add extra stimulation as he moved.

"Fuck yes . . ." For a moment, his eyes closed as if he were savoring the sensations. He thrust again, and when his tip peeked through the top of my breasts, I lifted my head toward it and licked it.

He let out a feral growl. "Yes . . .Victoria . . . more."

My hands squeezed my breasts tighter, my fingers pressing between them to slide along his shaft. When his tip poked through, I licked it. Again and again, and each time, I could hear his breath become heavy, harsh, his groans louder.

"I'm gonna come . . . I'm gonna come . . ." He gripped the headboard and fucked my breasts hard and fast. He threw his head back. "*Fuck.*" Cum shot out, hitting my mouth and chin and neck.

"Drink it, baby." He shifted, and his dick slid into my mouth.

I gripped him as I did as he asked the best I could. Finally, he sat back.

"Jesus fuck." He collapsed beside me.

"Was that okay?" I don't know why I felt I needed reassurance, but I did. I wanted to give him the pleasure he'd been seeking.

"Are you kidding?" He turned toward me. "You make me come so hard. You're like a fantasy."

I liked that, and yet, it wasn't enough. I didn't just want to be sexually compatible. I wanted his heart.

We lay quietly for a moment, and then he rolled on top of me. He kissed me, gently at first, enough to let me pretend there was emotion behind it. Slowly, the heat picked up.

Once again, he took my hands and pressed them over my head as his lips and teeth teased my nipples.

"Oh . . ." I arched into him.

"You like that? Are you ready to come again?"

"Yes."

He moved until his dick was at my entrance. "Look at me, Victoria. Watch me fill you."

I opened my eyes, finding him staring down at me. Slowly, he slid in. "Do you feel me?"

I nodded, wrapping my legs around his hips.

"I feel you." He bent over and kissed me again, soft, sweet. We moved together, taking our time until nature took over. I hit the pinnacle, soaring into sublime pleasure. With a thrust and a whisper of my name, he followed me over.

When our breaths settled and he held me close, I felt confused. At first, the sex felt physical only. A desire for fantasy fulfillment. But this time, it felt like something more. Something sweeter, deeper. Especially as he held me and kissed my temple.

I was in deep trouble. I liked it here in his arms. Too much. If I were smart, I'd end this part of our relationship. I'd make him sleep on the couch and not touch me again.

But let's face it, I wasn't smart. I was dumb enough to get what I could from him for as long as I could get it.

19

Alex

I was well and truly fucked. After a week in Victoria's , I'd experienced things I never thought I would. I never wanted to. It was why I'd never lived with a woman. Oh, sure, I'd been in close quarters with people I'd been assigned to protect, but I never ate meals with them, and I sure as hell never slept beside them in their bed. Yet here I was, essentially living and sleeping with my client, my friend's daughter. Yep, I was fucked and apparently didn't seem to care.

Good Christ, waking up next to Victoria felt so good. Too good. I'd spent forty-eight years avoiding this feeling, and to be honest, it hadn't been hard. In my life, I'd met interesting women and sexy women, but never one like Victoria. She lit up all my senses. She challenged me. Made me laugh. She brought out a fierce, protective side of me. When she touched me, I felt it deep in my bones. The need to be around her went well beyond lust. It felt like my soul was tethered to her.

And it was wrong. So fucking wrong. I had to do something. What

I should do is stop being her bodyguard. I should focus on getting this case resolved so I could return to England.

But my fucking heart argued that I still had three weeks that Archer had given me to work this case. Three weeks I could wake up to Victoria's beautiful face. Three weeks to banter with her. Three weeks to bury myself in her body.

My mind knew that I was playing with fire. It knew that my desire for Victoria wasn't going to burn out and there was no future for us, assuming I could be brave enough to pursue one. I couldn't have a life with her that included Henry being ignorant of it.

See, I was fucked.

What was most crucial to understand was that I wasn't needed here. Saint Security had plenty of capable men and women to protect Henry and Victoria for as long as Henry wanted protection. The only reason I was involved at all was because Henry specifically asked for me. But our friendship was being challenged by his foolhardy behavior, and it would be blown apart if he knew what I'd been doing with Victoria.

What I needed to do was to find some time and space away from her to clear my mind and my heart.

I was one lucky sonofabitch when Dax called and told me they'd picked up a guy skulking around Henry's house the night before.

"He's the usual low-level goon, but he's trying to play it tough."

"I want to talk to him." This was my chance to get away to sort my shit out and end this case.

"There's no need. I'll send—"

"I've met Pitney. Maybe that will give me an advantage."

"What about Banion's daughter?"

I thought of the safest, quickest way to deal with her. "We take her back to her father's." It was the right move as long as I could convince her to go along with it.

"I thought she didn't want to stay there anymore."

"It's just a day, maybe two." That was true of the case, but not of my time with Victoria. This had to be it. I had to end it now to save my heart, my soul, and my job.

"Alright. Do you want me to set up the transfer?"

"Would you? And let's keep the extra surveillance, moving them with her to her father's. If someone is scouting Henry's place, something might be up."

"Got it."

When I hung up with Dax, I left the bedroom where I'd taken the call and went to the living room where Victoria sat at her disk on a video call.

For a moment, I watched her, wondering how she'd he gotten so deep inside me, especially in so little time and with the big problem of her being Henry's daughter. Yep. I was fucked if I didn't get out now.

I went to the kitchen and made a cup of coffee, checking my email while I waited for her to finish her call. As she and her team wound down their meeting, I brewed another cup for her. By the time it finished brewing and I brought it to her, she was off the call.

"Such service. I might have to keep you around." She gave me a flirty smile that sent a wave of panic through me because my first thought to her words was that yes, she should keep me around.

I pushed that back. I pushed it all back and forced myself to be no-nonsense, professional. "Something's come up that I need to deal with."

She quirked a brow over the rim of her cup. It made me wonder if my voice sounded as desperate and terrified as I felt.

"Is someone coming to replace you?"

"There will be someone else, but also, it will be better if you go to your father's." I braced myself for her response, expecting her to fight me on it.

She sighed in resignation. "For how long?"

"A day. Maybe two." I kept my eyes on hers so she wouldn't suspect my deception.

"Can you tell me what's going on?"

I leaned against the back of her couch, wanting to look calm. I didn't want her to worry. "We picked up someone outside your dad's place last night."

Her brows shot up. "Is he okay?"

"Yes. He's fine."

Relief shone on her face. "Is it safe for us to be there if someone is casing the place?"

"Yes. There will be extra security. No one is getting into his place without serious injury."

"Okay." She stood and moved toward me. I wanted to grab her and pull her close but forced myself not to.

"So, what do you have to do? Will you be safe?" She looped her arms around my neck because I wasn't strong enough to stop her. Her nearness and concern for my safety did strange things to me. Things I liked. Things I shouldn't feel.

"I want to talk to him. See what we can find out about Pitney's plans toward your father or anything else we could use to get him off the street."

"Does it have to be you?"

It didn't. "I'm in charge of this for the time being, so I should go."

"Time being." Her arms loosened and I didn't like it. I held her tight and looked at her, not knowing how to respond without giving in to something I couldn't or hurting her.

She let out a breath. "Of course, for the time being. When this is all over, you'll go back to your life."

You could come with me. No, she couldn't. Jesus fuck, I was going mad. "Why don't you pack up what you need for a few days?"

"I thought you said one or two days."

"That's what I meant." Except I didn't. This was it for me and her. I should tell her that, but as I looked into her beautiful face, the words escaped me.

"I'll call your dad and let him know you're coming."

She stared up at me, and I wondered if she could see the lies in my eyes. I wouldn't be surprised if she did. She knew I could be an asshole.

Unable to help myself, I leaned forward and kissed her. Gentle. Sweet. Filling my chest with a need so strong I nearly gave in.

When I pulled away, I released her and went looking to pack up my own things. "Get packed."

I heard her leave the room and only then did I look up. I was such an idiot. How had I let this happen? Why did I let it go so far? I felt like a fucking asshole.

I pulled out my phone and called Henry.

"Alex, is everything alright?" Henry's voice was stressed. "We had some trouble—"

"Yes, yes. Victoria is fine."

"Thank God. I guess you know a man was found sneaking around the house."

"Yes. That's why I'm calling. I need to go talk to him, so I'm bringing Victoria back to your place."

"Oh . . . well, I'm glad she'll be here. I'll feel better. Will she stay?"

Yes, but she didn't know that yet. "Maybe. Right now, I need a couple of days. I've got extra men assigned."

"I wanted you—"

"I know, but you should have seen by now that all the men on this team are good." God, for once I needed him to relent.

"I guess it's just a few days."

"Yes. And I need to talk to this guy if we're going to put Pitney away."

"Where is he?"

I vacillated on what to tell him. Saint Security stopped working with less reputable and unsavory people years ago, but depending on the job, on occasion, our actions still skirted the laws. Instead of sending this guy to the police, we held him, questioning him. We knew Pitney wouldn't send the cops looking for him or he'd have to explain why his henchman was staking out Henry's.

We didn't torture, but we could definitely scare people just enough to find out something more substantial than fraud to put him away. If I could get that type of information, then maybe Henry and Victoria could have some breathing room.

They'd still need protection unless we could find a way to cut off Pitney's power. That was something I needed to look into. But first, I'd talk to this guy and learn what I could. If he cooperated not just with us, but with the D.A. too, we could protect him.

Then I could return to London and resume my life.

A pang of sadness clenched my chest at the idea of my old life. I ignored it.

"He's in custody." I answered Henry's question.

It wasn't a lie even if I knew Henry would think police custody.

"I've made a mess of things, haven't I?"

I pinched the bridge of my nose. It was too late for Henry to second-guess himself. "Pitney is a sick fuck, Henry. You're just trying to make the world better. "

"I am. I want a better place for Victoria. I don't want her to suffer anything with the Pitneys of the world. She has her life ahead of her. Someday, she'll marry and have kids . . ."

A dark mass of jealousy balled in my gut over the man Victoria would give her life and love and body to.

"I hope to be a grandparent someday. I'd like the world to be better for them. God, can you imagine me being a grandparent?"

I felt sick again. His words were a reminder of how old I was and how fucked up it was that I was having sex with his daughter. Thank God she was on the pill. Jesus, if she got pregnant . . . I couldn't even consider that.

20

Victoria

I grabbed several pairs of underwear, tossing them on top of the clothes I'd already packed. Alex said one or two days, but he seemed uncertain, so I packed for a week.

As I selected shoes to bring, I worked to deal with the unsettled feeling I had. Something about Alex was off. After a week of playful, sexy, insatiable Alex, today, he was distant. I told myself it was probably because we were about to see my father. He wanted to start practicing now like there was nothing going on between us. If my father knew about our relationship, he'd be upset. Well, not *relationship*. I suppose *affair* was a better description. Ours was a time-limited connection. In fact, maybe that time was up. Perhaps his behavior was starting the detachment process. It made sense. If this meeting he had to go to meant putting an end to George Pitney's threats against my father, then I wouldn't need Alex anymore.

The way my heart squeezed in my chest reminded me that the obnoxious man had found his way into my heart. If things were different, I might have tried to find a way we could spend more time together. He could show me all the wonders of the world. But I knew that wouldn't happen, not with his being my father's friend.

I went into my bathroom to gather my toothbrush and other grooming needs. I tossed my birth control pack into my makeup bag. It occurred to me that I'd need a new pack tomorrow as I took my last inert pill this morning.

Wait? I looked at myself in the mirror. If I was on inert pills this week, why didn't I have my period? How had I missed that my period hadn't come?

Alex. The man was a distraction. But God, to lose sight of something as important as my period?

I swallowed as the significance of missing my period hit me.

No. I didn't need to worry about pregnancy. Period or not, I was on the pill. I took it religiously—well, usually. I might have taken a pill a day late during my travels. Maybe that was why I was late. My body was confused. Plus, I was under a lot of stress with my father and Pitney. And many women had late or missed periods without being pregnant, right?

For a moment I stood, paralyzed, uncertain as to what to do.

Take a test.

Right. I needed to find out for sure whether I was just late or pregnant, except I couldn't be pregnant. Seeing the *Not Pregnant* on the test would make my worry evaporate.

The next question was how was I going to get a pregnancy test? I wasn't going to send Knightly or Mrs. Tillis out to get one for me. I could probably arrange for one to be delivered, but I wasn't sure how discrete delivery people were, plus, I couldn't be sure who he'd give it to at the house.

I needed to go to a drugstore, but Alex wouldn't let me do that alone. I could sneak out of the house, but with extra men watching, I wasn't going to get far.

I gripped the sink, panic starting to grow. Maybe I should tell Alex. I dismissed the thought even before it finished forming. His head would likely explode at the idea of knocking up his friend's daughter. Plus, he was dealing with Pitney's man.

Maybe I could have another Saint Security guy take me to the drugstore, but that too wasn't feasible. No doubt, Alex would tell my next bodyguard that under no circumstances could I leave the house.

Next idea was to call someone I knew and ask them to bring me a test. I thought of Samantha, but her hands were full with her mother and son. And if she showed up, Alex's men might search her.

Ugh! There was only one answer. I had to convince Alex to take me to a drugstore and let me shop in private. Yeah, right. But I had to try!

I did my best to look and act normal as I brought my packed bag to the living room.

Alex was standing at the window, his hands in his pockets. My heart filled with yearning and then ached that I couldn't have him. This was probably the end of our time together.

I wanted to seduce him one last time, but he'd pushed me away earlier. I tried not to feel hurt by that. I knew he'd already moved on.

"I'm ready, " I said.

He turned to look at me with an unreadable expression. It would have been nice if this was a little bit hard for him.

He picked up his bag. "Your dad is glad you're going home."

"It's just for a few days." I waited for his reaction, but he turned his attention away from me.

"Right." He took my bag and motioned with his head to precede him. I had a feeling he was hiding something. Was it that he was keeping me in the dark about the case or that this was likely our last moment together? I'd have thought he'd tell me our one-and-done had finally come to an end. He'd burned out his interest in me. Or maybe he figured I should just know that and wasn't going to bother to tell me. He could be an insensitive oaf.

I suppose this would be better than an awkward goodbye.

I didn't like uncertainty, so I decided to confront him. "This is goodbye, isn't it? Even if my dad remains in danger, I'll have a different bodyguard from now on, right?"

His brow furrowed. "Why would you think that?"

"Am I wrong?"

He looked down at the hands clasped in his lap. "No."

I didn't say anything as I waited for him to elaborate. He didn't. I guess that was that.

"I need to stop at a convenience or drug store."

For a moment he looked confused. Had he expected me to beg for more time? Or did he need a minute to catch up to the new topic?

"No."

"Yes. I need things that I don't want others to get for me. They're personal."

"No."

"Yes. Should I ask Ian to take me instead?" It was petty, but I was desperate.

The comment had the desired reaction. Alex's eyes narrowed and his jaw tightened. "Fine, but I go in with you and you do what I say."

Hmm, that wouldn't work. I needed to think of a plan where he wouldn't be looking over my shoulder as I grabbed a pregnancy test. A test I didn't need, except to reassure myself that I wasn't pregnant.

"Pull up to the next drugstore," Alex told our driver.

Crap, what was I going to do now?

When the car pulled to the curb, Alex told me, "Wait here for a moment. " He stepped out and appeared to scan the area. "Alright, come on."

I scooted out of the car and entered the store wondering what the heck I was going to do. I headed down the feminine hygiene aisle. Panicking, I grabbed tampons and pads. I mean, that's what I was going to need when my period finally came.

Alex's cheeks turned red as he saw what I was buying. And with that, an idea formed.

"Here." I shoved them at Alex.

"What?" His hands wrapped around the items, his expression horrified.

"I need you to hold those while I look for vaginal cream."

Alex's eyes darted around the room, probably not looking for Pitney's men but instead making sure no one could see this manly man holding tampons and pads.

I grabbed a douche and yeast infection cream and handed them to Alex too. "I need these after all that sex."

"Good Christ."

"Oh, I need to check for nipple cream. You've sucked mine raw." I didn't know if such a cream existed, but I felt sure he didn't either.

"Jesus fuck, Victoria."

"Oh, look, UTI relief." I grabbed a box. "I should get some. So much sex can lead to a urinary tract infection."

"God damn."

"What?" I stared up at him innocently.

"This!" he hissed, still looking around like one of his burly buddies might see him.

"What about it?" I rolled my eyes. "Too manly to hold feminine products? Here." I started to take the items from him. "Go stand by the door while I get what I need. Heaven forbid you be caught near menstrual pads." This was it. If this didn't work, I was going home with all this stuff but without the one thing I really needed, a pregnancy test.

He scanned the store. It wasn't empty, but the few people there looked harmless enough.

"Fine." He strode toward the main door.

Yes! Victory. I quickly grabbed a pregnancy test while his back was to me and brought it with everything else to the self-checkout. I scanned and bagged everything, then paid.

With the pregnancy test well-hidden between the douche and tampons in the bag, I walked up to him. "Ready?"

His eyes narrowed at me. "You enjoyed that, didn't you?"

I grinned. "A little."

He looked at me then in a way that made my heart stall in my chest. It reminded me of the way he'd looked at me the night he told me he couldn't stop thinking about me.

I went up on tiptoes and kissed his cheek. "It was a great adventure, Alex."

He gave a short nod, then opened the door and escorted me to the car.

Once home, Knightly greeted us. "Mr. Banion would like to see you," he said to Alex.

Alex looked at me, and I felt the weight of this moment. There would be no goodbye kiss. No intimate acknowledgement of the last few weeks.

"Take care of yourself."

I sucked in a breath as I felt tears come to my eyes. "You too."

"This way." Knightly directed Alex to my father's office.

Alex followed, looking back at me just as he was about to walk through the office doors.

I gave a small wave. He sent me a wan smile in response. Then he was gone.

I sighed, heading upstairs with my bag of products. I went straight to the ensuite bath connected to my room and dumped the bag on the floor. I snatched the pregnancy kit and read the directions.

"Are we really going to do this?" I asked my reflection in the mirror.

I was probably overreacting, but knowing would alleviate the worry. I followed the directions, leaving the test on the box as I distracted myself by going to unpack. Three minutes later, I stood at the threshold of the bathroom, too nervous to walk in and see if my life was about to change.

No. I was being ridiculous. I was worrying for nothing.

I stepped into the bathroom and looked at the test.

PREGNANT.

21

Alex

I should have been relieved by how quickly Victoria accepted that this little affair we had going had come to an end. I admired her ability to speak it out loud when I hadn't had the guts to be clear with her. She had understood what I hadn't been able to articulate. She didn't cling and ask for more time. She didn't pout, nor did she get angry. She accepted and moved on. It was exactly the perfect response. So why did it piss me off so much?

She'd ensnared me with her beauty and wit and intelligence until I was halfway in love with her. I didn't much like holding all those girly products, but when I realized she was fucking with me, still teasing even though we were done, I'd nearly changed my mind.

But her ability to revert back to normal, to not feel any loss over the end of us, told me she didn't feel the same for me. Why the fuck would she? I was old enough to be her father, after all.

My mind was in a whirl of these thoughts when I left Henry's home and headed to a safe house Saint Security had up in the Bronx so I could meet with the man found skulking around Henry's house last night. The fact that I was bothered by how easily Victoria was able to walk away from me was an indication of just how important it was that things between us ended now. Clearly, I was in too deep.

When I arrived at the house, Dax was already there to meet me. From the outside, the location seemed like a normal residence, but on the inside it had been soundproofed and was loaded with electronics. Places like this were usually used to protect witnesses or other people in our charge from immediate danger. But this time, it was acting as a holding cell for the man who could be holding the key to taking George Pitney down. Or maybe not. If he was a low-level goon, chances were he knew nothing.

"Anything new?" I asked Dax as we went to the kitchen.

"He's still keeping mum. You want some coffee?" Dax pulled a mug from the cupboard. I nodded because I could use a little caffeine. I hadn't slept as much last week.

I gave my head a quick shake to make sure Victoria didn't take root again.

Dax quirked a brow. "Is that a yes or no?"

"That's a yes. Thanks."

Dax used the pod brewing system and made two cups of coffee, bringing them both to the table. He slid mine across to me and then sat.

"We know his name is Tommy Langhorne who was very recently married to Amiee Pitney."

My eyes widened, not expecting that.

"Amiee is George's niece. Officially, the kid works in sales within their real estate arm."

"That gives him a good excuse to be skulking around the neighborhood." I took a sip of my coffee.

Dax nodded in agreement. "He must be dedicated if he's doing it at two thirty in the morning. Pitney had to know that we were there, so the fact that he sent his niece's husband sounds like it could be a test of the kid."

I nodded in agreement, but then again, maybe not. "He doesn't like the kid if he's willing to let him get arrested or caught by us. Maybe he wants to get rid of him."

"That's possible too." Dax sat back, draping his arm over the back of the chair next to him. "The kid is trying to be tough, but I think you'll see right away that he's scared shitless. I'm surprised he hasn't pissed his pants yet."

That was good news to my ears. "I want to talk to him, but first I want to lay out some ideas that should help us close this thing up sooner rather than later."

"I'm all ears."

"We need information that can help us nail Pitney, but you know as well as I do that he can get Henry from prison."

"Yep."

"So we need to destabilize the organization."

Dax studied me. "You talk like it's organized crime."

"The business may be legit, but we both know that Pitney operates much like how the mob does. And we also know that if Pitney, the head of the snake, is removed, another one is going to grow in."

Dax nodded. "You want to figure out who that is?"

I leaned forward. "I want to find the one who is greedy and power-hungry enough to usurp Pitney. We find him and do what we can to make sure he takes the lead."

Dax thought about that. "How can you know that your friends and anyone else will be safe with a usurper?"

"First, the usurper isn't going to want to carry around Pitney's baggage. In fact, they're likely to throw Pitney under the bus. Make everything seem like it's squeaky clean. Second, Pitney's actions against Henry are more personal. He's annoyed by what Henry's publications are printing."

"And what happens when Henry publishes unkind things about the new guy?"

"I'll worry about that." I hadn't quite figured out how I would handle it. I hadn't had any luck persuading Henry to change how he did business so far, but if this worked, I hoped that it would motivate him to rethink getting into deep shit again.

"Have you identified anyone yet?" Dax asked.

"I want to talk to Tommy-boy here to see what more we can learn about the organization beyond what we have on paper."

Dax nodded. "By the way, we have gone ahead and started surveilling his wife as well." He pulled out his phone, tapping the photo app and handing it to me. There were pictures of a svelte long-legged blonde woman getting coffee at an Upper West Side java joint, and another of her getting her nails done at a fancy spa.

"Do you think she doesn't realize her husband is missing?"

Dax shrugged. "Hard to know. She doesn't look concerned, which is either really cold or she thinks he's been working all night."

I frowned as I scratched the day-old stubble on my chin, making a mental note to shave later. Disappointment that I wouldn't be with Victoria filled my chest. "Wouldn't the woman be suspicious if her salesman husband was working all night?"

"Remember we're talking about George Pitney, her uncle. I imagine she knows the overtime hours that some of his people have to work."

I nodded. "Let's keep eyes on her. I think I'm going to talk to her, but let's start with Tommy."

"A man who likes to tip his hand. I like it. What do you think you can get from her?"

"Anything that I don't get from her husband." Hopefully, something that would get me out of New York before my three weeks were up.

"It's possible she's totally and completely innocent of what her uncle does. Making contact with her can put her in danger."

I rolled my shoulders because I never liked putting innocent people in danger. "Well, we should make plans to protect her if necessary." My concern for Henry and Victoria outweighed Tommy's wife. Did that make me an asshole? Maybe. But I've had to make these kinds of decisions for many years now. Some were the right decisions and some weren't, but I've learned to live with them all.

Dax picked up a file sitting on the table and handed it to me. "Here's what we've got so far."

I picked it up and read it as I moved to the basement door. I picked up my bag. Normally, I'd have put it in one of the bedrooms since I planned to stay, but I took it with me down to the basement where Tommy was being held.

Outside the room he was in, two Saint Security men sat, watching him on the screen. "Pay up, Walters. He still hasn't pissed himself."

Walters saw me approach. "Double or nothing. I feel like Sterling will have him shitting too."

Deal. The two men shook hands.

I rolled my eyes but smiled. I'd done shit like that before.

"Good luck," Walters called as I opened the door and entered the interrogation room.

Tommy was as attractive as his wife in a soft, pretty boy sort of way. The few notes I'd quickly scanned from Dax's file told me that he too came from money, although not the type of money Pitney had. Dax's notes said they were looking into any connections between Tommy's family and Pitney's. Perhaps they were cronies, or maybe Pitney had something over Tommy's family.

Tommy sat in an uncomfortable metal chair at a drab, institutional metal table. His hands were zip tied, but an empty plate and cup sat before him, indicating that he had consumed the food and beverage he'd been brought.

He looked up at me with tired and weary brown eyes. As if remembering what was going on, he shifted, straightening and adopting a tough guy scowl. "I'm not talking to you."

I gave him an affable smile as I put my bag on the table. I unzipped it enough to put my hand in and rummage around.

Tommy's eyes narrowed and his complexion turned green. "What are you doing?" I knew he had to be imagining all sorts of terrible things in my bag. Hammers. Saws. Pliers to pull out his fingernails. We didn't use those things, but he didn't know that.

With my hand still hidden in the bag, I found my grooming bag and a razor. I pulled it out. "I'm giving you a shave, Tommy boy."

"Shave?"

I nodded as I walked over and sat on the edge of the table next to his chair, tugging at his dark T-shirt collar. "Not much hair there. Maybe I won't need it."

He jerked away from me. "For what?"

I almost felt bad for the poor kid. He couldn't even be twenty-five, and now he was being subjected to the enemies of his brand-new uncle-in-law.

"The electrodes stick better on clean-shaven skin."

His brows shot up to his hairline. "The electrodes?"

I shrugged and pointed my thumb back over my shoulder toward the door. "Those guys are tired of waiting. They want to know what you know. So, they called me." I smiled again.

"Will it hurt?" His voice quavered.

I looked at him with pity, hoping he saw someone who was showing sympathy toward him. "Well, it doesn't feel good. But really, that's the least of your troubles. When you shoot electricity through a person, there's always a chance your heart will stop. Not that we want that. Because we don't, Tommy. All we want is information." I reached into the bag behind me, pulling out my shaving cream. "You've been a tough nut. I admire that." I depressed the top, squirting the foam on the tips of my fingers. "We've had some people who were able to still keep their mouths shut after all this. If you stay strong, Tommy, maybe you will too."

He shot up from his chair and rushed to the corner of the room, standing like a six-year-old boy in trouble by the teacher. "You can't do this. This is illegal. Help!"

I continued to sit on the edge of the table, shaking my head and tsk-tsking. "You should've thought about that before you went to work for your wife's uncle. Surely, you know about his questionable activities. You must be all right with it. This," I said, holding up the razor, "is the possible outcome of going into dirty business with George Pitney. He didn't tell you that when he recruited you? That doesn't seem very nice."

Tommy tried to hold his hands up in surrender, but they were still bound at the wrist. "I don't know anything about his business. I'm a salesman."

I cocked my head to the side. "What were you selling at two thirty in the morning on Riverside Drive?"

"N–n–nothing. I was just out for a walk."

I sighed. "Well, if you're going to stick with that story, I'm going to have to give you a shave." I wished I had a pair of scissors in my bag so that I could cut his shirt open and smear the foam over his chest. It definitely would make him wet his pants. Maybe shit, too. Perhaps Walters needed to up the ante.

"It seems I forgot my scissors." I wiped the foam into his drinking glass. "Excuse me while I go get some."

"What do you need scissors for?" Tommy was about to hyperventilate, which wasn't good. I couldn't talk to people who passed out.

"Don't worry, Tommy. When you leave here, you will still have your manhood."

His hands shot down to cover his groin.

"But I need to cut open your shirt so I can shave you. For the electrodes. Remember?" I stood and headed to the door.

"No, no, no. Wait. George just asked me to go down and look around the house and see what sort of security it had."

"What house?" I moved back into the center of the room.

Tommy shrugged. "Some media guy. George doesn't like what he's been publishing."

Now we were starting to get somewhere. "How many times have you done this?"

"Just once."

I figured he was telling the truth because certainly, our men would've seen him. "And what, specifically, were you supposed to report back to Uncle George?"

"Just about the security system. Oh, and count the number of men who could be there watching the house."

I crossed my arms over my chest and cocked my head to the side, wondering why George would send this kid down to do work he knew he'd get caught doing. George had to know we were there.

"And how many did you count?"

Tommy shrugged. "I don't know. I mean they were people, but I didn't know if they were security or not. You know, like parked on the street. I didn't see anybody when I hopped the fence to go into the back until they grabbed me."

"Why does George want this information?"

Tommy scraped his hands over his face. "I don't know, except that he's mad at him for printing all those stories."

I walked over to Tommy, who tensed as I approached. I rested my hand on the wall as I leaned into him. "Why did he pick you for this job? Clearly, this is not in your job description as a salesman."

Tommy looked at me, and I knew any second, he was definitely going to piss his pants. I shifted back a little bit. "I'll ask you again, Tommy. Why would he pick you?"

He sighed. "I like to gamble and go to strip clubs. But I don't want my wife to know."

Now it made sense. "So George found out and told you he wouldn't say anything if you did this for him."

Tommy nodded. But it still didn't make any sense on why George would send someone totally inexperienced. He ran the risk of Tommy getting arrested. Tommy probably would've withstood the police interrogation, and maybe that was what George was counting on.

Or maybe it was a test for us. Maybe George had sacrificed Tommy to be certain about who Henry was using as protection and how we were operating.

"What does your wife know about all this?" I asked.

His head shook like a bobblehead doll. "Nothing, and I don't want her to know. "

"What does she know about Pitney's business? And why doesn't she seem concerned that you've been gone all night?"

He watched me for a long moment, and I suspected he was trying to find a good lie. Finally, he sighed. "She thinks I'm a wuss for not taking her to France. So when I had this opportunity, I told her I was going to do work for George."

"And that turned her on, did it? She gets wet thinking of your going to the dark side?"

He simply shrugged. That told me she knew about George's activity. She would be the next on my tour of interviews.

I stepped back and motioned to the chair. "Have a seat, Tommy. I'm going to go have a chat with your wife."

"No. You can't do that."

"I promise that she will be safe. No electrodes will be involved. But you need to finish talking to the men here and let them know everything you know about George Pitney's questionable activities."

The kid's legs gave way, and as he sank to the floor, tears streamed down his cheeks. I felt bad for him, but I didn't let on. After all, this was Pitney's fault, not mine.

"I don't know anything. I just married into the family a few months ago. But I know enough to know that George will kill me. Maybe Aimee too."

I squatted down in front of him. "Tommy, look at me."

He lifted his gaze to mine. "Are you being hyperbolic, or do you really think you're in that kind of danger?"

"He'll really kill us."

"If that's true, we need to know all the reasons you think that could happen, and me and my men will protect you and your wife. We will be very generous." I stood and grabbed my bag, shoving my razor and shaving cream back in it. "You have to decide now, Tommy. I'm on my way to talk to your wife, but I'm in communication with everyone here, so I'll know whether you're cooperating or not. But I'll tell you this. Your chances of coming out of this alive are much better with me and my team than with George Pitney. I think you know that."

I turned and walked out of the room. Outside the door, Dax and two other men stood where they had been watching the interview on a computer screen.

Dax shook his head as he laughed. "Electrodes? That was a good one."

I shrugged. "I had to improvise somehow."

The two younger men looked at me. "Dude, that was awesome."

I shrugged. "I must've lost my touch a little bit. He still hasn't pissed his pants."

I left them to finish questioning Tommy and had my car drive me to where our surveillance team had spotted Tommy's wife, Amiee, having lunch with some of her girlfriends.

I entered the fancy restaurant and made a beeline for her table before the host could stop me. "Mrs. Langhorne?"

She and her friends looked up at me.

"I need to talk to you about your husband."

"My husband?" She looked at her friends with an uneasy smile. "If you want to talk to my husband—"

"I've just finished talking with your husband and now I want to talk to you."

This time, she let the worry shine through. "Oh, God, was he arrested?"

"Arrested?" her friends exclaimed.

She realized what she said. "No, he can't be arrested." She tried to cover up her gaff with a laugh.

"He wasn't arrested. But I really do need to talk to you. Alone." I looked at her two friends. "You don't mind, do you?"

Aimee nodded. "I'll catch up with you guys later."

The friends seemed reluctant to leave but finally scooted out of the booth.

I slipped in across from her. "You don't seem particularly concerned that your husband didn't come home last night."

Her hands shook as she took a sip of water. She clearly wasn't finding George Pitney's world sexy now.

"He was working."

"As a salesman in the middle of the night?"

She shook her head. "I don't know what he was doing, but I knew he was doing it for someone."

She was nervous about telling me who he'd been working for. "Your uncle doesn't like your husband very much, does he? It's the only thing that makes sense about why he would send Tommy out like a sacrificial lamb."

Her eyes rounded. "Sacrifice? Is he . . .?"

I waved my hand. "Your husband is fine. He's with me and my team. We work for Saint Security."

Recognition showed in her eyes.

"You've heard of us, then?"

She nodded. "Everyone knows about you. I think my parents worked with you when they took a trip to someplace that was dangerous." The fact that she didn't know where parents went told me that she liked living in wealth but wasn't too interested in the details on how it occurred.

"I can see why George might not care what happens to your husband, but surely, you knew the risk. You thought your husband was too boring. Does it excite you to live like a mobster like your uncle?"

Her eyes cast downward, suggesting regret or maybe shame. "I was mad at Tommy. I didn't want him to go, but we were supposed to be taking a trip to Paris, and he told me we couldn't go because he needed to work. He said he needed to make more money. I know I don't look smart . . ." She paused, and I realized she wanted to know my name.

"Sterling." It was the name I used with people I didn't think I'd see again. It was the name I'd used on the plane with Victoria. *Dammit.* I pushed thoughts of her way.

"As I said, Sterling, I might not be the brightest bulb in the toolshed, but I know that if we don't have money, it's going somewhere. And I know the type of group that Tommy and his friends are in. He's either gambling or whoring it away. So I told him to grow up and be a real man."

And Tommy took that to mean joining her uncle's illegal operations. He wasn't the sharpest tool in the shed, either.

She leaned forward, looking side to side as if she wanted to make sure no one could hear us. "My uncle isn't a good man. If he finds out about this—"

"As I said, Mrs. Langhorne, I'm pretty sure your uncle knew exactly what was going to happen."

She sat back. "Why would he do that? He would risk Tommy talking."

"Because Tommy doesn't know that much, does he? And my guess is before long, he's going to summon you and tell you to cut ties with Tommy. And I imagine if you don't . . ." I let the sentence hang.

By the way her breath hitched, I knew she knew what I meant. Tears started down her cheeks, and I began to feel bad. Talking with people like this had never bothered me that much before. It was a means to an end. But Amiee and Tommy were definitely in over their heads. It was another reason to get rid of George.

I reached my hand across the table, putting it over her forearm. "We can protect you and Tommy. That is, if you love Tommy and want to stay married to him."

She took my hand, gripping it in both of hers, holding it like it was a lifeline. "You could do that for us?"

I placed my other hand over our linked hands. "We can."

"But we don't know very much. In order to get your protection, we need to know stuff, right?"

"You probably know more than you think. Every little bit we learn, we can use."

"To get my uncle?"

I shifted, wondering if I should be trusting this woman with so much information. For all I knew, she was going to run back to George and tell him all we'd discussed. But even if she did, it wouldn't change anything. George knew that we had Tommy. He probably had eyes on Amiee right now, which meant he currently had eyes on me. I didn't like that so much, but it was what it was.

She pulled my hands to her lips, giving my knuckles a kiss. "Bless you, Sterling." The move was a little off putting. Was she an Oscar-winning actress or sincerely relieved that she was being given an opportunity to escape from her uncle's orbit?

I'd need to keep in mind that she might be fucking with me, but for now, I was going to move forward with the idea that she wanted out. She and Tommy were going to be the answer to getting George Pitney put away and making Henry and Victoria safe.

22

Victoria

I sat in the window seat of the makeshift office I'd made in my grandfather's old bedroom, just as I had done for the last three days. I should've been working. I should've been going to the doctor. I should've been doing something, but instead I was sitting, staring out the window without really seeing. I was a mixture of depressed and anxious. I knew that I'd been developing feelings for Alex, but I didn't realize just how strong they were until he was gone. And by gone, I meant completely. The closest thing I'd heard from him was through my father, who at dinner last night explained that Alex and his team were working on some plan that hopefully would free my father as a target of George Pitney.

But he hadn't contacted me. I supposed he wouldn't. Our adventure was over and he'd moved on. I wondered if his next conquest was Pitney's niece who was caught in a restaurant kissing his hand. There was an intimacy to it that broke my heart. Was she part of a honeypot scheme? Is that what it was called when operatives had sex as part of their jobs to get information? Did Alex do that . . . sleep with women as part of his job? Or was she just convenient, like I'd been on the plane and in my home?

The anxiety came from the unexpected pregnancy. I rubbed my hand over my belly, both in awe and terror that a life was growing inside me. After the initial shock, I spent hours on the Internet trying to figure out how it was possible that I was pregnant. I was shocked at the number of stories about women getting pregnant on the pill, as well as a host of other birth control methods. There were even stories of failed vasectomies. Why wasn't this better known? I decided that someone needed to write an article about it, and I surreptitiously included it in the list of ideas that I sent to my senior editor to consider.

All that research really was a distraction. What was done was done, and no matter what, research wasn't going to change it. But I wasn't sure what to do about it. My conscience told me that the right thing to do would be to tell Alex. He was a part of this and had a right to know. But we weren't in love. He wasn't a man who wanted to make a life with someone.

And then there was the fact that he was friends with my father and paranoid beyond hell that my father would find out. That begged the question, is ignorance really bliss? Would it be better for him to live the rest of his life not knowing that he had created a child?

The feminist in me reminded myself that the child was also partly his responsibility. But I was financially secure and had a stable home, so I didn't need Alex for anything. But would my baby miss having a father? I grew up without a mother, and while I was curious about her, I didn't feel that my life lacked anything because my father was such a loving and attentive parent. Still, now that I was pregnant, I'd been thinking more about my mom. I had been a boo-boo baby, so I had some understanding of how she and my father must've felt discovering that she was pregnant. What I couldn't understand was how she walked away and never looked back. Even now with the uncertainty and terror, I knew that I would be in this child's life. I already loved it. What did it say about my mother that she simply walked away from me? She hadn't loved me. She hadn't wanted to be a wife and mother. And considering the wealth of my family and how easy her life would have been had she stayed, she very clearly didn't want any of that.

Just like Alex. I knew he was a good and decent man, but I also suspected that he too would walk away. He didn't want to settle down, and he didn't want my father to know about us. So, did I protect him from the stress of all this by not telling him?

And of course, the questions didn't stop there. What would I tell my father? If I didn't reveal my relationship with Alex, the only solution was to tell him that I'd hooked up with somebody in England.

While I had some time before I needed to explain things to my child, I had to consider what I'd tell him or her about their father. I didn't want my child to feel abandoned by learning that his father didn't love us, or at least him or her. So maybe I could tell the baby that their father died.

I let out a groan, hating that my child wasn't even here yet and I was already planning to lie to it. Maybe I needed to go away for nine months and consider adoption. The child didn't need to be brought into the world with such complications. But the idea of handing the child over to other parents, no matter how perfect and lovely they might be, didn't feel like something I could do. I had the means and resources to be a good mother, and maybe instead of worrying about all this other crap, I needed to focus on the baby.

It would be nice to have somebody to talk to about all this. But I definitely wasn't going to talk to my dad, Knightly, Mrs. Tillis, or Caroline. I still wasn't allowed to leave the house, so it wasn't like I could go talk to a counselor. I definitely wasn't going to talk to my staff about it. The only one I could call was Samantha, but it didn't feel right to put my burdens on her with all she was going through.

Then again, she was a single mother. I didn't know how that came to be, and chances were that our situations were different, but maybe she could give me some advice. At the very least, she could be a sounding board to help me sort through all these feelings and thoughts bouncing around in my head like a pinball machine.

I checked my watch, discovering it was nearly nine in the evening. Was that too late to call her? Taking a chance, I dialed her number. She surprised me by picking up on the second ring.

Even before I said anything, I felt guilty about calling her. She was going through so much. I hadn't bothered to check in on her while I was living in a bubble with Alex, yet here I was, in the middle of my own chaos, reaching out to her when she probably didn't have much more to give.

"Tori?"

"Hey, hi. Sorry to call so late."

"No. This is a good time. Both Mom and Pax are out for the night. This is my time to have a moment to myself."

Oh, hell. I was encroaching on her respite time.

"Tori? You alright?"

"I'm trying to decide whether I should talk to you about the thing I called you for, but that would be selfish when you've got so much going on."

"You can talk to me."

I ran my fingers through my hair, letting out a long breath. "I'm in a bit of a conundrum."

She was silent for a moment. "By conundrum, do you mean trouble?"

"If by trouble you mean pregnant, then yes."

"I take it, it's not planned."

"No. It's really weird because deep down, I'm happy about it even though my life is a hot mess right now. Is that strange?"

"No. It's not strange at all." She spoke as if she understood what I meant from personal experience. It was a reminder that she'd lived a life I didn't know anything about, and I hadn't been there for her, for the good or bad of it.

"I know I want to keep the baby, but it complicates everything."

"Does the father know about the baby?" she asked.

"Not yet. And I'll be honest, I'm leaning toward not telling them at all. How bad is that? It's really bad, isn't it?"

"I suppose it depends. Is he abusive?"

I had no doubt that Alex could kill somebody, probably with his pinky. But I didn't think he was abusive. "No. But he'd been clear that he didn't want to settle down and have a family. It was just supposed to be a little affair."

She was quiet for a while.

"It's actually more complicated than that."

"The man who was with you the other day? Your dad's friend?"

My first instinct was to tell her that Alex was my bodyguard, but then that would put into question why I would go to her house with a bodyguard and potentially put her and her family at risk.

"I suppose it doesn't really matter who it is. The question is where are things now? Is this affair still going on?" she asked, making me relieved I didn't have to try and explain my situation with Alex.

"No. It ended about three days ago, and I haven't seen or heard from him since."

"And do you expect to?"

My heart pinched tight. "No. At least not in a situation that would lead to something."

She was quiet for a minute again. "Conventional wisdom is that you need to tell him because he has a responsibility, and maybe he would want to know. Babies can change things."

I nodded in agreement because it changed me.

"But at the same time, you have to think about what's best for your child. Do you want your child to grow up with a father who is only there out of duty and not love or is absent because there's no love?"

"That's what I've been debating." I wanted to ask her if that had been her situation. But she would have shared it if it were relevant or she wanted me to know.

"In the end, Tori, it's all about what's best for the baby. Everything else about you and the father, goals and expectations, all that isn't as important as what is best for your baby. As you know, plenty of kids grow up without one or the other parent and turn out just fine. There's plenty of kids who grow up with two parents who are messed up. So, if you just focus on what's important, loving and caring for your baby, the rest will work itself out."

Her opinion didn't alleviate my guilt about not telling Alex, but it did make me feel like less of a bitch for considering it.

After I got off the phone with Samantha, I went and changed for bed. I'd read that I probably wouldn't feel the symptoms of pregnancy until six weeks, but already, I was feeling fatigued. Then again, maybe it was the stress.

I settled into bed and closed my eyes to sleep. Like all the other nights since Alex left me here, he drifted into my dreams. The two previous nights were more of a nightmare with him and my father yelling, my father at Alex, and Alex at me for getting knocked up.

But tonight, Alex entered my dreams wearing shorts, a T-shirt, a ball cap, and hiking boots. He squatted down next to a small body of water that he'd hiked to. Between his legs stood a boy, maybe two or three years old, also wearing a ball cap and looking up at me with pale blue eyes.

"Look, Mommy, there's a frog."

Only then did I realize I was there as well, also in shorts and a T-shirt and a ball cap.

"What does a frog say, son?" Alex asked him.

"Ribbit-ribbit."

Alex laughed and turned to look at me, his expression full of joy and happiness.

I stared at him in confusion even as happiness bubbled up. "I thought you didn't want this."

He stood, lifting our son and putting him on his shoulders. "Are you kidding? This is the greatest adventure of my life."

I shot up in bed, blinking into the night. It had been a dream. It wasn't real. But could it be? Would it be possible that Alex and I could be a family? My heart ached for just that.

Alex had been clear that he was a one-and-done bachelor, but he'd broken those rules with me. He'd confessed that he couldn't stop thinking of me. Maybe it wasn't love, but it was something more than a hookup, right?

But was I brave enough to tell him the truth about my feelings and the baby? And if his feelings were more, would he be brave enough to face my father?

23

Alex

Four days after leaving Victoria at her father's house, great gains were being made in dealing with George Pitney. Tommy and his wife were tucked safely away in another safe house in another part of the city, and they were doing the best they could to help us in exchange for arranging for them to get away from her uncle. They didn't know much about George's business and even less about his criminal activity, but neither was the information they could share unhelpful. They didn't know what we were planning, but through our questioning, we were able to learn who would be good candidates to challenge Pitney to take over the company. Aimee even indicated she had heard discussions between her uncle and a member of the board that suggested animosity between them. It almost sounded like members of Pitney's board, and many of his high-level managers and VPs, were about at their wits' end with him. There seemed to be some suggestion that Pitney's behavior was changing, which to my mind wasn't a good sign. It was easier to deal with people when you could predict how they'd act. It sounded like Pitney was becoming irrational and paranoid.

I contacted Henry to ask what he knew of the few names Tommy had given me of people who seemed unhappy with Pitney and would like to take over. I figured with all of Henry's investigative journalism experience, he was a good source of information as well. The one name that showed up on both their lists was Jack Moore.

We decided Dax would be the one to approach Jack. We wouldn't let him know our plan, but we'd assess and work to manipulate the situation that would put him in charge. Dax was the best person because although I'd come from an influential family in New York, I'd been gone a long time. Dax hadn't been from a rich family, but he married into one of the biggest. The Clarke family was right up there with Henry.

With a plan and things to do, I buried myself in work. Research, strategy, surveillance, questioning Tommy and Aimee, and making sure they didn't change their minds. This distraction was welcome but unfortunately not foolproof at preventing me from thinking of Victoria.

How hard could it be to stop caring for someone? I truly believed that by going cold turkey, cutting off any contact between us and going on with my life, was the answer. I still believed it was the answer, but I was learning that it was going to take a whole lot more time and effort than I had thought.

It didn't help that she showed up in my dreams. In them, she was sometimes calling me out as the coward that I was. Other times, she was sweet and sassy, and those were the times when the longing nearly brought me to my knees.

But if I were honest with myself, the worst times were the mornings waking up alone in bed. The first two mornings, I automatically reached out for her, prepared to pull her to me and wake her up with sweet kisses and slow sex. Yesterday was the first day that I woke up and remembered where I was. I was in a Saint Security safe house, babysitting spoiled brat newlyweds.

Today, we made headway on the plan, and with the information that Tommy and Aimee gave us, we are actively pulling together evidence that we hoped the D.A. would use to pick Pitney up and put him in jail. The charges were still fraud and other stupid charges, but something was better than nothing.

I've been keeping Henry in the loop about what was going on through phone calls, purposely not stopping by the house so I wouldn't have to see Victoria. But now we were at a crucial stage of this mission, and I needed to talk with Henry. Mostly, I needed to get him to back the hell off his investigative reporting until Pitney was put away and Jack Moore was installed as the head of the company.

As my driver pulled up in front of Henry's home, my heart beat a million miles a minute. I wasn't sure if it was because I so desperately wanted to see Victoria or that I was terrified I would run into her. She was smart and young and had a business to run, so I doubted she thought about me much now. But if I saw her, it would ruin the minuscule progress I'd made this week in trying to move on.

Knightly let me into the house and led me to Henry's office. I didn't let out a breath until the office door closed behind me and Victoria wasn't in sight.

"The end is in sight." Henry poured himself a drink and then one for me too. "We should celebrate."

"Let's not get ahead of ourselves." Still, I accepted the drink he offered as I needed it. I couldn't stop glancing at the door, wondering if at any moment Victoria would walk in. "Things are progressing about as we expect. Moore is strong, pissed off at Pitney, and power greedy. He's the best choice to challenge Pitney."

Henry shook his head. "He doesn't have any scruples either."

"Yeah, but he also doesn't want to kill you. And as long as you don't piss him off, he won't want to. Look, Henry, we're not going to find a Mother Teresa type. If we're going to take Pitney's power away, Moore is our best bet."

Henry took a sip of his whiskey but made a face of distaste. I'm pretty sure it was the idea of maneuvering Jack Moore into a position to usurp Pitney and not the whiskey that he didn't like.

"If Moore makes this move, that's news," Henry said.

"Report it like everybody else would. Factual without editorial commentary on his less than angelic acts. There's a lot riding on this,

Henry. I know that you have no problem risking your life or my life—"

Henry bristled. "Risking your life is what you do. All of you at Saint Security—"

"Yes, we signed up for this, but there are others who haven't." I didn't say Victoria's name because saying it would make her too real again and I had been working fucking hard the last few days to eliminate her from my mind and my heart. It wasn't going very well, but I was determined to succeed.

"We captured one of his men—"

"Captured? You make it sound like a military op."

Maybe I was telling him too much. "He's the guy who tried to access the house. He and his wife are working with us. And when this is all over, we're going to give them new identities and send them off. This is serious shit, Henry. This couple is too young and too naïve to be doing what we're asking them to do. Please don't make it harder for them by fucking this up."

Henry flinched but nodded.

He sat for a moment, drinking in silence. Finally, he said, "You like living like this, don't you?"

"Like what? Like my friend is going to get himself and his family killed? No, Henry, I don't."

"Touché. I meant the planning, strategizing, spying, danger."

I shrugged. "It keeps life interesting."

"And dangerous."

"Sometimes."

Henry studied me. "I used to think that if you got married, a woman could settle you down a little bit. Even now, you're so raw and rough around the edges. I guess it would take a special woman to do that."

I immediately thought of Victoria and how she had bewitched me like no woman ever had. "Yeah, well, that woman doesn't exist. If she did, I'd have certainly met her already."

Henry laughed and shook his head. "You won't find love with one-night stands."

"I don't see you happily married, Henry. You're saying you've been a monk all these years?"

The smile on his face faltered a little bit. It had me wondering if perhaps there had been somebody. But if that was the case, where was she? Had he loved and lost? Yeah, well join the club, man.

"I have Victoria, and she's the greatest thing that ever happened in my life."

If he'd stabbed me in the gut, the guilt wouldn't feel as fierce as it did at this moment when I thought of the things I did with Victoria, his daughter, the greatest thing that ever happened to him.

I downed my drink. "We chose different paths."

Henry cocked his head to the side. "Don't you ever wonder what it would be like to be married and have a family?"

"Nope. Never." At least until I met Victoria. And even then, any of the thoughts that tried to break in about a future with her were immediately blasted away because there was no future. Not with Henry's daughter.

"Why not? Don't you ever get lonely?"

"No, Henry. Settling down isn't conducive to the life I want to lead. It was the reason I walked away from my father, and that reason hasn't changed. Besides, if I'm lonely, I can always find a friend." I waggled my brows like a douche man whore to make my point.

Henry looked at me over his glass as he took a sip. When he brought the glass back down, he asked, "Doesn't it get old? Mindless sex with a woman whose name you don't know and will never see again?"

I shook my head. "Nope." Well, until it met Victoria. "You know, Henry, maybe if you got laid, you wouldn't be making enemies in high places. Maybe that's your problem. You need to get laid."

"You always were the vulgar one."

I laughed even though I wasn't liking how I was coming out in this conversation. "You must be forgetting that I knew Henry Banion back in college. There were no shortages of notches on your bedpost."

"Yes, but then I grew up."

I pointed at him. "Because you had to. You got a woman knocked up, and you ended up having to do the right thing."

He scowled at me. "I didn't change my ways to be a father because it was the right thing to do. I did it because I love Victoria. I'm not joking, Alex, when I say she's the center of my world. You've met her. You've seen the woman she's become. I'm so fucking proud of her."

I felt like I'd been given a slap on the hand, and in retrospect, I probably deserved it. "Well, I don't have that."

"That you know of. Who's to say that there aren't a bunch of little Alexes running around in this world, considering the number of women you fucked over the years?"

The idea of it sent a chill down my spine. "Now you're just being mean."

He shrugged. "It could have happened. It could still happen even for a geriatric like you. I've heard of men as old as seventy and even eighty getting women pregnant." Henry looked upward as if he was imagining something. "What I wouldn't do to be there on the day a woman shows up at your door with a round belly or a child and tells you you're the father."

"I thought you liked me. Why would you wish something like that on me?" But even as I said the words, I had a flash Victoria round and glowing with my child growing inside her. I shook my head to get rid of the vision.

"What would you do if a woman showed up on your doorstep with your child?" Henry seemed genuinely curious.

I shifted uncomfortably because I didn't like the idea that my response would show just how much of an asshole I was. "I'd do the right thing. I'd provide for them."

"But you wouldn't marry her. Be a family."

"I'm not going to marry a woman I don't love. That's not good for anyone." I couldn't figure out why Henry was harping on this. He wasn't married. He didn't marry Victoria's mother. Was he projecting his own issues onto me?

"And you've never found a woman you've loved?"

"No. Never. Thank God." *Except Victoria*. I sighed. "You know me, Henry. What would I do with a wife and child?"

"You would love them, Alex. But maybe that's the problem. You don't know how to love. Or maybe you just don't want to love."

The words hurt more than I could ever have imagined. Even more so because he was right, at least about one thing. I didn't think I could love, but now I knew differently. Even so, I didn't want to love. I was willing to risk my bones on dangerous excursions in my life and my job, but not my heart.

"You hit the nail on the head. I don't want to love."

24

Victoria

"And you've never found a woman you've loved?"

"No. Never, thank God. You know me, Henry. What would I do with a wife and child?"

"You would love them, Alex. But maybe that's the problem. You don't know how to love. Or maybe you just don't want to love."

"You hit the nail on the head. I don't want to love."

Alex's words reverberated through my head. I was the biggest fool in the world. Had I really thought that Alex would want to be a family? That he'd want me and his child?

This pain and the feeling of being an idiot were my own fault for eavesdropping. But when I'd heard that Alex was here, I made my way downstairs, hoping to have a chance to talk to him, to tell him about the baby. I suppose deep down, I knew I was being foolish. But after that dream of all of us together, Alex happy as a father, hope had found its way inside me. Every memory I had of Alex, I'd been able to twist into the possibility that he cared for me. What an idiot.

Sharing his repulsion at the idea of marriage and kids stole my breath. The walls felt like they were closing in on me. I had to get away, and yet I knew the moment I stepped out the front door, Alex's men would be on me, preventing me from leaving.

I moved away from the door to my father's office and managed to make it to the living room at the front of the house. The room was rarely used, so I felt certain I'd be alone as I processed Alex's words and figured out my and the baby's future.

I sank down onto the couch butting up against the front window. I turned my body so that I was leaning back against the plush arm, pulling my legs up and wrapping my arms around my knees as I rested my head and stared mindlessly out the front window. The more I thought about it, the more I realized how much I'd been deceiving myself. There was no way Alex was going to change his mind and want a family. Not if that meant being with Henry's daughter. He'd been clear that my father would never know about our affair. Whatever feelings he had for me, if there were any at all, they did not outweigh his friendship with my father.

The tears streamed down my face as I grieved for the life I and my child might've had. Especially the baby. I reminded myself that I was raised by one parent and for all intents and purposes, I'd had a good life. A great life. I could do the same for my child.

I also told myself that I was a strong, independent woman and that I would be fine on my own. But there would always be a hole in my heart that only Alex could fill. I would live with that for the rest of my life.

The wave of emotion washed through me, and I buried my face in my knees. The sound of two men talking had me stifling my tears, and I tilted my head to hear who was talking in the foyer. My father was saying goodbye to Alex. Alex was leaving without seeing me. If there was any question about how he thought about me, that definitely answered it.

From my vantage point, I could see Alex as he descended the stairs in front of the house. He was doing something on his phone, and he stopped for a moment, turning to look back up at the house. Our eyes caught, and I thought I saw something in him, but then he turned away as Ian, along with several other men, joined him in front of the house. I didn't think my heart could break anymore, but it did. It shattered, and I was certain that it was going to lie in pieces for the rest of my days.

As I watched Alex talk to his men, it occurred to me that if they were at the front of the house talking to him, then they weren't at their positions around the house. If I wanted to get out, this was my moment.

I jumped up from the couch and went to the entry to the foyer, poking my head to look down the hall and across to my father's office. It was empty. I scurried out and made my way to the elevator, stepping in and hitting the button for the garage. I decided that this would be the best point of exit since it was around the corner from where the men were talking. I probably should have gotten my purse, but I had my phone, attached to which was a card holder where I stashed a credit card and a hundred-dollar bill in case of emergencies.

When I reached the garage, I scanned the area, making sure Knightly wasn't preparing to leave on some errand or returning from one. No one was around, so I rushed over to the garage door. If I was going to get caught, this would be the time. The door wasn't necessarily loud, but it wasn't quiet either.

I pressed the button, and as soon as the door rolled up enough for me to fit underneath it, I ducked under and trotted out to the sidewalk. I immediately turned left and then picked up speed to run up to the next block. I went left, which thankfully was a shorter block. Then I went right, heading up toward Broadway.

I ducked into a Starbucks to catch my breath. I pulled out my phone and ordered a car, hiding in the coffee shop until it pulled up to the curb. I slid into the backseat, only then realizing I didn't know where I was going. The only place that came to mind was Samantha's. Again, I felt a wave of guilt at thrusting my problems on her when she was already overwhelmed caring for her mother and her son. But I decided she could just put me in a room by myself somewhere. That was all I really needed, time away and alone.

I imagined that when my father and Alex realized I was gone,

Samantha would be the first place they'd look. But I knew there was time. Everyone in the house thought I was upstairs working, so they wouldn't notice I was gone until I didn't show up for dinner. If I played this right, I'd be back before that. How I'd get in without anyone knowing I'd been gone was a problem for me to solve later.

When I got to Samantha's house and knocked on the door, Maria answered and smiled at me. "Miss Layton didn't mention you're coming by."

"I'm being rude again. If she's busy, I can just sit in the living room or somewhere."

Maria frowned, and I was sure she thought I was going crazy. But she invited me in, led me to the living room, and let me know that she would tell Samantha I was there.

A few moments later Samantha entered, her expression full of concern. She sat next to me on the couch. "Oh, dear. What happened? Did you decide to tell him after all, and it didn't go well?"

"I did decide to tell him, but I didn't have the chance. I overheard him and my dad talking, and my father was teasing him about the possibility of a wife and kids, and I'm pretty sure Alex would rather drink broken glass than be a father."

"Wow."

I nodded and wiped away the tears that couldn't seem to stop falling. Samantha reached over to the coffee table where a box of tissues sat. She handed me the entire box, and I was pretty sure it still wouldn't be enough.

"When he left, he didn't bother to see me. And when he was out front, he saw me in the window and just turned away. Like I was nothing. He even told my father that he had never loved a woman and he was grateful for it. God, Samantha, how have I been so stupid? I had this dream of us being a family, and somehow, I'd talked myself into believing that was a possibility when all the evidence was pointing to the opposite."

Samantha took my hand in hers, giving it a squeeze. "I'm sorry."

I leaned over, resting my head on her shoulder. "What you said was right. I can't think about how this has shattered me. I need to think about the baby. Alex told my father that if he unexpectedly got a woman pregnant, he would provide financial support, but that would be it."

"What a gem," she quipped.

"Fortunately for me, I don't need his money." I turned my head to look up at her. "I'm trying to tell myself that I'm doing him a favor, but there's something about it that still doesn't feel right."

She gave me a stern look. "I know how you're feeling, Tori, but based on what you said, I'm sure he'd see it as your doing him a favor by not telling him. He doesn't want it. Why burden him and create more stress for you?"

"Is that how it was with Pax's father?"

She flinched, and it made me regret asking about something that clearly hurt her.

"Never mind. It's none of my business. I'm sorry."

"Pax's father and I were done, or more accurately, he was done with me, before I even knew I was pregnant. By then, I was out west making a life for myself, and similarly to what's going on with you, I made the decision that telling him would just bring on more stress and turmoil than any of us needed."

I was glad that my father had been able to help secure her job out west so that she could find distance from the man who'd hurt her and forge her own life. Now she was back in New York, and while it was a big city, that didn't mean one didn't run into people they knew.

"Now that you're back home, do you ever worry that you'll run into him again?"

She swallowed and looked away. "I don't get out much, so not really."

I rested my head on her shoulder again. "Did you love him? I only ask because I'm wondering if it's true that time will heal my wounds."

She was quiet for a moment. "I wish I could tell you that was true, but if you love him, I suspect there will always be a part of you that loves him and grieves for his loss. But you do learn to live with it."

Well, that was something.

We sat quietly for a moment. My pain didn't go away, but I did have a sense of gratitude to have Samantha with me.

"I'm sorry I have been such a shitty friend," I said to her. "I was a terrible friend, and now here I am, laying my problems on your doorstep when you're already carrying so much."

"I've been a shitty friend too, Tori. When I left New York, I broke off with everyone except my mom. I'm sorry about that."

I sat up and looked at her. "Do you plan on staying in New York?" It was only after I asked it that I realized how insensitive the question was since I was essentially asking if she'd stay after her mom died.

She shrugged. "I don't know. I don't think so. Moving will take a toll on Mom, but we're thinking of selling the house and maybe getting a little bungalow on the beach. My mom always liked the beach, so it would be nice for her. And Pax loves it too."

If she was talking about the beaches in Long Island, that wasn't too far away. Again, I was selfish in wanting to keep her close.

"I didn't ask about your job. Did you have to leave your position?"

She shook her head. "Right now, I'm telecommuting, and it's working out pretty good. I'm sort of thinking of doing something like you did. Starting my own business. I'm a little uncertain about it, but my mom's all for it, and when she's not too tired, she spends her time developing business plans for me."

I smiled. "That's great. Something you two can start together. And I have no doubt that whatever you do, you'll be successful. You always got better grades than I did in college."

She smiled. "Yes, but you are always more outgoing and assertive, traits that I don't really have."

We continued to chat about all sorts of things. Some from our past and tentatively about our futures. When Maria came in to ask if I'd be staying for dinner, I realized that I had dominated so much of Samantha's time.

"You're welcome to stay. Sometimes Mom joins us. Or maybe it will just be me and Pax."

"Where is Pax?" I hadn't seen him at all.

"He's on a play date this afternoon. But I expect him back shortly."

Samantha's smile seemed genuine, welcoming, and I wanted to spend more time with her. But it was time to go.

I stood, and Samantha joined me. I gave her a tight hug. "Thank you so much. Please let me know if there's anything I can do to support you as much as you support me."

"You're not staying?"

"No. I should go. I didn't let anybody know I was leaving, and Dad will start to worry."

Samantha led me to the door, and we hugged again before I walked out. Once on the front stoop, I ordered another car to bring me home.

The black sedan pulled up in record time, and the driver stepped out, looking at me over the hood. "Ms. Banion?"

I nodded and walked over to the car, opening the back and sliding in. The driver got in and pulled away from the curb.

As the car drove through the city, I sat mindlessly looking out the window. My brain was filled with thoughts, and yet I wasn't able to hold onto any one of them. So, I just let it go blank, welcoming the respite.

Fifteen minutes later, I snapped out of my reverie and realized that the scenery didn't match my neighborhood. Instead of being on the upper East Side, we were wandering through a section near the park on the West Side.

"Excuse me, but I need to head over to Riverside." I rattled off my address again.

He glanced at me through the rearview mirror but didn't respond. What did that mean?

A chill ran down my spine. What was going on?

For a moment, I wondered if Alex had realized I'd disappeared, and this was one of his men picking me up. Maybe he was trying to make a point of how careless and reckless I'd been with this cloak and dagger type pickup.

We pulled up in front of a large, opulent residence. As I studied it, I didn't recognize it. No one I knew lived there.

My nerves tingled in warning. I didn't know what was going on, but I knew I didn't want to stick around to find out. I reached for the handle to open the door but it wouldn't open.

Panic shot through me. "What's going on?"

My door opened and a man leaned down, looking in. He wasn't someone I knew or recognized.

"Welcome, Ms. Banion. Mr. Pitney is excited to have you as a guest in his home."

25

Alex

Victoria's face haunted me for the rest of the day. Not that I'd ever been completely free of her, but seeing her watching me from the window, her expression seared in my brain. I couldn't be sure what she was feeling. She was too far away to assess her expression completely, but I knew it wasn't happiness or contentment. I prayed to God that whatever was weighing on her had nothing to do with me. Why would it? The ease with which she'd walked away from me told me that our time was a brief affair. So her discontent had to be about something else.

It occurred to me that maybe she was getting more threats from Pitney's camp. Jesus fuck, I was falling down on the job because I should have talked to her. But I was too much of a coward. I could walk into a jungle full of militants, but I couldn't face Victoria.

I did have a moment to wonder if perhaps she'd overheard my conversation with Henry. Everything I told him about not wanting a wife and family, about providing for any offspring I might accidentally produce, but never loving, was true. Or at least it had been until

I met Victoria. But why would it bother her? It wasn't like she wanted me.

God, sitting and talking to Henry like that, I was sure I was getting an ulcer. I stared him in the face and told lie after lie, knowing I couldn't tell him the truth because the truth would ruin us. The sooner I got back to England, the better because I was getting tired of the guilt and pain and yearning. Thank fuck our plans were moving forward with little to no glitches. I'd be home in no time and then I'd forget Victoria.

Yeah, right. Like that would ever happen.

But it had to. There was no scenario in which I could keep Henry as a friend and love Victoria as my partner. In the middle of the night, I had moments in which I thought I should choose Victoria over Henry. But then I remembered that for her, our little affair was an adventure.

Perhaps this was God's way of punishing me for the cavalier way I went through life, particularly related to women. I'd never fucked with a woman's heart or had been cruel to them, Lorraine notwithstanding, considering she stole from me. But perhaps my lifestyle offended God.

Then again, the pain that had taken up residence in my chest was a reminder of why I had chosen to live my life the way I had. I was experiencing the very thing I had been trying to avoid.

"Alex?"

Goddammit, my brain was elsewhere again. I turned to Dax. "Yeah?"

"Elliott met with the D.A. today, who is very interested in what we've brought him so far, but he's still hemming and hawing over pursuing prosecution."

"Did he at least say he was going to look into what we'd found?"

Dax nodded. "The other thing is, my wife and I are going to be heading home in a couple of days. The way Elliott's talking, it sounds like that's the timeframe we have on this little investigation. Of course, all the protection will remain in place for Banion, but this plan to put Pitney away has only about seventy-two hours left."

"Then we'd better start moving faster." My phone rang. I pulled it out of my pocket, seeing Henry's name on the screen. At the same time, a second call was coming in from Ian. "Can you call Ian and see what he needs? I want to take this from Henry."

Dax nodded, pulling his phone from his pocket as he turned to leave me in my area I set up in a conference room at Saint Security.

I poked the answer button. "Henry."

"Tell me she's with you."

Immediately, my heart jackhammered in my chest. The panic in Henry's voice, along with his inquiring about Victoria, was all it took to know that something was seriously wrong. "Victoria's not with me. She's at home with you."

"We can't find her anywhere."

Emotion and panic burst through me, surprising me with its intensity. I sucked in a deep breath to calm my nerves and be the professional crisis manager that I was. Jesus fuck. Victoria was gone?

"Calm down, Henry. Tell me what's going on."

"I thought she was working in her office, but when she didn't come down to dinner, I had Mrs. Tillis go up and check on her, but she wasn't there. She wasn't in her room. She's not anywhere in the house and she's not answering her phone. That's not like her, Alex. She wouldn't let me worry like this."

I stepped out into the hall and waved my hand toward the woman working on a computer in one of the cubicles, planning to have her put out a call to search for Victoria.

"Alex."

I whirled around to see Dax. "Ian says Victoria's gone missing."

Fuck, fuck, fuck. "I'm on my way, Henry. We'll find her." And when I did, I was going to give her a good tongue lashing because I had no doubt that she disappeared because she wanted to. There is no way anybody could've abducted her from the house, which meant she'd snuck away. Where would she go?

"We need someone to go to her place, and I need Samantha Layton's phone number." Her home and Samantha's were the two obvious places, so I'd start there.

Dax was off to send someone to her apartment. I found Samantha's number and a few minutes later had her on the line, asking if she'd seen or heard from Victoria.

"Yes, Tori came by earlier today. But she left a little before dinner. Why?"

I looked at my watch, realizing that the ride from Samantha's house to Victoria's was only about twenty minutes, less if traffic wasn't too bad. Now it was nearly an hour later. "Did she say she was going anywhere else besides her father's home?"

"No." Concern grew in Samantha's voice. "She didn't want anyone to notice she was gone, so she was in a rush to get back. She ordered a car and went home."

"What sort of car?" I grabbed a sheet of paper from a nearby desk to jot down Samantha's information.

"The usual black sedan. What's going on?"

I put a note to contact all the private car services to see who picked Victoria up. I added the ride share companies as well. "Victoria hasn't come home and she's not answering her phone."

On the end of the line, Samantha gasped.

"If you hear from her, tell her to call her father or me. And you call us as well."

"Yes, absolutely."

I handed the woman working near me the note, telling her to pull up the companies and find out about their drivers who picked up at Samantha's home. "Can you find out about surveillance cameras in that area as well?"

With that assigned, I rushed from the building, arranging my own ride with one of our men, and headed to Henry's. The minute the car stopped, I bounded out and up the steps.

Knightly opened it as if he were waiting for me. "He's in a state, Mr. Sterling. Have you found her yet?" His concern was more than just as an employee. He clearly saw Victoria as family.

"I haven't found her yet, but we're looking."

I entered Henry's office. When he saw me walk in he rushed over, gripping my forearms. It'd been the same response

Victoria had when she thought something had happened to her father.

"Tell me you found her."

"Not yet. We do know that she went over to see Samantha."

Henry's brows drew together. "Samantha?" He gave his head a quick shake. "Oh, yes. I forgot she's back in town."

"According to Samantha, she left around five."

Henry's arm jerked up as he checked his watch. He looked at me, his expression stricken. "It doesn't take more than an hour to get from the Layton house to here."

"I know. But we have to stay calm—"

"We have to be out looking for her."

"We are. You need to stay here and keep yourself together in case you get a call or we hear from her. Alright?"

My phone buzzed in my pocket, and my first instinct was to ignore it because I needed to focus on Henry and Victoria. But of course, I pulled it out of my pocket in case it was Victoria or news about her.

I looked at the caller ID, but the number was blocked. A sense of dread filled my chest as I poked the button "Who is this?"

"Alex Sterling, long time no talk."

My gaze shot to Henry as I recognized George Pitney's voice.

"I have something you want."

A new sort of unease spread through my belly. Why was Pitney calling me if he had Victoria? Did he know about us?

"And you have something I want."

Strangely, I had a tiny sense of relief that only one of my worst fears was coming true. Pitney wanted something I had, not to blackmail me.

"What's that?" I asked, stepping back and turning away from Henry. I needed to focus and couldn't do that with Henry's agitation radiating around me.

"My niece and her nitwit husband."

"Who?" I decided to play dumb.

"Don't fuck with me, Sterling." The words came out heated,

followed by an intake of breath like he was regaining control. "I know you met with my niece. She seemed to take a shine to you."

That explained how my picture with Aimee ended up on a gossip website. "She was worried about her husband disappearing and wanted Saint Security's help," I lied.

"Let's not play games. I have Banion's daughter. I'm willing to give her back in exchange for my niece and her husband."

That was it? Something was up. Why wasn't he asking for Henry to back off his investigations and publishing news on him?

"I don't know where they are."

"I don't believe that, but even if it's true, you can find them, right?"

I had to play this like all this was just another job. "Sure. For a price."

He paused, and I imagined he was trying to figure out what, if any, game I was playing. "Fine."

"How about I come over and we can negotiate the work?"

"How about you find them first?"

"You know it doesn't work like that." I was careful not to use his name. As it was, I could feel Henry's eyes boring into my back. "I need a picture of the nitwit and information about when he was last seen. Same with the wife. Then I'll know the scope of the job and can quote you a price."

He paused again. "How do I know you're not fucking with me?"

"You don't. But why would I do that? Or if you don't trust me, call someone else."

"Two hours." He hung up the phone.

I held the phone up to my ear to give me a moment before talking to Henry. I had to be careful about what I told him.

"Are you taking a job when you need to find Tori?" he snapped at me.

"No." I pushed the group text and sent Dax a message to let him know we needed to meet to discuss this current situation with Pitney.

"Dammit, Alex."

I shoved my phone in my pocket. Turning, I put my hand on Henry's shoulder. "Do you trust me?"

"Yes. Absolutely."

"Then trust me on this. If all goes well, Victoria will be home in just over two hours." I patted his shoulder and then strode out of the room to the front door.

"What? How?" Henry called after me.

"I've got to get to work."

TWO HOURS AND A PLAN LATER, I strode into George Pitney's home. His butler-slash-goon led me to an office near the back of the house. I scanned the room, noting a door at the rear that our infrared scan of the home suggested was where Victoria was being kept. My nerves sizzled to think she was just feet away.

"Want a drink?" Pitney said by greeting. He sat at his desk looking like the king of the world. He was the epitome of smarm and asshole. He looked normal for an asshole, but I watched for signs that he was losing it, becoming irrational, as I'd heard.

"Nope. What's the job, George?"

He smirked as he sipped his expensive booze. "I have to say, I was surprised to find you working for Banion. You always struck me as someone who was repulsed by goody-two-shoes."

I shrugged.

"But then I learned that you and he were old college buddies. I know you have a history with him. Does he know about your history with me?"

"What business is it of his?" I was okay with his going off on a tangent. My job was to keep him occupied, his attention away from the room next door.

"Does he know you're here? I know you're working for him."

"He knows what he needs to know. If you know he hired me and you have his daughter, what's all this bullshit about finding your niece?"

"I just want to know where your loyalties are."

"They're with whoever pays me. You and Henry might not get along, but to me, your money is the same color of green."

George laughed. "You have no scruples about who your client is."

"Finally, you understand. So, what do you want from me, George? Is it just finding the niece because you've got Henry by dick here? I can't imagine that this is why I'm here."

George's laugh this time was louder as he stood. "I always liked you, Sterling. No-nonsense and effective. You helped me a lot when I was in a scrape."

Not really. He thought I took care of another thorn in his side, but in fact, we helped that guy get a new identity. He'd gone from being a Wall Street-type who found out too much about Pitney to a small business owner in Nowheresville, Kansas.

"You paid well," I said.

"How much for you to deal with Banion?"

Bile churned in my belly. He was asking me to kill Henry. Thank fuck I was wired up and we had a team in a van recording all this. Surely, the D.A. could use it. "What do you mean by deal?"

Pitney looked at me with a you-know-what-I-mean expression.

I shrugged. "I don't read minds. You want a scandal? A government investigation into his business? What?"

Pitney's eyes narrowed, and I imagined he wondered if I was wired. "I should think that whatever happened to poor Snyder would work."

Snyder was the poor sap now living in Kansas under another name. But Pitney believed he was dead. We weren't murderers, although we weren't saints, as the name suggested either. There was a time in which we "dealt" with people, but normally, they were murderers or genocidal leaders. People the government wanted to get rid of but didn't want it linking back to them.

I nodded. "He's dead."

"Right." Pitney opened the drawer of his desk.

I surreptitiously checked my watch, wondering if I needed to waste more time.

"How much?" Pitney pawed through an envelope of cash. I considered asking for a check, but he was smart. He didn't leave a paper trail.

"What about the niece?" I asked.

"I don't care about them."

"So that was just a ruse to get me here?"

"I wanted to know how loyal you were to Banion. Not at all, as it turns out."

Sometimes, I hated this game. "What about his daughter?"

"When Banion is dealt with, she can go home." He glanced toward the door. "She's a beauty. Voluptuous." He waggled his brows.

My fists clenched, ready to punch the image of her body out of his head. "Surely, you don't have to take something like that. I imagine you have women draping all over you." I hoped to hell the compliment would take his sight off Victoria.

"Too right. How about one hundred thousand now, and another two when it's done?"

I shook my head and held up my hand showing five fingers.

He arched a brow. "Five hundred thousand? Two hundred now—"

I held up three fingers.

He stared at me but then acquiesced. "Fine. Three now, two later." He stood and walked to the door, sending a surge of panic through me. Instead of opening the door, he moved a set of books on the shelf aside to open his safe.

He tossed several stacks of bound bills on his desk. "Will you need a bag?"

"Yep."

"I'll have Tanner bring us one. In the meantime, how about a drink? We can toast to our new partnership."

I wanted out, but I also wanted to play it cool and make sure enough time had passed. "Sure. Why not?"

26

Victoria

I never entertained the idea that I could be kidnapped, but if I had, I never would have imagined I would be held captive in an opulent library by a wealthy businessman on the Upper West Side of Manhattan. Weren't kidnapped victims usually held in dark, dingy basements?

Here I was, standing in the middle of George Pitney's impressive library, annoyed at myself for being in this position and nervous about what Alex was going to do to remedy it. Considering George Pitney's history, I should've been more nervous about what he planned to do to me, but perhaps I focused on Alex because the other option was too scary to consider.

When Pitney's minion pulled me out of the car and brought me to the room, Mr. Pitney entered from another door at the side of the room. It appeared that the library was attached to his office. He greeted me with a smile, acting like I was a long-lost friend or special guest whom he'd been eager to see instead of the victim he'd forcibly brought into his house.

"What am I doing here?" I demanded.

He laughed and clapped his hands in delight. "Right to the point, Ms. Banion. I like that about you. You are here because your father has become an annoyance, and I want to make it stop. I believe you are the solution to my problem."

I rolled my eyes at him, not sure where the bravado was coming from. "And you have to resort to kidnapping me? Are your negotiation skills not up to par?"

There was a quick flash of irritation in his eyes, enough to see how lethal he could be and how maybe I'd be better off keeping my mouth shut.

"You should be grateful that I have brought you here. You are in a comfortable room while I take care of business. I could've very easily made this difficult for you, but you're not a part of this. Your father is. As you can see, there are plenty of books to read to bide your time, and we have a small bar over there where you can have water or any other drink that we have in stock. I will be just through that door. At the door through which you've come, Guenther will be standing guard. Don't get any ideas that you can escape."

I glanced at the window.

He smiled with humor, much like I imagined a cat did at its prey. "The window has alarms. Now that we've gotten that all out of the way, I have a phone call to make. If you behave and things work out, you will walk out of here no worse than when you came in."

He didn't wait for me to say anything. Instead, he nodded toward Guenther and then left the library, entering the side door into his office. Guenther gave me a hard scowl, probably to scare me into submission, and then left me alone in the library.

I immediately rushed over to the window, looking down and noting the long drop to the ground and, as I suspected, no way to ease myself down. That was if I could bypass the alarm, which I couldn't. I didn't know the first thing about disarming alarms.

I looked across to the building next door, thinking maybe somebody would be there. I could flag them down. But all the rooms were dark. On the off chance that someone might look over, I decided to search the room for a pen and a piece of paper. Maybe I could put a sign in the window letting them know that I was being held captive and to call the police.

I searched every shelf, the one desk that had no drawers, and even in the cushions of the couches and chairs. While there was plenty of paper in the books, I couldn't find a single pen. Was that on purpose? Were they afraid I'd use it as a weapon? I didn't know how to do that either. I bet Alex could both disable an alarm and kill with a pen. I hoped he found me and then didn't throttle me for being reckless.

I went over to the door of Pitney's office, pressing my ear to it to listen to what he was arranging with my father. The only thing I heard him say was "Two hours."

A chill went down my spine, wondering what that meant. Maybe it was a meeting between him and my father. I hoped it wasn't the time of my demise. I sent out a silent prayer, hoping that my father would call Alex and others from Saint Security. My father was just the type of man who could be reckless, especially when it came to protecting me. I hoped he was smart and called Alex instead.

For the first half-hour, I wandered around the library, checking out the books and other items Pitney displayed there. I might've been impressed if I weren't scared out of my wits.

For the next hour, I plopped myself in one of the plush chairs and just sat, contemplating my life. I thought about the decisions I'd made in the past and the goals I had for the future. I rethought my decision to keep Alex from knowing about the baby. So much of my decision to keep the baby a secret was out of fear. Perhaps I needed to be brave, be willing to hear his rejection so that I could go through life with no regrets, without any questions of what if.

Finally, bored, I got up and made my way around the room again, wondering if it would be weird to find a book to read while I waited. As I browsed his collection of Lord Byron poems, wondering how such a jerk would have romantic literature on his shelf, I overheard talking in the other room. Had my father come?

I ended my quest for a book and made my way toward the door, pressing my ear to it. Not my father, Alex. My heart soared. He was here to save me. I didn't know how, but I knew he would.

I was about to open the door when George said, "I just want to know where your loyalties are."

"They're with whoever pays me. You and Henry might not get along, but to me, your money is the same color of green."

I stopped short. Was that Alex?

"How much for you to deal with Banion?"

My heart raced. Was George hiring Alex to kill my father?

"What do you mean by deal?"

God, it sure sounded like Alex.

"I don't read minds. You want a scandal? A government investigation into his business? What?"

Okay, so maybe I misunderstood. Still, why was Alex entertaining this? Did he even know I was missing? Did he care?

"I should think that whatever happened to poor Snyder would work," George said.

"He's dead."

I gasped. Oh, my God. They were talking about killing my father.

I wasn't able to hold down the bile that rose from my belly in horror. I rushed over to the trashcan in the corner, emptying the contents of my stomach. Alex wasn't a hero. He wasn't the man I thought he was. He wasn't the man my father thought he was. He had just made a deal with the devil to kill my father.

I had to get out to warn him. I started to back away when a hand closed over my mouth and I was bound tight against a hard body. I began to thrash.

"It's Dax Sheppard. Saint Security," he hissed quietly. "I need you to relax and keep quiet."

Was I being saved? But he worked with Alex. I continued to struggle.

"We're not going to be able to get you out of here and to your father if you do not cooperate with us." His voice was terse, his hand tighter on my mouth.

"If you can keep quiet, I'm going to release you, and then we're going to get out of here. Do you understand?"

What alternative did I have? Maybe they worked with Alex. Or maybe they figured out Alex wasn't good either. Either way, I was in the proverbial rock and hard place. I nodded against his hand.

Dax released me, and I whirled around, shocked at the three men in the room with me. I hadn't heard them enter. What had they done to Guenther?

One man was over at the door. Dax guided me toward it. The other man, who I realized was Ian, came from the window to stand with us.

Dax nodded to the man at the door who'd been looking out as if he was looking for Guenther. He nodded to Dax.

"We're heading out, moving quickly. Keep up and don't make a sound," Dax said.

Dax ushered me out behind the unknown man and Ian. He hurried me down the hall and through a door that led to a back stairway. We proceeded down two sets of stairs and stopped at the door as the first man looked through it. With another wave, he ushered us through and down another flight of stairs to what I determined was the employee entrance from the garage.

We'd made it this far, but I held my breath. Surely, Pitney had men guarding exits. But the next thing I knew, I was in a beat up old car, lying in the backseat as it pulled out of the garage.

I lay, stunned. This wasn't the kind of experience I'd ever expected to have.

Several minutes later, Ian looked over the front seat. "Are you okay?"

I nodded. "Just a little bit in shock, I guess."

Dax handed me a bottle of water.

I took a sip. "How did you know where I was?"

Ian smiled. "That's our job."

I drank my water, thinking about whether or not to ask them about Alex. "Is my father safe? Mr. Pitney wants him dead."

"Everything's going to be fine," Dax said, paying more attention to the streets than to me or the others in the car.

Several minutes later, we pulled into my father's garage. Someone must have alerted my father that I was coming as he met me at the elevator. I threw my arms around him.

"I want to throttle you for pulling a stunt like that. But I'm so happy to have you home." He held me tight. I'd never been so happy to be home and safe with my dad.

"I'm so sorry." Now that I was safe, the adrenaline dropped and the tears and the shakes overwhelmed me.

My father brought me upstairs, taking me into his office and setting me on the couch as he went to the bar in the corner.

"Do you want water or something stronger?"

I really wanted something stronger, but I thought of the baby. Alex's baby. The tears burst out again.

My father hurried to me with a glass of water. "What did that bastard do to you? Do I need to take you to the hospital?"

It was interesting that all this emotion wasn't coming from the fact that a man like Pitney had kidnapped me but from learning the truth about Alex. He wasn't here to help us. He was here to work for Pitney.

I gripped my father's hand and looked him in the eyes. "Alex is not the man you think he is."

My father tilted his head to the side. "Alex is the one who found you. He rescued you."

I shook my head. "No, he didn't. He was there, but he wasn't saving me. I heard him, Dad. I heard them talking to Pitney. Alex took $500,000 to kill you."

My father jerked and shook his head. "That can't be. Are you sure?"

"They talked like Alex had worked for him before. Mr. Pitney asked him to do to you the same that he did to someone named Snyder."

My father rose and began to pace, something he did when he was thinking. "Snyder. There was a Snyder who went missing nearly a decade ago. He's presumed dead at the hands of Pitney." My father's expression was perplexed. "I've known Alex for a long time. He was protecting us."

I shook my head. "He was probably spying on us."

My father scraped his hands over his face. "Ever since he went to work for Saint Security, I'd always thought he was a little different. But I thought deep down, he was good."

"He told Mr. Pitney that all he cared about was the money. He said Pitney's money was as green as yours."

My father closed his eyes, digging the heels of his hands into the sockets of his eyes. When he looked at me, I saw a mixture of sadness and anger. "I'm so sorry, Tori. I can't believe that I had begged him to come and protect you, and all along, he was willing to sell us out to Pitney."

I let out a sigh of relief that he understood. But that relief was short-lived when I realized I needed to tell my father the rest.

"There's more, and you're not going to like it."

He came over, sitting on the couch and taking my hands. "Whatever it is, Tori, we'll deal with it. I'm here for you."

I looked at him and finally understood the betrayal Alex had talked about, but now I didn't believe he wanted us to be a secret because he cared about my father. Now I believed that he wanted to keep my father from knowing about us so he could stay on the case. To continue to play both sides.

I swallowed. "Dad, I had a little thing with Alex."

His brow furrowed. "What thing? A crush?"

I shook my head. "No. He was on the plane—" I stopped short as realization dawned. "Oh, God. It wasn't a coincidence that he and I sat together."

"I'm still not following, Tori."

"We were seated together on the plane. It couldn't have been a coincidence, could it? I mean, what are the odds? He must have called Mr. Pitney after you called him, and he tracked me to the plane. Made sure we sat together. I didn't know who he was. He acted like he didn't know who I was, but he had to, right?"

"God, Tori. I'm so sorry."

I closed my eyes. I thought I'd been an idiot before. Now I felt like the biggest dummy in the world. "Dad."

"Yes, honey."

"That thing with Alex wasn't a crush. It was more than that. I mean, not love, but—"

"What are you talking about?"

I let out a shuddering breath. "I had an affair with him."

It took a moment, but when it sank in, his hands bit into mine. "That bastard seduced you?"

Is that what Alex had done? Was he playing me this whole time?

27

Alex

Fuck. Shit. Damn. I sagged against the wall outside of Henry's office as my world crumbled around me. Henry wanted to kill me, and to be honest, I couldn't blame him. If my friend fucked my daughter, I'd be pissed too. Strangely, the thing that impacted me the most, though, was that Victoria thought I was a murderer. She believed I was betraying Henry by working with Pitney to kill him. Clearly, she'd overheard the conversation I had with Pitney, and she took it as truth. It was proof that her feelings for me were nothing more than lustful attraction. If she had cared for me, surely, she would know that it all was an act. An act to distract Pitney while Dax and the team helped her escape.

God. The plan had worked like a dream. Very rarely did we execute a plan that went without a hitch. The minute my phone buzzed in my pocket with two quick phone calls telling me they'd successfully gotten Victoria out, I'd made my exit, heading straight to our van up the street that had been monitoring the visit. I handed over the pack of money Pitney had given me to a teammate who was charged with getting it recorded and to the D.A. Hiring a hitman surely carried more weight than fraud, so I was feeling good about finally putting that fuckhead Pitney away. Not that I didn't have some bad feelings. I was pissed off that Victoria had put herself in such a dangerous situation.

I parted from the team and made my way to Henry's house to make sure everything was all right and then give Victoria a piece of my mind.

Knightly let me in, and his smile was ecstatic, happy Victoria was home. He told me Henry and Victoria were in his office but that he was rushing off to get champagne to celebrate. I made my way to his office but stopped short as I heard them talking, recognizing the tone of the voices weren't of a happy reunion.

I couldn't fucking believe it. Not only did she believe that I was in league with Pitney, but she had managed to make sure Henry believed it too. I was about to walk in on them and clarify what I'd been doing with that discussion with Pitney. I'd been buying time. I'd been setting him up. And then she'd done the unthinkable. She revealed our affair. There was nothing I could say or do to overcome that. Even if they believed what I'd been doing when I met with Pitney, there was no getting over the fact that I had slept with his daughter. Our friendship was done.

I pushed off from against the wall and strode out the front door and down the steps. I made my way up the block, needing to walk off the anger, the frustration, the pain. I wanted to be angry at Victoria and Henry, but the truth was that I'd brought this on myself.

"Sterling? What's up, man? Did you get the daughter?" Jacobs, one of the Saint Security team, stepped from the bushes at the edge of Henry's property.

"Miss Banion is home and all is well." I imagined at any moment, Henry was going to be calling Elliott or maybe even going to the top and calling Archer to tell him I'd fucked a client. God, my life was a shit show. I'd lost Henry. I'd lost Victoria's respect. And now I was about to lose my job. Not that I wouldn't be able to find other work, but it would probably be with a more unsavory crowd, like George Pitney, and I wasn't going to do that. It was ironic that I wanted to do good, but Victoria thought I was a murderer.

"Where you off to?""

"I just need to take a walk. If anything happens or you need anything, get in touch with Dax or Elliott."

His brow furrowed, suggesting he could tell something was up. But he gave me a curt nod and stepped back into the shadows.

My phone vibrated in my pocket, and I had no doubt that it was Pitney. My phone had been blowing up for the last twenty minutes, likely starting the moment Pitney realized Victoria was gone. But why? He should have been arrested by now. He was on tape hiring me to kill Henry. With the fuck was wrong with the DA? I'd served Pitney up on a platter, so why was he blowing up my phone?

I turned the corner, heading up the long block away from the river. I wasn't going anywhere in particular. Just walking, my mind swirling like a whirling dervish, thoughts ricocheting off every corner of my brain. I wasn't able to string them together to figure out my next plan.

I was midway up the block, when arms came around me, gripping me hard. I moved to free myself when a bolt of electricity blasted through my body.

"Motherfucker!" I tried to struggle, but these guys were bigger and there were three of them. A needle prick stung the side of my neck. I was about to die. There was no fighting against being drugged, so I just gave in and then everything went black.

I WOKE IN A DARK, windowless room, my hands tied behind my back, my ankles tied to the legs of the chair like I was in a fucking espionage movie. But this was no movie. This was real. Interestingly, this wasn't the first time I'd been in a situation like this. Of course, it hadn't happened since my mercenary days when I was younger, and I usually had a team that knew I was gone and would come get me.

I scanned the room, simultaneously trying to work out the kinks in my neck and shoulders. There was no dealing with the headache likely from the drugs, but it was possible I'd been slammed around a bit. I had no doubt that I was here courtesy of Pitney, who I guess didn't want to give me the cushy room he had given Victoria. But he wouldn't. Not when he figured out that I'd set him up and saved Victoria. He'd know that I was working with law enforcement. Being the slippery fuck that he was, he obviously had gotten away. And because I was so lost in my head during my walk, I hadn't noticed it when a van pulled up and Pitney's men grabbed me.

Pitney was in real estate, among other things, so he owned a lot of properties throughout the boroughs and beyond. But he was also smart, so it seemed unlikely that he would take me to a location in which his name was on the deed.

I strained my ears to see if I could hear anything that would reveal my location. I heard nothing but the sound of my own breathing. It made me think of that tagline from the movie about no one can hear you scream in space. That's where I was. In a dark void.

The door swung open, letting in a blast of light that had me wincing, shutting my eyes, and turning away.

"Sleeping beauty is up. Let the boss know."

Pitney's goon Guenther made his way into the room, stopping to stand before me. He crossed his arms and gave me a menacing stare. "You think you're so smart. Don't you?"

I shrugged. "Smart enough. How is your head, Guenther?" When the team had gone in to rescue Victoria, the plan had been to incapacitate him much in the same way he'd incapacitated me. His head had to hurt like hell, just like mine did.

His fist shot out, catching me in the chin with such force that one leg of one chair lifted and then smacked back down. It hurt like a mother fucker, but I used all the skills I'd learned in the military and then later in security to ignore it.

"You'll hurt more than that when Mr. Pitney's done with you."

I wouldn't lie. A small shiver of fear slid down my spine. While there was no proof, there were certainly rumors that George liked to toy with the people he was pissed at. I imagine I was about to go through a long torture before my death and dismemberment. When they were done with me, there would be nothing left. I will have been eliminated from the face of the earth, like I'd never existed. And who would care? Sure, the Saint Security team would be pissed. Maybe I'd get a plaque on the Wall of Honor, but how long would I really be missed? My father probably thought I was already dead. Henry and Victoria would be pleased.

I shook my head, trying to stop myself from going into a downward spiral of self-pity. If this really was it, I wanted to go out in a blaze of glory, not like a pathetic, whiney bitch.

Pitney entered the room, and all semblance of a successful businessman was gone. I understood what Tommy and Aimee meant when they said he looked possessed sometimes. Pitney looked like the devil himself. Yup, this was it for me. Being resigned to death brought me a strange sense of calm. I wouldn't fight for my life, and that gave me a lot of freedom to speak my mind.

I grinned up at him, even though the split lip I had hurt like a motherfucker. "I'm really glad that my last memories in life are going to be knowing that I helped put an end to you."

Guenther's arm drew back.

"Not now, Guenther. There'll be time for that later."

Pitney grabbed another chair from the corner of the room and set it in front of me. He sat down, smoothing out his tie like he was dignified. "That's only true if I am caught, and I don't plan to be. But whether I am or am not, I get to spend the rest of my days thinking about how I made you scream. How I made you beg for your life. And then how I ended it. In all the world, I'll be the only one who knows where your remains are."

It was going to be difficult for him to leave the country, although I imagine he'd already had a plan for it. He probably had money stashed in countries around the world that didn't have an extradition treaty with the United States. So, it was possible that he could get away and live out his days, but it wouldn't be as the big businessman he was now. Whatever money he had stashed away would have to last him a lifetime because even as we spoke, all his legitimate accounts were likely closed unless the DA was still being a pussy.

"But before I kill you, I will kill your friend and then have my way with his daughter before I kill her too."

Rage erupted through me. My restraints bit into my wrists as my reflex worked to punch Pitney in the throat and end him here and now. "You will be dead before you get close to them."

He laughed. "So, you do care about people. We had a wager on whether you were totally heartless or not. Looks like I owe Guenther some money." He studied me for a moment. "Maybe you won't live long enough after all. I'll bide my time. Eventually, they will think they're safe. They'll decide they don't need so much security. And when that happens, I'll be there."

"You're all talk, Pitney. We both know that if you're not going to prison you're leaving the country. You're not an idiot. You won't come back."

His eyes flashed with lethal anger. "Rest assured, Sterling, that they are going to die before their time, and I am going to let them know that it was at my direction. You get to go to your death knowing that."

I knew the Saint Security team was the best in the world, and they would do what they could to keep Henry and Victoria safe. But Henry and Victoria could be reckless, which meant it was quite possible that Pitney would be able to follow through on this threat. He might be in jail or out of the country, but one of his goons could carry it out.

Pitney turned away from me and toward a man I didn't recognize standing at the door. "Could you bring me my tools?"

Another blast of fear shut down my spine. How odd that I was now in the situation that I'd put Tommy in, although I'd been bluffing? I knew Pitney wasn't. There was no information for me to divulge that would allow me to avoid his wrath. No. His plan was to torture me until I died.

I'd been through torture before, and I wasn't too thrilled about this being the way my life would come to an end. I'd have much rather died of exposure in the Himalayas, or maybe been eaten by a shark in Hawaii. At least then I'd have been doing something I loved.

The man returned with a box that he set on the floor next to Pitney. Pitney pulled out a variety of items one at a time, examining them, clearly wanting me to examine them too. Knives. Mallets. A picana, a wand that delivers an electric shock. A large plastic bag. I couldn't be sure if that was to put my body parts in or maybe he was going to wrap it around my head and suffocate me. Mentally, I sucked in a breath and let it out, resolved that things were about to get real.

A table was brought in and placed in front of me. My hands were freed as two men held me down and set my right hand on the table.

Then Pitney picked up a hammer. "How about we start with this little piggy?"

Even I knew piggies were toes, but this time I opted not to point that out. I don't know why? My hand was just as important, if not more so than my toes. Luckily for me, I was left handed, so he wasn't totally incapacitating me by fucking up my right hand. I didn't have much time to consider it when the hammer came down on the tip of my pinky finger.

At the first blow, time ceased to exist. I drew inward, gathering strength to endure. As he continued, I felt outside of myself and was proud of the way that with each strike of pain, I let out a slew of expletives on Pitney. My favorite was "motherfucker, cock sucking ass wipe."

I couldn't say how long it went on. He moved from the hammer to the picana, zapping me with the high voltage but low current rod. Then he gave Guenther a turn. He much preferred to use his own hands.

The pain continued, but it was almost as if my body couldn't respond to it. By the time the darkness came, it was a relief. I welcomed it, wrapped it around me until I was gone.

28

Victoria

I knew my father would be upset, or at least weirded out by the knowledge I'd slept with Alex, but he was downright crazed. I truly believed that if Alex were here, my father would carry through on his threats and kill him. Or he'd try. Based on what I heard today, my guess was that Alex would be able to thwart the attempt.

I had more to tell him, obviously, because of the baby, but I decided now wasn't the time. Based on his reaction, maybe there would never be time. I knew that was unrealistic. I couldn't hide a pregnancy forever. Now that I'd told him about me and Alex, it seemed unlikely that I could attribute the baby to somebody else. My father's head was going to explode when he learned I was pregnant.

I still couldn't believe what I heard Alex say to Mr. Pitney. Was there some sort of explanation that would make sense of it? The two men were talking alone, so there was no reason for them not to be honest with each other. Clearly, they knew each other as it sounded as if Alex worked for him before. "Dealt" with someone before. All points appointed to Alex not being the man we thought he was.

As my father ranted and raged, I tried to work through Alex's involvement. The only thing that made sense was that my father had called him and asked for help with Pitney, then Alex contacted Pitney. That had to be how we ended up next to each other on the plane. Was having sex part of the plan or just a nice side benefit for him?

Even as I thought these thoughts, something inside me told me it couldn't be true. But what other explanation could there be?

My father pulled out his phone.

"What are you doing?"

"I'm calling that motherfucker and telling him to come over here so I can kick his ass."

I rose from the couch and went over to him, putting my hand over the phone. "To what end, Dad? It doesn't change anything. Just let it go. We both just need to let him go." My heart squeezed in pain, which was weird considering how betrayed I felt. How could I have fallen for a man like that? And now I was having his child.

I could see in my father's eyes that he couldn't let it go. He had to do something. "I'm calling his boss. Surely, there are rules about not sleeping with your client."

Since that was better than inviting a lethal man into our house to try and beat him up, I acquiesced.

As he made his phone call, I drank my glass of water and continued to try and wrap my brain around the man I thought I knew and who he really was.

A few moments later, Knightly entered carrying flutes and a bottle of champagne. "I thought we might celebrate the return of Miss Banion." Knightly read the room immediately, and his brows furrowed. "What's wrong?" He scanned the room as if he was looking for something. "Did Mr. Sterling deliver bad news?"

Both my father and I jerked our attention to him.

"What? What do you mean?" my father asked.

Knightly shifted uncomfortably. "I let Mr. Sterling in a little bit ago. Told him you were in your office and I went to get champagne. Did I do something wrong?"

I smiled reassuringly at Knightly. "No, you didn't." But if Alex was here, why didn't he visit with us? Was he still here? Was he planning on carrying out Pitney's plan?

Fear nearly choked me. "I think we should call the police."

"I can ask one of the Saint Security men to come in." Knightly's expression was still baffled.

"Yeah, but can we trust them?" my father asked.

"What did Alex's boss say?"

"Only that he'd look into it. I'm not sure he took it very seriously."

I wondered if Saint Security operated like the police, who had a reputation of protecting their own. If Alex had been playing both sides, he'd have been putting his own men in danger from Pitney. Would they protect him knowing that?

"Ask one of them to come search the house."

My father stared at me. "How do we know that they're not working with him? He has been in charge of this whole operation."

"I suppose it's possible, but if you think about it, it's not very likely. Saint Security has the best reputation in the world. What are the odds that he could get all the people on his team to be party to George Pitney?"

"We can't underestimate the influence of Pitney."

"Maybe not. But I would imagine that they will feel betrayed, just like we do, when they learn what he did. But to be safe, let's not tip our hand. We'll just say we heard something in the house and ask him to search."

My father thought about it for a moment and nodded. Okay, we'll start with that." He turned his attention to Knightly. "Can you ask one of them to come in?"

Knightly nodded but still appeared perplexed as he left to call in a Saint Security guard from outside.

A few moments later, a man we knew as Jacobs entered my father's office. "I understand you think there's a problem?"

"We were hoping that you might search the house. We thought we heard something funny and wanted you to check it out," my father explained.

Jacobs nodded affably. "Sure thing. You didn't have Alex search when he was here earlier?"

My father and I glanced at each other and then back at Jacobs.

"You saw him here?" I asked.

"I saw him when he left. He said everything was fine and then headed off."

The relief on my father's face matched my own. Alex wasn't lurking about, ready to kill my father. I realized we needed to say something to Jacob, but I still didn't want to tip my hand.

"It was after that. Would you mind looking?" Even though we knew now, no one was in the house, the search of the house didn't seem like a bad idea. When Alex was here, he searched the house all the time. Now I wondered why. Perhaps he was doing his job as he was supposed to but was tempted away by Pitney. He essentially said as much in their conversation. He went where the money was. That didn't explain how he ended up on the airplane, but at this point, the how or why didn't matter. All that mattered was staying safe.

Jacobs completed the search and left.

"I know it's late, but you still haven't eaten. Caroline has prepared a meal for you," Knightly informed us.

I'd totally forgotten about dinner. By the way we both picked at our food, neither Dad nor I were very hungry. But I forced myself to eat because I knew that's what the baby needed.

I wondered for a moment what Alex's parents were like that they ended up raising a son like him. I knew his father had disowned him. At the time, I thought it was a rotten thing to do, but maybe he did it because Alex wasn't a good person. Maybe he was born that way.

I pressed a hand over my belly, making a promise to my child that I was going to do my best to give it all the love and support it needed to grow into a happy, productive citizen of the world.

After dinner, my father tucked himself away into his office, and I probably should have done the same. But I decided that since I'd been kidnapped earlier, it was okay if I took the evening off. Instead, I hid myself away in the living room with a pad of paper as I tried to sort my thoughts and map out a plan for my future. A future that for the time being would probably require me to stay with my father.

When I yawned, I checked my watch and realized I'd been there for nearly two hours. It was time to put the hot mess of my life away and get some rest. I had just stood and stretched when there was a knock on the front door. I knew nobody could get up to the door without first passing through security. For a moment, I wondered if it was Alex. He wouldn't have been stopped unless they knew what he'd done. Now I second-guessed our not explaining things to Jacobs.

I went to the entryway of the living room and watched as Knightly opened the door. "Mr. Shepperd. Mr. Jorgenson." Knightly pulled the door open, allowing them into the foyer.

"Is Alex here?" Dax asked. The fact that they were looking for him here suggested they didn't know the type of man he was, or they did and they were here to stop him from killing my father.

"No. He was here earlier but left before seeing Mr. and Ms. Banion."

From where I was eavesdropping, I could see Dax's brow furrow. He looked at Ian. "And Jacobs saw him leave."

He nodded. "Yes. He said Alex was on foot. He told Jacobs that all was well and then he continued up to the corner."

"Are you here to terminate that motherfucker?" My father strode into the foyer.

Both Dax and Ian's brows shot up to their hairlines.

"Excuse me?" Dax bristled.

"That asshole seduced my daughter." My father seemed more concerned about Alex sleeping with me than his being hired to kill him.

Dax's brows drew down while Ian's went impossibly higher.

"Then is Victoria here?" Dax asked.

My father stepped up to him. "Why? Do you want to be the next—"

I rushed out, pressing my hand against my father's chest. "I'm sure that's not what he means."

Dax and Ian looked at me and my father like we'd gone mad.

"What's going on here?" Dax demanded.

"Like you don't know," my father scoffed. "I trusted him."

Dax turned to me, clearly ignoring my father. "Have you heard from him?"

"Don't talk to her." My father moved to push Dax away.

Again, I held a hand out to stop him. "The last time I heard Alex was when he took money from George Pitney to kill my father."

Neither Dax nor Ian looked surprised by that.

"You're okay with that?" my father hissed.

Ian's expression was perplexed. Dax looked at us like we were idiots. "That was the plan."

My father backed away, pulling me with him. "Knightly, call the police."

All of a sudden, Dax laughed. "Jesus, you thought that was real?"

"Alex is good," Ian said.

The pit of my stomach clenched. Had I gotten it wrong?

"The guy is on vacation trying to save your ass." Dax glared at me. "Both your asses, which is no easy feat considering you're both reckless and don't seem to care about putting anyone else in danger—"

"How dare you," my father bellowed.

That sick feeling in my stomach grew.

"Alex knew you'd be forever in danger even if Pitney went away on fraud charges. So what did he do? He got Pitney on tape hiring a hitman while simultaneously sending in a team to rescue you. The man is a fucking genius. He risked his life for the both of you and you think he's a murderer?"

"No wonder he left," Ian murmured.

Oh, God. Had Alex overheard us? Why didn't he come in and set us straight?

"He still fucked my daughter."

Dax looked at me. "Did he put his hands on you when you didn't want him to?"

I shook my head.

"She's a grown woman, Banion."

"He was my friend. It's wrong. Perverted."

Dax shook his head. "That's between you all. I have more important things to do. Come on, Jorgenson."

The two men started for the door.

"Wait." I rushed over to them. "Why are you looking for Alex?"

"Why do you care?" Dax continued out the door.

"He's missing," Ian answered.

I followed them down the steps. "Missing? How?"

"If we knew that, we wouldn't be here." Dax's phone rang, which was the only thing stopping him from getting into the waiting car. "Sheppard."

I watched as he took his call, waiting to find out what was going on.

"Mother fucker!"

"What?" Ian asked.

"Pitney wasn't at the house for the arrest."

"He's on the run," Ian commented.

Dax shook his head. "What are the odds that he found Alex?"

Oh, God.

"Alex is too good for that," Ian argued.

"Not if his head wasn't in the right place." Dax glared at me. "Let's take a walk around the corner. See if we can find anything or a witness to where Alex might have gone or if Pitney found him. Contact Elliot to request access to any surveillance cameras in the area." Dax and Ian started up the street.

I'd been wrong about Alex. The guilt of that burned deep in my gut. More than that, I was in a panic. If Pitney had Alex, it meant he knew about the sting he pulled. He'd kill Alex for sure. Alex would die because of me, because I'd been selfish and escaped protection. He'd die without knowing I loved him and was having his baby. Even if he didn't care about me or the child, he deserved to know. And now, it was probably too late.

"Will you call me when you have news?" I called out to Dax and Ian.

"If Alex wants to contact you after we find him, he can. *If* he can." Dax's words were a slap to the heart. I pressed my hand to my chest like that would ease my pain, fear, and guilt. But it didn't. It wouldn't. It would live there until this was resolved. Maybe even forever.

29

Alex

Pain pulsed through every cell of my body. It clued me in that I wasn't dead. Or maybe I was, and I was now in hell.

I worked through the pain to focus on my surroundings. Listening, I heard nothing. Had Pitney gotten tired of torturing an unconscious man?

With incredible effort, I opened my eyes. The room was dim, not dark. A shadow appeared, looming over me, and instinctively, I flinched, recoiling from whatever Pitney was going to deliver next.

"You're safe now, Alex. You're in the hospital."

The voice was familiar, but I couldn't place it.

"It's Dax. Are you with me, Alex?"

I emerged from the fog, my vision clearing to see Dax standing over me.

"How the fuck did you find me?"

He let out a laugh. "Tommy and Amiee didn't have a lot of information until it counted. They were aware of several properties owned by Pitney but under a different name. We started with the ones closest to an airport where he might make an escape and lucked out.

I'll tell you what, man, I think if we arrived any later, things might be different for you."

I tried to nod, but it hurt too fucking bad. "Thanks."

"Of course. I'm just glad we found you in time." Dax handed me a glass of water. "You should drink something."

I lifted my left hand and noted a significant bandage on it. I took the glass with my right hand and sipped, but my teeth hurt. I ran my tongue around them, wondering if I still had them all. Miraculously, I did. "And Pitney? Is that fucking pussy of a D.A. finally arresting him?"

Dax shook his head.

That was when I knew I had to be in hell. "What the fuck?" The vehemence with which I spoke sent more pain through me.

Dax gently patted my shoulder until I winced. "He's dead. Most of them are. The ones who aren't are recuperating in a hospital under police custody."

"What happened?"

"I'll give you the details later. Suffice it to say that Pitney did not go gently into that good night." I could imagine the scene even though I wasn't conscious during it. I knew how operations like this worked. It wasn't quite like the movies, but the end result was the same. Carnage.

"Your old buddy Henry is having a field day with the story."

Thinking of Henry brought me to Victoria. The memory of hearing them talking about how I was a murderer and how angry Henry was to learn about my relationship with Victoria filtered back, causing a different type of pain. It rooted in my chest, and I imagined it would live there forever.

"Are they safe?"

"Yeah, they're safe." Dax's expression looked as if he had a bad taste in his mouth. "Seriously, Alex, if those are the types of friends you have, I can't imagine your enemies." Then he flashed a grin. "I guess I can, as Pitney was one of them."

I shrugged. I hadn't had many friends in life. I suppose when I was working, I grew close to my team, but that waned once our mission was done. Henry had been the only one who stuck.

"Seriously, they believed that you accepted money from Pitney to take Banion out. Even as we were rescuing her, she totally believed that." He shook his head. "I mean she's pretty, but . . ."

"But what?" What a weird statement.

"Jorgensen and I set them straight on your part of the plan that involved saving Victoria. But Banion is still pissed about your little tryst with his daughter."

Oh. So the secret was fully out. "You know about that. Are you here to fire me?"

Dax let out a hearty laugh. "No. I'd be the last person to fire you for fucking a client. I did the same."

Oh, right. His wife had been a client at one point. "What did Archer do?"

"He gave me a promotion. They had me open the office in Las Vegas. Look, it's not a good idea to sleep with the clients, but no one's going to fire you over it unless it becomes a legal issue. And speaking of the clientele, Banion's daughter has been holding vigil outside your room for the last two days."

"Two days?" Was that how long I'd been out?

Dax nodded. "I'll be honest, I'm kind of surprised you've woken up already. Pitney certainly did a job on you."

"I can feel it in every inch of my body. I feel like shit."

"You look worse. Anyway, the daughter is outside and would like to see you. I've prevented her from doing so, but only because I got pissed off at how easily she questioned your character."

"I don't want to see her." That wasn't true. I absolutely wanted to see her. But what would be the point? Even if she knew now that I wasn't a murderer, it didn't change our situation.

"I don't blame you. But I will say the woman is clearly wracked with guilt. You might let her say her peace. It would make her feel better, not that she deserves it, but I thought I'd mention it. I'll be honest, the last two days of watching her and occasionally talking with her, I've come to the conclusion that she's in love with you."

It took a moment for his words to filter in. "She doesn't love me. If she did, she would have known that I wouldn't kill her father." And if she did, she wouldn't have so easily walked away. I suppose it was dumb to hold that against her since I was the one who ended things. But it had been fucking hard. For her, it wasn't.

"Yeah, I get that. If you don't feel the same, there's no reason to talk to her. You can just lay here and recover."

"It wouldn't matter if I felt the same."

Dax arched a brow, and only then did I realize I'd said the words out loud.

"Are you saying that you do feel the same? That you love her?"

"Like I said, it wouldn't matter. She's Henry's daughter."

Dax stared at me for a long moment, and I got the feeling he was trying to decide whether he was going to talk to me about something.

"Listen, I'm not the type of man who gets involved in other people's love lives—"

"You don't have to make an exception for me."

"Even so, I feel like you and I are alike in a lot of ways. The job is our life. Attachments only make us vulnerable. And let's face it, the traditional idea of marriage and kids sounded like a real snooze fest."

It turned out that Dax and I were a lot alike.

"But here's what I discovered. Life with Vivie and the kids has been the most exciting adventure of my life. Yeah, I'm not walking into a jungle in a Third World country trying to take out a despot or rescuing someone caught up in a political game. But I'm okay with that because after a while, the mind and the body grow weary. Tell me the truth. There was no real fun in dealing with Pitney."

"I'm happy for you, man. And I'm sorry if I've delayed your return home or taken you away from your family."

Dax rolled his eyes. "That's not why I'm telling you this. What I'm trying to tell you from someone who's been there, who's lived the life you lived, is there is no greater happiness or adventure than letting the love of a good woman into your life. Now whether or not Henry's daughter is that woman, I don't know. But if you love her, I'd encourage you to explore that. Sure, she's your friend's daughter, but

I'm confident that bridge is burned no matter what. Ungrateful bastard."

"I did sleep with his daughter."

Dax rolled his eyes. "Maybe it's a little weird, but she's a grown woman. A grown woman who has been sitting outside your room for two days."

I wouldn't deny the nice feeling in my chest knowing that caused, but it didn't change anything. "I appreciate what you're saying, Dax. Really. And I know that my friendship with Henry is done now that he knows the truth. But Henry and Victoria are the only family they've got. They're very close. I don't want to come between that or put her in a situation where she might have to choose one or the other. And that's assuming she felt anything for me, which I'm convinced she doesn't. If you could just tell her that I don't have any ill will toward her and I want her to go on and live a happy life and send her on her way, I'd appreciate it."

"All right."

I hurt like a motherfucker, but the idea of lying in bed all damn day felt worse. "Do you know how long I need to be here?"

Dax laughed again. "Jeez, man, you only just woke up. Let me go get rid of Banion's daughter and let the nurse know that you're up."

"Thanks, man."

"Of course. Oh, I'll be heading home with the family tomorrow. If I'm lucky, Vivie and I made another baby on the strip." He waggled his brows.

Dax was one of the most kickass men I knew, so it was a little bit strange to see him all gaga over his wife and family. Even so, it was nice too. He looked happy, happier than anyone I met except maybe Noel and Archer, both of whom had families too.

Perhaps that feeling deep in my gut was a pang of envy that I wouldn't have that.

I WASN'T JUST lucky to come out of George Pitney's clutches with my life, but I had all my body parts as well. In a feat of surgical magnificence, the doctors were able to save my hand, although it would never be the same. I supposed rock climbing was out in my future.

I had bruises and contusions, a couple of fractured ribs, and burn marks, but nothing else had been broken. Thank fuck. Not that I wasn't a 100 out of 10 on the pain scale, but I could have come away a lot worse than I had.

I was pretty out of it for the rest of that day and the next, but the following morning, despite the continued pain, I was ready to get out of the bed and go home. I was informed that I couldn't fly back to England, but if everything checked out okay today, the doctor would allow me to at least go to the Saint Security corporate apartment to finish my recuperation. The nurse had just finished checking all my stats when I heard a commotion outside my door.

The nurse made a face. "It must be that woman again."

"What woman?"

"The one that your colleague said wasn't allowed to see you, but every day, she comes by and insists that she should."

"Is it Victoria?" She was the only woman I could think of who would continually demand to come in, maybe even make a scene doing so.

"I think so. I'll get rid of her."

"No. You can let her in." I'd given permission before I had fully thought it through. I didn't have any reason to see her, but I'd let her have her say as Dax said she needed.

Victoria pushed into the room, looking over her shoulder as if she was expecting someone to grab and pull her out again. When she first turned to me, her expression was full of anger and frustration. But the minute she saw me, she burst into tears.

"I look that bad, eh?"

"No. I just couldn't believe you were okay until I saw you." She came toward me, reaching for my right hand, but I pulled it away.

"Say what you need to say, Victoria. I'm tired and I feel like shit."

She nodded and sniffed. "Yes, of course. Thank you for seeing me. I just . . . I needed to tell you how sorry I am."

"You needed. I'm in the fucking hospital overcoming a beating, tasering, and a hammer to my hand, but you need something. That's how it is with you and Henry, always what you need, not giving a shit about anyone else."

She drew back at the anger in my voice. And I was angry, not only because she believed I was capable of killing her father or that she betrayed me by telling Henry the truth about us. What I was the angriest about was the desire to pull her close and bury my face in her long, dark hair. It was fucked up that after all of this, I couldn't stop loving her. But apparently, the heart didn't work like that. I was hurt and angry, yet still yearning for something I couldn't have.

30

Victoria

I'd been so grateful to hear that Dax and his men had been able to find Alex and bring him back to safety. But it had been difficult to get information on Alex because Dax and others on the team seemed to resent me and my father. I guess I couldn't blame him for that. Alex had gone to great lengths to keep us safe, and we'd questioned his character. Not only that, but my running off and getting caught by Pitney had put him in danger. I'd regret that for the rest of my life.

When we received word that Alex was in the hospital, all I wanted to do was to go to him. I needed to see with my own eyes that he was alive.

My father couldn't stand that. "He was my friend, Victoria. Do you know how unsettling it is to hear that he slept with my daughter?"

I felt for my father, but I couldn't deny what I felt as well. "I imagine it is unsettling—"

"It's fucking perverted. The job is done. Just let him be and let him go home."

I shook my head. "I can't do that, Dad."

"Why the hell not?"

I sighed. "Because I love him."

"Oh, for Christ's sake, Tori. You can't possibly be in love. Sex isn't love. Besides, Alex doesn't know how to love."

"I never said he loved me. He probably doesn't, but I love him. I want to go to him. I will go to him." I considered telling my father about the baby, but I decided that Alex needed to know first.

My father pulled in a breath, puffing himself up. "I refuse to let you go."

I let out a humorless laugh. "I'm a grown woman. I don't need your permission."

I hated the way he looked at me, the heat, but also the pain, the feeling of betrayal he must be experiencing. "You're a grown woman who continues to accept an allowance from me. What if I cut you off?"

His words felt like a stab to the heart, not because I wanted or needed his money, but that it was coming down to this. Him threatening me.

I hoped my expression was soft and not angry. "You have to do what you have to do. I don't need your money. And in fact, if you want the money that you've given me for the last few years back, I have it saved. I can return it to you. But I am going to Alex."

"So that's it. You're going to choose him over me."

I shook my head. "You're the one who's choosing. Sorry, Dad, I've gotta go."

LITTLE DID I know that I would be blocked from seeing Alex for three days. On the final day, I couldn't take it anymore. My despair at not seeing him rose in anger until I was making a scene in the hallway outside Alex's room. I knew it wouldn't matter. The Saint Security guard posted outside his door wasn't going to let me in.

When the nurse came out, she gave me a disapproving look but then told me that I could go in and see Alex. The guard looked at her in question, and she informed him that Alex said he'd see me.

I hoped that was a good sign. I entered his room, half afraid the guard would yank me out. When I finally saw Alex, my heart stopped. His face was battered and bruised. His hand was in a large bandage. I wanted to run to him and soothe his pain.

He pulled away and looked at me with such disdain, it nearly brought me to my knees. But I was determined to say the things I hadn't been brave enough to say before. But before I got to that, I had to apologize.

"You needed. I'm in the fucking hospital overcoming a beating, tasering, and a hammer to my hand, but you need something. That's how it is with you and Henry, always what you need, not giving a shit about anyone else."

I recoiled from his anger, at his accusation even as I knew he was right. "I suppose it is selfish of me. I've been wrong about so many things, but especially about you. I believed something that wasn't true, even though I should've known better."

Alex just watched me, his expression unchanging. "I can see why you might not know better. But Henry should have. I guess that doesn't matter now since you outed us, anyway."

So he had overheard our discussion or someone told him that my father knew. I looked down in shame. "I don't have a good excuse except I was scared and confused." I looked up. "I'm sorry that I doubted you. I know you're a good person. I should've believed in you. I should've known better."

"Why? Why should you know better? You don't know me. Fucking someone doesn't mean you know them."

I flinched at the hard words in the harsher tone. I sucked in a deep breath as I prepared to tell him the truth. What I wanted to do was leave. I'd made my apology. But I needed to tell him everything, even if he rejected me. "I should've known better because I love you."

One brow arched. "I'm not sure you know what love is."

"I know what I feel, Alex," I said on a frustrated breath. "And I know it won't matter to you. I know that you are a bachelor for life. I know the idea of a wife and family is repulsive to you."

This time, his brows drew together quizzically.

"I overheard you telling my father that he was being mean to suggest that you settle down." I could feel myself getting agitated, so I took a moment to settle my nerves. "The point is, I understand where things between us stand, but I wanted you to know that before this all happened, I'd fallen for you. I love you and I betrayed you, and for that I'm very sorry."

He watched me for a moment. "Okay."

I closed my eyes because I wanted more. I'd wanted him to forgive me, but even without that, it would be nice if he said something more than just okay. I couldn't read his expression. Did it matter at all that I loved him?

I swallowed as I prepared to give him the last bit of news. "Okay. Well . . . there's one more thing, and I'm only telling you this because you should know. You have a right to know."

His expression remained unchanged.

"I'm not asking for anything. You don't have to do anything."

He smirked, or what I thought might be a smirk in his bruised and battered face. "I can't do anything anyway, Victoria."

I let out a breath. "I'm pregnant."

His breath hitched, but I still couldn't tell how the news impacted him.

"I know this isn't what you want, and it's okay. I can raise the child—"

"Did Henry tell you to keep it away from me?"

"What? No. My father doesn't know."

His jaw tightened. "Will he hate it because it's mine?"

What? "No. My father is angry." He was beyond angry, but I knew he'd come around. He was hurt and betrayed, but he was a good man. "He'll be so happy to be a grandfather."

Alex turned his head away, looking off. I wondered what was going on in his mind.

Finally, he turned back. "I'll provide whatever you need."

It was what he told my father he'd do. My heart burst in my chest, proving I'd been unable to protect myself from his rejection.

"I don't need anything," I said harshly, covering up my agony with anger. Knowing I was about to weep and not wanting him to see it as it would likely anger him since I brought all this on myself, I turned, reaching for the door.

"It wouldn't have worked."

I stopped and looked at him over my shoulder. "I guess we'll never know." I pulled open the door and strode out of Alex Sterling's life.

31

Alex

Wh

hen I told Henry I'd support a woman who got pregnant by me, I had no expectation that it would ever really happen.

I'm pregnant.

The words continued to reverberate in my head. Shock was my first response, followed by longing. A wish that things could be different. But they couldn't.

Was I a bad person for forfeiting my rights as a father? Detestable. Worse than my own father. But if Victoria and the child were to be happy, truly happy, I had to be out of the picture. Her life was with Henry. They were a real and true family. I couldn't come between that.

As long as Henry would love the child, then they would be fine. More than fine. Henry, unlike me, was capable of love. Oh, sure, I believe I felt it, but was that enough for Victoria to stake her life on? To risk losing her father over? No.

As I watched her exit my room, my breath, my very life, was leaving with her.

My cheeks felt damp. Using my uninjured hand, I wiped away tears. Jesus, I was crying.

My door opened, and I quickly brushed away the evidence of my emotional collapse.

Elliott entered. "Do you feel as bad as you look?"

"Worse." I prepared to be fired. Dax might have gotten away with sleeping with a client, but I doubted I would. Henry would hound Elliott or Archer until I was gone.

He sighed. "I never thought anyone would get one up on you."

I shrugged, then winced at the shot of pain. "Yeah, well, my head wasn't in the right place."

He came to stand next to my bed. "Because of the woman?"

Fuck, was there anyone who didn't know about me and Victoria? I nodded. "Are you here to fire me?"

His brows bunched. "Fire? Hell no. If that was happening, that would be Archer's job, not mine. No, I'm here to make a proposition."

"Really?"

"I know you're going to need some time to recover, but when you do, what would you say to taking over the New York office and I could take over London?"

"Why?"

He ran his hand through his hair. "I could use a break from this place. I was thinking that with your woman—"

"She's not my woman."

I love you.

I'm pregnant.

"Well, maybe you'd like a change too."

If I had a future with Victoria, I'd jump on this in a moment. But now, all I wanted was to go home and try to put all this behind me.

"I don't know."

"Listen. You don't have to decide now. You've got another four to six weeks of recovery. Plenty of time. Until then, I've got to get a report from you for Archer. Are you up to it?"

I nodded and then spent the next two hours recounting my ordeal with Pitney.

"Think about the switch," Elliott said as he left after taking my report.

I saluted him, even though I knew the answer would be no.

Exhausted, I slept until I heard another commotion outside my room. Had Victoria decided to try again?

The door burst open, and Henry barged in. "You're not going to die until I've told you what a fucking pervert you are."

"You can't be in here—"

God, I didn't need this now, and yet I knew I owed it to him to let him kick my ass. "It's okay," I said to the Saint Security guard. I wasn't sure why I had a guard when the one I had wasn't that good if Henry got past. "I'm sorry I didn't die."

"Fuck you, Alex. I didn't say I wanted you dead. I said you couldn't die until I gave you a piece of my mind." His eyes scanned me. "Jesus, you look like shit."

"You'll be glad to know that Pitney did a solid job at kicking my ass."

He shook his head and threw up his hands. "Why? You fucked my daughter. Why would you do that?"

I guess Victoria told the truth in that she hadn't told him yet about the baby. I scraped my good hand over my face. "I didn't know she was your daughter."

"Bullshit."

"She sat next to me on the plane and . . ." And, well, Henry didn't need to hear those details. "When I did learn who she was, I felt sick."

"Right, because it's fucking perverted. And yet you didn't stop."

"I tried." God, I was tired.

"But you let your dick lead you into debauchery—"

"It wasn't like that, Henry. She's not like the others."

He laughed derisively. "Oh, right. Are you going to say you love her now? That she's—"

"Yes."

Henry's mouth clamped shut. "What did you say?"

"I said I love her. I never told her that. She won't ever know it unless you tell her." I held my hands up in surrender. "I don't want to get between you two."

"Oh, so now you're a saint and I'm the bad guy?"

"Jesus fuck, Henry. What do you want me to say?"

"How about you're sorry?"

"I can't do that."

He stepped closer to me, and for the first time in our lives, Henry could overpower me and kick my ass. The look in his eyes suggested he might. "You fuck my daughter and you're not sorry? You betrayed me, and you're not sorry."

I shook my head even as it hurt me. But it would hurt more to say that I was sorry for any of it.

"I'm sorry that I hurt you, that I've lost you as a friend—"

"For what? You say you love my daughter and yet she's home bawling her eyes out."

My gut clenched. "I'm sure you told her I was no good for her."

"Of course I did. But she's got it in her head that she loves you. I told her this was your way. Fuck 'em and leave 'em. You did that to my daughter, you fucking bastard."

"Mr. Sterling, is everything okay?" the nurse poked her head in the door.

"It's fine."

She looked at Henry with skeptical eyes.

"Really." *Even if he kills me, it's okay.*

She exited.

"So this is it. You're going to recuperate and go back to London, fucking and leaving more women."

"Henry . . ." I didn't know what to say. "If I stayed with her, it would ruin what you two have. If I leave . . . she'll get over me and you'll be back to normal."

"Stayed." He jerked back. "Is that even an option?"

I closed my eyes. "If I thought it could work out . . . if I wouldn't be a wedge between you, then yes." I laughed. "The other night, God, it feels like a million years ago, you were hassling me about being in love. And I said all the things you expected me to say, but they were lies. They were lies because of Victoria. But she's your daughter, and I knew there was no fucking way I could make something with her."

He stared at me. "You mean to say that you've finally fallen in love and it's my daughter? For real? For fucking real?"

I nodded.

"Fucking hell." He turned away, running both hands through his hair. He whirled around.

"You think I'm too old?"

"I don't think you're too old."

Really? I hadn't expected that.

"It feels creepy because you're my friend." He continued to stare at me. "Fuck, fuck, fuck . . ."

I simply lay there wondering what was going through his head.

Finally, he came up to me, poking me hard in the chest. A blast of pain shot through me, making me wonder if he knew I'd been shocked by a cattle prod there.

"Okay, big guy. If you love my daughter and want her, prove it. Be with her. Make her stop crying. Make her happy or I will kill you."

I looked at him, wondering if I was hallucinating. "What?"

"I'm not going to be the asshole here. If it's true love, go for it." He laughed like he was calling my bluff. "I bet you weren't expecting that, were you? I won't be the excuse you use to hurt my daughter, Alex. So now you have to decide whether you're brave enough to be the man she needs, the man she thinks you are."

A mixture of relief and terror washed through me. Relief that he'd accept me in Victoria's life and terror that I wouldn't be able to be the man she deserved. I'd already failed her by not stepping up to be a father.

"And on that, I'll let you wallow in your pain." He went to the door, opening it. Before he walked out, he looked over his shoulder. "By the way, thank you for saving her life and for risking yours to make us safe." He was out the door before I could acknowledge his thanks.

"Wow." I lay in bed not sure what to think, except that Henry had just given me permission to love Victoria. To be with her. Except . . . what if I failed? What the fuck did I know about love?

There is no greater happiness or adventure than letting the love of a good woman into your life.

Dax's words filtered back into my mind. Was this how he felt with Vivie? Did Noel and Archer feel this? And what did I have to look forward to if I didn't step up and grab love? The life of adventure I'd had before didn't seem so appealing. Oh, sure, I wanted to travel and explore, but it would be so much more exciting with Victoria by my side. Victoria and our child.

The answer was clear. It had always been clear, but I'd been too afraid to act on it.

I pressed the buzzer for the nurse. "Yes, Mr. Sterling."

"I've got to get out of here." I fought the excruciating pain to sit up and swing my legs over the bedside.

"You're not discharged. The doctor will be in—"

"I have to go now." I slid out of the bed, my feet hitting the floor, jarring every bone in my body.

"Mr. Sterling." She attempted to get me back in bed.

"Get the doctor. I need to leave."

"You stay here." She went to the door. "Make sure he doesn't leave," she told the guard.

He looked in, his brows raised as I waved him in. He stepped in, letting the door shut as the nurse went to get the doctor.

"What's your name?"

"Doug."

"Doug, I need to leave. You need to help me drag my ass out of here. Where's my clothes?"

"I think Mr. Shepperd dropped a bag off." He pointed to the corner. "Your other clothes were bloody and taken for evidence."

"Right. Help me get dressed. We have to hurry."

"I don't think—"

"Don't think. I'm your superior and I'm telling you that you need to help me break out of this place."

I made a mental note to let Elliott know that I'd bullied Doug into helping me so he wouldn't lose his job.

Getting dressed was like rolling in broken glass, but I did it. Doug checked the corridor. "I don't see the nurse."

"Good. Let's go." I felt a million years old as I hobbled with Doug's help to the elevator and down to the garage where Doug arranged for a car.

Once in, I drew in a breath to manage the pain. I gave the driver the address. "Try to avoid potholes and quick stops, but more importantly, get me there quickly."

He eyed me through the rearview mirror. "You sure you're okay?"

"No. But if I have a chance of being okay, it requires you to get me to that address ASAP."

32

Victoria

I think I set the world record for the number of tears cried. It was impossible that there were any still left in me, yet they continued to fall. Just when I thought I had them under control, I would think of Alex and the agony of this whole situation would hit me, and the floodgates would open again.

When my father arrived not long after I returned from seeing Alex in the hospital, he wasn't much help. He didn't seem crazed like before, but he continued to rant and rave, telling me what a terrible person Alex was. How I should've never gotten involved with him. How Alex used and abused me.

I knew that wasn't the case. I wasn't used or abused. If anything, I was the one who abused him. It wasn't like he tricked me or seduced me. I got into this thing with my eyes wide open knowing that he was a man who didn't want any attachments or entanglements. It was my own fault that I was where I was now.

"You're just making it worse, Dad. If all you're going to do is badmouth Alex, you can just leave."

My father stopped short mid-pacing and looked at me. It was as if somebody snapped their fingers in front of his face and brought him out of a trance.

"Oh, hell, Tori. I'm doing a terrible job trying to comfort you."

"Yes, you are."

He sat next to me on the couch where I'd perched myself when I arrived home and started my cry-fest. I was glad to be home and at the same time, it brought back memories of the week that Alex and I had been here alone, holed up in our own little cocoon.

"I'm sorry, honey. I've handled this all wrong. I've taken my anger on him out on you. I should have never threatened to take your allowance or made it seem like you had to choose between us." He tugged me in close, kissing me on the head like he used to do when I was a little girl.

"Thank you."

"It just kills me to see you crying over a man like Alex."

So much for letting it go. "This isn't Alex's fault. Just because he doesn't ever want to love anybody, doesn't make him a bad person. You've never loved anybody. Are you a bad person?"

He tensed. "It's not the same. No one has loved me, and I let them down." There was a disconnect in his voice that had me looking up at him.

"Have you loved anybody, ever?" I asked.

In a flash, I saw sadness, maybe even regret, but then as quick as it was there, it was gone. "We're not here to talk about me."

"Why not? It will take my mind off my troubles."

He gave me a wan smile and squeezed me close. "As your dad, I wish I could give you a Band-Aid and make all this go away. I know it will take time, but you're a strong woman, Tori. You deserve better than Alex."

I wondered if now was the time to tell him about the baby but ultimately decided against it. Things between us were good, calm. I didn't want to ruin it.

"Let me make you some tea or something."

I nodded. "Tea would be nice."

He went to the kitchen, and I sat on the couch, staring out the window. A memory of Alex, his wicked eyes watching me as he sauntered over and then had his wild way with me on the couch popped up. Immediately, tears gushed again.

With my dad and tea, I pulled it together a little bit longer, but then when my father left, I was back on the couch weeping again. Maybe if I got it all out now, the healing would begin sooner. Eventually, the crying wore me out and I fell asleep, grateful for the respite from grief.

I was woken by a loud bang on my door. Was it real or a dream? I lifted my head to listen. It sounded again, and I rose from the couch, heading to the door. I looked through the peephole and gasped.

I undid the locks, swinging the door open. "Alex."

He was leaning against the wall and looked as if at any moment he might fall over.

"What are you doing out of the hospital?" I looked up and down the hallway, wondering how he'd gotten here. He certainly couldn't have come on his own.

I started to lift his arm so I could hook it around my shoulders to help him in.

"Fuck. Don't touch me."

Immediately, I stepped away.

His expression turned remorseful. "Fuck. Sorry. Shit . . . That wasn't the first thing I wanted to say. You can help me on my left. It doesn't hurt as much on that side."

I did as he said, helping him into my home and setting him on the couch.

"Let me get you a glass of water." I hurried to the kitchen, grabbing a glass and filling it from the tap. I returned to the living room where I found him sitting, his hands resting on his thighs, his head reclined back, and his eyes closed. He might've looked like he was asleep except it appeared that he was doing breathing exercises. I wondered if that was how he managed to make it through all the terrible things Dax had been sure to tell me had happened to him while he was in Pitney's grasp.

"Alex, let me call somebody and have you taken back to the hospital."

He lifted his head. "No."

I stood in front of the couch watching him, wondering why he was here.

"I want to find out," he said, his eyes looking a bit glazed.

I stared at him, uncertain what he was talking about. "What do you mean? Find out what?"

"I told you that we wouldn't work, and you said that we would never find out. But I want to find out."

My heartbeat picked up, but my head warned me not to read too much into this. "Why? Nothing's changed."

"Henry's changed his tune . . . I think. He's still pissed, but now he's pissed because I've made you cry. He wants me to fix it."

See, this was why I couldn't get my hopes up. "You're here to appease my father?"

His brows furrowed as if he didn't quite understand what I was asking. "No."

"You just said that the thing that changed was my father—"

He shook his head, using his good hand to rub his eyes. "Fuck. I'm not talking right." He shifted, his face grimacing in pain.

"For God's sake, Alex. Let's get you back to the hospital."

"No! Fuck . . . sorry." He let out a long sigh and then patted the cushion to his left. "Can you sit for a minute? Please? I'll get my thoughts in order, and I'll do this right. I promise."

Skeptically, I moved and sat on the couch next to him.

"First, I love you." He could've started dancing a jig and I wouldn't have been more surprised.

"What?"

His hand reached over, palm up, asking for me to take his hand. It was instinct more than will that had me putting my hand in his.

"I love you. I can't say for sure when it happened, but it was before we left this place."

"But you said—"

"I know what I said. I was a coward. Henry was right, I was afraid to love. And of course, there was the complication of your being Henry's daughter, but mostly, I was terrified. You are a young and vibrant woman with so much ahead of you. I'm an old man, older now after spending some time with Pitney. I've felt things I haven't felt before, but I was afraid to tell you, especially since you saw this whole thing as a fling. A great adventure. You said so, remember? In the drugstore when you bought all those girly products?" He frowned. "This is an aside, but why did you need all that if you were pregnant?"

My lips twitched upward. "I embarrassed you with all those products so that you would go away and I could get the pregnancy test. And I only said that what we had was a great adventure because it seemed clear that it was over. I was going back to Dad's and that meant we couldn't be together."

He thought about that for a moment, but his expression was a bit lost. I wondered if he was foggy from medication or maybe he had a head injury.

"I'm sorry you had to go through all that without me. I should've been there, but I know why you didn't want me to know. I made no secret about how I had set out to live my life."

I nodded, relieved that he understood.

"I wanted a life of adventure and no strings, but then I met this smart, feisty, kickass, sexy woman on an airplane, and she's turned my world upside down. She's brave too, because she told me she loved me and was having my child knowing that I would reject her. That guy is such a fucking asshole."

I let out a laugh and could feel tears coming again, but this time they were happy ones.

"Both Dax and Henry said things to me that helped me realize what I really want." He shook his head. "That's not true. I knew what I wanted. I wanted you. I just was afraid to ask for it. Afraid for me, but also not wanting to fuck up things for you and Henry. I don't know, maybe they're all just excuses. I know I'm not worthy of you. I'll be honest, Victoria, I don't know if I can make you happy or the baby happy, but I want to try. For me, not Henry. If you still love me and will forgive me."

I sniffled, giving up on controlling the happy tears. "You're a big galoot sometimes. Did you know that?"

His lips twitched up. "Galoot. Does that mean charming and sexy?"

"Not usually, but in your case, yes." I squeezed his hand. "I love you, Alex, and I forgive you. Do you forgive me? All this pain you're in, it's all my fault."

"We stopped him, though. You and your dad are safe. I'd die to make that happen, so this little bit of excruciating pain, I can deal with."

His words didn't alleviate my guilt. I vowed I'd take care of him, help him be as strong as before.

"You're my hero."

He snorted.

I leaned closer to him, wanting to kiss him senseless but not wanting to hurt him. "Can we kiss and make up?"

He nodded. "It will hurt, but it will be worth it."

As gently as I could, I brushed my lips over his. He let out a long exhale, and I could feel his body relax. I settled in next to him, careful not to bump his injuries.

We sat in silence for long moments, so long that I wondered if he'd fallen asleep. But then he said, "Do you think our kid will like to hike?"

The dream I'd had earlier came back to me. "I'm sure he will."

FOR THE FIRST FEW DAYS, I cared for Alex twenty-four, seven. He joked that it was preparation for when he was old and infirm. He continuously reminded me that when I was his age, he'd be seventy.

"And you'll still be a charming, sexy galoot."

For the most part, we were in our bubble again. Alex would rest and I'd work. Then I'd make dinner, and we'd watch a movie or a show about exotic places on Earth. While he received a few calls, no one came to visit. I talked to my father and invited him over, but he declined. He said he was happy if I was but that he still wasn't ready to see me as Alex's partner. I was grateful that he was coming around. I hoped that by the time I told him about the baby, he'd be ready to give us his blessing.

I'd arranged for some in-home healthcare that came and checked on Alex's progress and gave him exercises and a routine to help him get back on his feet. Three weeks later, he seemed almost his usual self. His ribs were still sore and his hand wasn't fully healed, but he was moving about normally, mostly without pain.

He finally made his way to the office, saying he needed to talk to his colleagues and his boss about going back to work. When he was gone, I wondered what would happen. His work was in London and mine was here, although it could be there. Would he want me to come?

Yes. Everything he'd said since he showed up on my doorstep suggested he would. But we didn't talk about the future. We talked about our days. We talked about the baby in vague, futuristic terms. But we didn't plan a future.

Instead of worrying about it, I buried myself in my own work, catching up on tasks I'd fallen behind on during the whole Pitney ordeal.

He returned midafternoon, poking his head in my office. "Got time for a break?"

"For you, absolutely."

He took my hand and led me to the bedroom. He put his arms around me, and I immediately felt his hard length. It was the first time I'd felt it since before I'd returned to my father's when I thought we were done.

"Hmm . . . are you sure you're up for this?"

"Don't I feel up?" He buried his face in my neck, kissing me, sending delicious chills along my skin.

"Yes."

"I do want to talk to you. I have an opportunity to stay in New York. To run the office here, and Elliott will go to London."

I felt giddy inside. "Is that what you want?"

"I want to be with you. If you'd like to come to London, we can go there. If you want to go to Timbuktu, we—"

"Have you been to Timbuktu?"

He smiled. "Yes. But I was thinking you'd want to stay close to your father. He'll want you to be close too, especially with the baby."

"I want to be where you are, but near my father would be nice."

He gave me a quick kiss, almost as if he couldn't wait to kiss me. "I will need to go to London to deal with my flat and my office."

"Will you be gone long?"

He shrugged. "Probably not too long." His hands slipped under my shirt. "Do you know how long I've waited to touch you?"

"Three weeks, same as me. But you needed to heal."

"You heal me, Victoria."

I knew what the word *swoon* meant when he said things like that.

"You can come with me."

"Huh?" I'd lost track of the conversation as his palms were rubbing my nipples.

"You can come to London with me when I pack up. You can work there while I deal with things."

"I'd like that."

His smile was brilliant, like I'd given him a gift. "Good. Now." He lifted me up and carried me to bed. "I hope you don't have to return to work because I have a lot of time to make up for."

I had a ton on my to-do list, but nothing was more important than him. "You're sure you're well enough?"

He stood by the bed and undressed. "I'm well enough, though you might have to do all the work."

I undressed then held my arms out. "Let me take care of you."

He lay with me, rolling until I was on top. I used my fingers to trace the remnants of bruises and burn marks on his body. I couldn't stop the guilt that he'd been hurt because of me.

"Hey?" He took my hand, bringing it to my lips. "There's no permanent damage."

That wasn't true. His hand would be permanently scarred and deformed. I looked at him, feeling sad and grateful all at once.

He levered up, slipping his left hand round the back of my neck. "Kiss me, Victoria."

I smiled and gave in to the love. I kissed him, turning the heat up to scorching.

He growled as his hands gripped my hips. "My fucking hot lady."

Soon, I was lost in sensations. His touch. His taste. His words of love. How did I get so lucky?

He lay back, and I rose over him, needing to feel him inside me. I sank down, letting out a long sigh as his body filled me. I'd known we were together the day he came to my apartment, but at this moment when his body joined with mine, I finally felt my heart fuse back into place. It was like I needed to feel the physical sensation of our souls joining.

"I love you, baby." His hands gripped mine as I rocked over him. "You're so fucking beautiful, did you know that?"

"You're biased."

"That doesn't make me wrong."

I leaned over and kissed him. "I love you."

"Take me to heaven, baby. The way only you can."

After that, we moved and touched and kissed without words. Slow and sweet at first, soon the need built, higher and higher, to a fever pitch.

"I'm there, Victoria. Come . . . take me with you."

I threw my head back as my orgasm peaked. "Alex!" I rode him in short, quick strokes.

"Yes . . ." He bucked up, his fingers digging into my legs as he emptied inside me. "Yes . . . God . . ." He tugged me down and kissed me. I could taste his love. I hoped he could taste and feel it from me as well.

I moved off him, knowing his ribs were still sore. "How do you feel?"

"Fucking awesome." He turned his head, grinning at me. "You should have done that day one."

"I'm sure it would have hurt more than felt good."

"Your touch never hurts." He took my hand and kissed it, a gesture that never stopped making me swoon. "You're okay with this?"

"Having sex? Yes. Did I make you think I wasn't?"

He rolled his eyes. "I meant us. Your father is still—"

"My father will come around."

Alex looked at me dubiously.

"Someday."

"And if he doesn't?"

"You're stuck with me, Alex Sterling. So stop looking for reasons to sabotage it."

"I just want you to be happy, Victoria."

"I am, Alex. So happy." I wondered if it would be too much, too soon, to tell him how I pictured us as a happy family.

Together forever.

33

Alex

In all honesty, I wasn't completely sure what I had said to Victoria when I arrived at her apartment. Between the drugs and the pain, it was a miracle I made it there at all. But I must've said the right things because when I was fully coherent, she was by my side, tending me, which was no easy task. Having her care for me like I was a feeble old man wasn't the way I would've liked to have started a relationship with her, but I felt fucking grateful to have started anything with her at all.

Three weeks later, I was stronger and understood what Dax meant that day in the hospital. My life was turning out to be a grander adventure than I could have imagined. The only downside was that Henry was keeping his distance, at least from me. He had told Victoria that if she was happy, that was all he wanted. But he was still grappling with the fact that his friend was in love with his daughter. I totally got it. I could see how weird that would be, so I didn't push it.

Now that I was mostly healed, I felt I could take my life by the reins and directed it toward a life of adventure with Victoria. She and

I hadn't talked about the future, probably because the focus was on getting me healthy again. We talked about the baby, but not necessarily about us. What she didn't know was that in my mind, we were linked forever. We were going to live a fucking fairytale happily ever after. Who knew that I had it in me? I didn't think I had until I met Victoria.

When I was finally strong enough to go out into the world, I headed to the Saint Security offices. For one, the D.A. wanted to interview me about the Pitney case. Pitney was dead, and I still hadn't asked for details, mostly because I didn't care. I was safe, and that fucker was dead. The D.A. needed my report to close out the case.

While I was there, I talked to Elliott about his proposed plan to switch offices. We got Archer on the phone, who supported the change, and the plans began.

I'd been nervous to tell Victoria about it. I wasn't sure how she viewed our relationship. For me, our lives together were a done deal, but maybe to her, I was just her boyfriend who'd knocked her up.

But the Gods were on my side as she was completely on board. That and finally being able to make love to her made me feel like my life was finally on the right track.

Victoria and I prepared to return to England for a few weeks so I could pack up my things and work on making the transfer to New York. At the last minute, Victoria couldn't come because she needed to meet the district attorney regarding the George Pitney case. The D.A. wanted to make sure that all the Is were dotted and Ts crossed about what a scumbag he was. Victoria was a key witness because Pitney had kidnapped her. Her abduction had set the ball in motion that led to my kidnapping and Pitney's eventual death. As far as I was concerned, that chapter in my life was over, and I was ready to live full-throttle with Victoria and our child.

That was another thing that totally blew my mind. I was going to be a father. It was fucking ridiculous how excited I was about that considering I hadn't planned to be a father. Victoria kept calling our child a boy based on a dream she'd had. But I kept visualizing a little girl with Victoria's eyes and sweet face. I couldn't wait for this little person to arrive.

So life was good. Well, almost. I had to go to London alone, and I didn't like that. It was a reminder of how devastating it would be to lose her. I'd be a liar if I didn't have moments of being afraid and wanting to protect myself from that. But she was my world now, and I was diving headfirst into the deep end of total love and commitment, knowing that if it went wrong, it would be the end of me. But that was where the adventure lay. At least one of the places.

But a week later, I was at the airport, having bought a ticket simply so I could meet Victoria at the gate. She walked off the plane looking like an angel, wearing worn jeans and an oversized sweater and her hair pulled up in a messy bun.

When she saw me, her face lit up, and it was like the world was right again. She rushed toward me, flinging herself into my arms, her legs wrapping around my hips and her arms around my shoulders.

She streamed kisses all over my face. "Take me home, Alex. I am so horny for you."

I laughed. "Well, hello."

She pulled back, looking at me, and the love I saw in her eyes felt undeserved and at the same time, it gave me life. "I missed you."

"Not as much as I missed you." I set her down and took her bag. "Let's get you back to the flat so I can take care of that problem of yours. I'm curious, how long has this horniness been an issue?"

She threaded her fingers with my good hand, moving in close to me. "Since the moment you left."

"Well, that's terrible."

She looked up at me, and I couldn't help but lean over and kiss her right there.

"What about you Mr. Galoot?"

"Well, me? I've got blue balls. I'm hoping you'll take care of them. I know you're very good at tending to men in pain."

Her smile was sweet and tender, telling me she was thinking back to those weeks when I'd been incapacitated and she'd so lovingly cared for me.

The minute my flat door closed behind us, I had her pinned against it, my lips devouring her sweet mouth and my hands roaming her body, searching for soft skin.

She moaned. "Yes, yes, yes."

In my mind, I should take her in to bed, but the need was so hot, so fierce it had to be dealt with here and now.

"Will I hurt you or the baby if I have you here?" I asked as I sucked her earlobe.

"No. I want you now. God, Alex . . . now, now."

I'd never heard such desperation in her voice. My woman was in need and I was damn well going to take care of it.

I stripped her bare, dropping to my knees. I kissed her belly. Then I hooked her leg over my shoulder, opening her wet pussy to me. I inhaled, feeling so fucking happy to have her with me. I wanted to dive into her, drown in her. I licked and sucked, and within moments, she cried out, her body shuddering.

I stood, undoing my pants and shoving them down. I lifted her leg again, this time hooking it over my hip.

"Look at me, Victoria."

Her eyes lifted to mine.

"I love you." I thrust in, filling her in a single move.

She gasped, gripping my shoulders. "Alex." Her eyes closed, and her head fell back against the door. "More. More."

I kept my eyes on her face, loving the sheen of perspiration, the pink in her cheeks, the way she gasped and moaned as I moved in and out of her. My dick was harder than granite, but I was going to make her come again. I was going to watch her reach for pleasure and then succumb to it. I'd seen many women come in my life, but Victoria was the most sensual, beautiful woman I'd ever seen, and when she came, it was perfection.

"Oh, God . . . yes . . . Alex . . ." She bit her lower lip, and her hips rocked against mine. She was there.

"Come, Victoria."

She cried out, her pussy clamping around my cock so tight I saw stars. I pumped into her again and again, each time causing a thump against the door. Anyone outside the door would have to know what we were doing, but I didn't give a shit. I was with Victoria, the woman who showed me love and adventure. The woman I planned to spend the rest of my life loving.

AFTER A WEEK of completing business and moving arrangements, we made a quick trip up to the Isle of Skye to see the fairy pools and then returned to London to board a plane back to New York.

As the plane hit its cruising altitude, Victoria leaned over to me. "I'm having the strangest sense of déjà vu."

I arched an eyebrow. "Are you now?"

She nodded. "I believe I've been here before."

I was extremely pleased that she was recognizing that this was a full-circle moment. We had first come together in a crazy mixture of passion and lust on a flight from London to New York. It was intended to be a one-off, nothing more.

This time, I was going to do it right. This time, it was going to be forever.

Victoria walked her fingers up my left arm. "Are you feeling like a little adventure, Sterling?"

"I'M ALWAYS UP for an adventure, and for you, I'm always up."

Her eyes glanced down to my lap. She looked up at me with delight in her eyes. "Well, then." She nonchalantly looked around as she unbuckled her seatbelt. She made her way up to the first-class restroom, and just as she was stepping through the door, she caught my eye, giving me the proverbial come-hither look. She closed the door behind her, and I sat for a moment, even though deep down I wanted to jump out of my seat and sprint to the bathroom. The passengers around us were all busy reading, working, or watching a movie.

Acting as normally as I could, I exited my seat and made my way up to the restroom. I opened the door, slipping in. Victoria was standing against the sink, her eyes filled with passion.

I brought my hands to her hips, settling my hard dick against her belly, wanting her to know just what she did to me. "So, we meet again."

She looped her arms around my neck. "Fancy seeing you here again."

I bent down to kiss her, tasting the sweet lips I intended to taste until my dying day.

When I pulled away, she looked up at me, her brow arched. "Should I be worried that you're not ravishing me already?"

"The ravishing will commence in a moment. First, I have something I need to talk to you about."

Her brows drew together. I was sure she was wondering why I didn't say whatever I needed to say back at our seats. But I couldn't. This was the best spot for what I needed to say to her.

My nerve endings tingled, and a bead of sweat slid down my back. I was nervous. "I told you I wanted to know."

Her smile was lovely. She nodded. "I'm glad you pulled your head out of your ass and decided to find out."

I flashed a grin, loving it when Victoria didn't mince words. "What I wanted to tell you is that I do know. Without a doubt, Victoria, I know we're going to work." I brought my hand to her cheek as her eyes rounded.

"I know that I was totally against a settled life, and a month and a half is a crazy time frame to know that I was wrong about that. But it's as clear as day that my life is with you and the baby. And what I'm taking a long time to get to is to ask you to marry me."

I remembered the ring I bought shortly after I arrived in London. I quickly pulled it out of my left pocket where I had stashed it. I held it up, hoping she liked it. It wasn't elaborate, overflowing with jewels. It was elegant, a single perfect diamond for a single perfect woman.

She looked at the ring and then me. "Oh, my God."

The nervousness picked up. Was this too soon? "You're killing me here, Victoria."

She blinked, and then a smile radiated from her face. He held up her left hand. "Yes. Yes, yes, yes. I want to marry you."

Thank fuck. I slipped the ring on her finger and then pulled her into a tight embrace, just holding her, savoring the fact that I would hold her like this until the day I died.

"You planned this?" she asked.

"I did. I almost asked you in Scotland—"

"This is the right spot. Where it all started."

I dropped my forehead against hers. "It did start there, Victoria. I remembered wishing I'd broken my rule and taken you home. Asked for your name and number. You grabbed my heart and never let go."

She smiled. "For a committed bachelor, you sure know how to make a girl swoon."

I smiled. "How about I make you come too?"

"I think it's the law. You have to consummate the engagement."

I was pretty sure that was just for marriage, but who was I to argue? Whatever it took to keep Victoria with me, I'd do. So I touched her in all the ways I knew she loved within the confines of the cramped space. I kissed her breathless. And then I joined my body, my very being, with hers.

"You're mine," I whispered against her neck. "All mine."

"I'm yours." She took my face in her palms. "And you're mine. All mine. Forever."

My heart soared. My adrenaline pumped. Dax was right. There was no greater adventure than love.

EPILOGUE

Victoria

I was getting married! They said fairytales didn't come true, but I was living proof that they did. The only hitch was in telling my father. Not only did I need to let him know that Alex and I were getting married, but also that we were having a baby. The time had come. It needed to be done or it would seem like we were purposefully keeping it from him.

A part of me wanted to spare Alex from my father's reaction, but Alex was insistent that he needed to be there when we told him. "It would be disrespectful for me not to be there."

I arched a brow at him. "You don't need to ask for my hand."

He smiled as he pulled me close as we reached the door of my place . . . currently, *our* place until we found a new one suitable for a family. We were ready to head over to my father's and I was nervous.

"I know you're your own woman, Victoria. It makes it an even greater honor that you've agreed to join your life with mine. And because we are joined, I need to be there with you. Henry needs to see that I am devoted to you. I am one thousand percent in. And if he doesn't like it or if he gets upset, well, it is what it is."

I kissed him. "Then let's go see my dad."

When we arrived, Knightly gave me a hug and Mrs. Tillis came out to greet us as well. They were cordial to Alex, but clearly, they were being loyal to Dad by being cool toward him.

"Your father is out on the back terrace," Knightly told us.

It was a good sign. My father was treating this like a family visit. If it was business or serious, he'd have us meet him in his office.

"Hello, Dad," I greeted as Alex and I stepped out onto the terrace. I'd been holding Alex's hand, and I gave it a quick squeeze before I released it and went to hug my father.

"How was London?" my father asked.

"Cold and rainy, but lovely as well." I gave Alex a smile over my shoulder.

Alex extended his right hand, scarred and deformed from what Pitney had done to it but for the most part functional. "Henry."

My father looked at his hand, and I thought for a minute that he wasn't going to accept it. Not because of how damaged it was but because he still wasn't ready to accept Alex.

Finally, he extended his hand, giving a single shake. "Alex."

It broke my heart that before me, the two of them would've greeted each other with a hug. But we had a lifetime to get back to that.

"Would you like something to drink? Coffee? I think we might have some fresh-squeezed orange juice."

We arrived between breakfast and lunch, so my father wouldn't feel obligated to invite us for a meal and we wouldn't feel obligated to stay for one.

"I'm fine. How about you, Victoria?" Alex pressed his hand to my lower back, a move my father was laser focused on.

"I'm fine."

My father extended his hand, gesturing for us to sit. Alex guided me to a chair and then moved another chair close to me, then sat down.

My father remained standing, leaning against the back terrace wall and crossing his arms as he looked at us. He was clearly feeling guarded.

Alex's hand took mine as if he knew I was nervous. My father's eyes narrowed as they looked at our joined hands.

"I'm happy, Dad." I led with that because he told me that was what he wanted most for me. To be happy.

His jaw tightened as he turned his head to the side, looking away. He unbound his arms, setting them on the wall behind him. "That's all I want for you, Tori."

I smiled, ready to deliver the first blow. "Alex and I are getting married."

My father's eyes tensed, darkening. He looked at Alex. "It's a little soon, don't you think?"

Alex shook his head. "When you know, you know. I know."

I couldn't stop the sappy smile at his using the words he'd said when he came to me telling me he wanted to know if we'd make it and then on the plane telling me he knew we'd make it.

"You didn't think to talk to me first?" my father asked.

"With all due respect, Henry, Victoria is her own woman. I don't need your permission to marry her. I don't even need your blessing, although that would be nice. All I need is Victoria's permission, which she's given me."

I hated how difficult it was for my father to hear this. Why couldn't he be happy for me? Yes, Alex was his friend. Yes, maybe it was a little weird that I had fallen for his friend and his friend for me, but still.

"Dad, what kind of man would you have liked me to marry?"

Alex looked at me with an arched brow. I squeezed his hand to let him know I knew what I was doing.

"Not a Lothario."

I rolled my eyes. "Don't be like that. You'd want me to be with somebody who is kind, loyal, treats me well, with a good moral compass, trusted. Alex is all of those things. You wouldn't have been his friend otherwise. He was the one you thought of when I needed protecting. So how is this different?"

"I'll tell you how it's different. It's different because he's not worthy."

Alex stood. I didn't think he was trying to challenge my father. It almost looked like he was trying to be the friend they'd once been to each other. "I don't disagree with that. I know this is unsettling for you, and I'm sorry for that. I also understand that you may never get over it. And I'll grieve about that. But I love your daughter. She's the most important thing in my life. I plan to make her happy until the day I die. And if your feeling betrayed by the situation is more important than supporting us, I'll understand. But it feels like it would be a fucking shame."

My father reared back in shock at Alex's words. To be honest, I was a little surprised too, although I knew Alex could be blunt.

I rose and went to stand with Alex, threading my arm through his. "I think what Alex is saying is that we could be a family if you could let go of this resentment you have."

"Or what?"

"Or nothing," Alex said. "There's no ultimatum here, Henry. No threats. Victoria and I are going to be happy regardless of how you treat me. I suspect it will continue to hurt her, but you can't help what you feel, can you?"

"You think I'm being unreasonable for finding it offensive that my friend from college, the friend I remember holding the record for the highest number of girls fucked in a single semester, is now telling me he wants to marry my daughter?"

"Yes. That was over twenty years ago, Henry. We've grown up since then. Hell, I've grown up since the moment I met Victoria."

My father turned, pressing his hands against the terrace wall as he looked out into the small yard.

Alex leaned over to me. "Perhaps it's time to give him the other news."

It was hard to tell how Dad would take this, but I sucked in a breath. "There's one more thing we need to tell you, Dad."

He turned around, his arms crossed again." "Don't tell me, you're taking her away from me and moving to London after all."

"No. We're staying here. Alex is going to be managing the New York office of Saint Security. And I'm going to continue to do the work I'm doing. But in a few months, we're also going to have our hands full. We're having a baby."

A range of emotions swept across my father's face. Part of it was the bitterness he felt toward Alex. Another part of it seemed to be disappointment because a child would definitely bind us permanently.

But then he looked at me with awe. "My baby is having a baby?"

Tears welled in my eyes, and I nodded. "You're going to be a grandpa."

The tug-of-war battled in his eyes. He didn't like that Alex was the father of my child, and at the same time, I could see that the news made him happy. It was always him and me against the world. Even when my grandparents were alive, it always felt like just the two of us. But now that I was having a baby, the family was growing.

"Fuck." He reached out, tugging me in and giving me a hug. "You're going to be a beautiful, wonderful mother, Tori."

I squeezed him tight, feeling grateful that his love for me overcame his dislike of Alex.

When he pulled away, he put his hands on his hips and glared at Alex. "If you fuck this up, I will come after you and I will finish what Pitney started."

"Dad!"

Alex flinched as his experience with Pitney was still raw, occasionally waking him up in the middle of the night from a bad dream.

But he nodded. "If I fuck this up, Henry, I will deserve worse than what Pitney inflicted on me."

My father extended his hand to Alex. Alex took it and they shook. We still weren't meshed as a family, but it was progress.

THERE WAS REALLY no reason to wait to get married. Perhaps it was vanity since I wanted to wear a pretty dress before my pregnancy showed. So, less than a month later, I was standing on the beach out at our house in the Hamptons, getting ready to join my life with Alex's.

I had to beg and plead to get Samantha to agree to be my maid of honor. I told her she didn't need to do the usual maid-of-honor chores. I just wanted her there with me on the best day of my life.

My father told me that it was selfish of me to do that when Samantha had her hands full with her mother. Luckily for me, her mother supported the plan and agreed to attend too. She said she wanted to fill her remaining days with proof that life was happy and good.

Then I had to convince my father to walk me up the aisle.

"Your own woman, Victoria. You don't need me to give you away."

"No. But you're a part of this. Our families are joining." I didn't understand his resistance. Sure, he still was upset about Alex, but this was my wedding.

He continued to hem and haw, but then I pressed my hand over my belly and my eyes welled with tears, which definitely was a manipulation. "Please, Dad. It would make me happy." Luckily, it worked.

So here I was, on the beach, on my father's arm, wearing a lovely lacy tea-length dress, walking toward Alex who was definitely the sexiest, most charming galoot on the beach.

The ceremony was small. Knightly, Mrs. Tillis, and Caroline were there, as family, not as help, since we hired caterers and others to put the day together. Alex invited his father out of duty and seemed surprised when the gentleman showed up. Perhaps this was the start of all our families coming together and growing.

Some of Alex's colleagues from Saint Security were there as well, including Dax and his wife. Dax had made some comment about wanting to see Alex start his great adventure.

Mr. Elliott attended, although was leaving early to get to the airport for his move to London. A few of the other team were there, and two men that I hadn't met, but apparently one, Archer Graves, was the CEO of Saint Security, and the other, Noel St. Martin, had been the founder.

I was happy that they were all there, but I was happiest of all when I reached Alex and took his hand and then took his name.

After the ceremony, we had a small reception but left an hour later.

Alex was in a hurry to start the honeymoon, and he ushered me into a car and to a private air strip.

"Where are we going?" I asked, giddy with happiness. He had been secretive about our honeymoon plans.

"Anywhere you want to go." The car pulled up next to a private jet.

"What do you mean?"

"I've chartered an airplane to take us anywhere you want to go."

I bit my lower lip as excitement rushed through me. "Hawaii sounds nice, but I suppose that's pretty stereotypical, isn't it?"

He nodded. "But there's Fiji, Bora Bora, Tahiti."

"Those are long flights? What will we do the whole time?"

He gave me his sexy, wicked smile as he tugged me close. "We'll think of something." He kissed me, and it was full of love and promises and a future full of happiness. "Now, Mrs. Sterling, tell me. Where are we going to start our next great adventure?"

EPILOGUE II

Henry

Today was my daughter's big day. Bigger than her first birthday. Bigger than graduating from high school and college. She was getting married. I wanted to be happy for her because she was beaming, but I struggled with the fact that she was marrying my college buddy. I'd spent nights clubbing and picking up women with him back in the day. He'd been a committed bachelor, scoffing at the idea of love and family. And that motherfucker slept with my daughter, got her pregnant, and was now marrying her.

As much as it felt off, I had to admit that Alex looked at Tori like she walked on water. And I couldn't deny that even after all the challenges we'd put him through, he saved her life and made sure that George Pitney was no longer around to threaten me or her. More than that, I wanted to be in my grandchild's life, so I'd do my best to play nice with Alex.

But truth be told, Alex marrying my daughter today wasn't what had me on edge.

"Ready, Dad?" Tori looked up at me, and for a moment I saw my little girl. The one I would toss up in the air and catch. The one I'd take to the zoo.

"The question is are you ready?"

"I'm more than ready." Her smile was like the sun, and as long as Alex could keep her smiling like that, I'd support this marriage.

We stepped out of the house on the beach in the Hamptons and made our way toward Alex. His eyes were on her and only her. God, this was weird.

I kept my eyes forward, focused on the minister. But with every step, all I wanted to do was look to his left. To the woman standing up for Tori.

The truth was, I was a hypocrite. I'd ranted and raged about Alex and Tori. It had to be wrong for my good friend to sleep with my daughter. It *was* wrong. I knew it was because I'd done something similar five years ago. I too slept with a woman over twenty years my junior. It was wrong for so many reasons, including that she was my intern.

But holy hell, never had a woman made me feel like I was Superman or excited me the way she had. I was the CEO of the company, but had I been exposed, the board would have sent me packing. My father was still alive, and he'd have likely disowned me for risking the company simply because I couldn't stay away from a woman.

But that wasn't the worst of it. No, what made me a hypocrite wasn't sleeping with a younger woman. It was sleeping with my daughter's best friend.

It wasn't the same as Alex sleeping with my daughter, I kept telling myself. But it was a lie. Still, I did what Alex should have done and that was let the woman go. There was too much at risk for her and me. And for what? Yes, she was smart. An absolute delight to talk to. She was sexy as fuck, which was wrong, right? I couldn't desire my daughter's friend. But I had. And because it was wrong and on the verge of ruining lives, I'd ended it. I'd found her an incredible job on the other side of the country.

She'd known too that nothing would come of the affair, so she'd gone willingly. Hell, I suppose it was possible she'd been hoping I'd get her great job and that was why she was fucking me. I mean, what twenty-one-year-old woman wanted to fuck a forty-three-year-old man?

We reached Alex. Tori took his hand, and I stepped back, not as if I was relinquishing my daughter to him but to avoid staring into my taboo past.

I took a seat in the front row and gritted my teeth as I did my best not to look. But Jesus, I couldn't resist her then. How could I now? My gaze drifted to the left of Tori. To Samantha.

Holy hell, she was even more stunning than I remembered. Her blonde hair was pulled back, but wisps blew around her face. She still had amazing green eyes and perfectly formed pink lips. The memory of her taste filtered into my mind. Kissing her had always been amazing. And when those lips had wrapped around my dick . . . Jesus fuck, I'd come like never before.

I shifted, crossing my legs to avoid the evidence of my lewd thoughts becoming apparent.

The minister presented Mr. and Mrs. Sterling, and Alex kissed my daughter, and it made my stomach churn. But I had to accept the truth. My daughter was now married to my best friend.

The small group of guests clapped and cheered. Samantha handed the floral bouquet back to Victoria, and she and Alex walked back up the sandy aisle toward the house.

Samantha followed them, her eyes straight ahead. Was she trying to avoid me too?

As she walked past me, her familiar sweet scent enveloped me, triggering me with wonderful sensations I'd experienced five years ago.

I couldn't fucking help myself. As she reached me, I stood. "It's good to see you, Samantha."

Her breath hitched, and she stared at me like she didn't know what to do. Finally, she swallowed. "You too, Mr. Banion."

Her calling me Mr. Banion made me feel like I was a hundred years old. Like I was a dirty old man lusting for his daughter's friend. Wasn't there a movie like that? I think that guy ended up dead.

She continued up the aisle, and I was powerless to look away. She was fuller, rounder than before. It made her even more beautiful.

"How are you, proud dad?" Alex's father patted me on the back. I was surprised he was here, considering he'd disowned Alex for not going into the family business.

"I'm happy for them."

"They look happy. Who knows, maybe they'll make it. You were lucky, Henry. Never getting married. Wives only make your life miserable."

I frowned at him. "Sons do too."

"How about champagne to celebrate?" he said, ignoring my comment.

"I need to check with the caterer." I headed toward the house and was disappointed that Samantha was nowhere around. I found her mother sitting in the shade on the deck. She was suffering from a terminal illness, and it had meant a lot to Tori that she wanted to come to the wedding.

"Tori is beautiful, and she looks so happy," she said to me.

"Yes."

"I was surprised to learn Alex was her fiancé, but love is mysterious like that, isn't it?"

I looked up to see Samantha coming out of the house carrying a glass of water. "Yes, it is."

"Oh, Samantha, you remember Tori's father. Well of course you do. You worked for him, didn't you?"

"Yes. Here's your water, Mom. There's a room inside where you can lie down."

I was an asshole. Here Samantha was, struggling to take care of her mother as her father took off with his secretary. Tori told me she now had a son, which I had to admit sent me to the bottle after I heard it. She'd left me and immediately was in the arms of someone else. Probably someone her own age. But clearly, someone who wasn't around.

All this made Samantha's life more difficult, and I was infatuated with her again when I should be helping.

"If there's anything I can do for either of you, let me know. Really, Gwen, Samantha, I'm here for you."

Samantha wouldn't look at me. Gwen took my hand, which looked so large in her frail one. "Thank you, Henry."

"Of course."

"Let me check on that room, Mom." Samantha went back inside and again, I couldn't not follow her.

"Samantha."

She stopped, scanned the area like she didn't want to be seen with me. "I'm sorry I'm here. I know you don't want me here. I tried to get out of it but Tori—"

"I know." I'd tried to get out of walking Tori up the aisle. I was planning to hide in the back to avoid Samantha, and yet here I was, hunting her down. "But I'm not upset you're here. That's not why I stopped you."

She had no reaction.

I looked at her, at a loss for what to say. The things that came to mind weren't appropriate. Things like I've missed you. I want to see you again. Things that couldn't be said. Things I couldn't want. At the end of the day, she was Tori's friend.

"What did you want, then?" she asked, looking past me to the deck where her mother sat.

I laughed without humor. "It's just good to see you."

For a moment, her eyes softened. She looked at me like she had five years ago when she foolishly thought she was in love with me. When I'd known that I was in love with her but still sent her away.

"You too, Henry." She waited a beat. "I've got to go."

I stepped aside. "Of course."

I watched as she made her way up the hall toward the bedrooms. *Let her go, Henry.* She had a life. A son. A sick mother. She didn't need the complication of me. So, I let her go. I let the one and only woman I'd ever loved go.

Henry and Samantha's story continues here.

Want to binge read the entire Heart of Hope series? ***Get it here.***

SEAL DADDIES NEXT DOOR (PREVIEW)

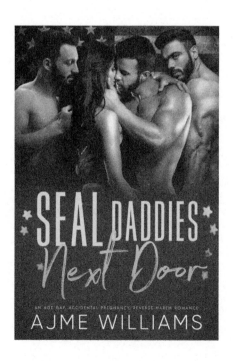

DESCRIPTION

**Becoming rich overnight led to a series of nightmares.
But the three *much* older Navy SEALs that entered my life as a
result were more like a fantasy come true.**

The electricity I feel with them makes me forget that the man who
surprisingly left me an inheritance has been murdered... *and I'm the
prime suspect.*

Reed, a protective single dad, has a rugged charm that could steal any
woman's heart.
Asher could cut glass with his razor-sharp features. Yes, he's
exceptionally strong but what draws me to him is his heart of gold.
Miguel has Spanish blood in him. His temper is unmatched, but
you'd never guess that when he cracks dad jokes.

These men fill my heart with joy... and my bed with heat.
My soul belongs to them, but do I even know who they really are?

Their traumatic past won't let them get too close to me, even though
the two pink lines on the stick bind us together.

I may not know who the dad is, but I'm taking a leap of faith.

They say I'm too innocent for my own good.

Am I naïve to think that I can trust them with my life, and with my
baby?
Our baby?

1

Juniper

02I

Item one: go on a date before Mama chews my ears off.

Item two: don't say anything stupid on the date.

Item three: don't run away if he calls you sugar.

Item four: okay, maybe run away, but tell Mama you ran because you got a case of the collywobbles. Do not, I repeat, do not tell her the date went to pot.

I'd had it up to here with my mama telling me I was gonna die a "lil' ole spinster." It used to be cute about five years ago.

But now, at the tail-end of twenty-nine, it was like I had this massive time-bomb strapped to my chest, and it'd explode any second.

I could almost hear her southern drawl in the back of my ears. For context, most of our conversations flowed along the same pattern these days.

"Well, sugar, I was just wondering if you'd met any nice fellas lately."

"Oh, Lord. Here we go again."

"Now, don't you go getting all huffy on me, Juniper. I just want you to be happy."

"I'm perfectly happy, Mama. I don't need no man to make me happy."

"Now, that's just plain silly. Everybody needs somebody."

"I've got plenty of somebodies in my life, Mama. I've got my friends, my books, and that dratted cat who visits me now and then. I think he likes me more than he does his folks."

"I don't know about that. That cat's not gonna take you out to dinner or dance with you under the stars."

"I can take myself out to dinner, Mama. And as for dancing under the stars, well, I'll ask the cat. Who knows, maybe I could bribe him into it."

"Hey, Ms. Davis?"

I looked up, pen in my mouth, at the little kid standing in front of me.

"What is it, Janie?" I smiled at her. Cute kid.

"Well, ma'am, I was just wonderin' if it'd be alright if I kept holdin' onto that *Faraway Tree* book for a spell longer."

"I know I missed the due date and all, but it's just so dang good, and I got a heap of homework that's been eating up my time somethin' fierce.

"Could I maybe bring it back in four days or so, pretty please?"

Janie's tongue grew sweeter than the tea in front of me with each word she uttered.

Her eyes enlarged in a dual attempt to convince me she was an adorable little Dachshund and that I had to excuse the late return.

It never failed.

I covered my lips with my hand in a poor attempt to conceal my grin.

"Okay, Janie, but this is the last time. Do you promise to read to the younger kids next week in return?"

She bobbed her head of golden hair enthusiastically. "I do!"

"Good girl. Off you go."

It was an unseasonably warm day here in the heart of Oakmont, Georgia, but I wasn't complaining.

I sat behind the circulation desk of The Quill and Hearth Library, a place as whimsical as its name. We actually allowed patrons to sip on sweet tea while they read their books.

I enjoyed the slow heat and the bird-like chattering of children. I loved the lower level for this very reason. It was a wonderland for the little 'uns.

We had a storytime event later that day. I could count on the little regulars to show up and demand a new fairytale. I'd been studying up for it too.

Maybe I could just talk about how Rapunzel should have gone renegade and used her hair to whip the shit outta that evil woman who'd caged her.

Or maybe I was just mad because I'd had a pretty sour conversation with Mama not ten minutes ago.

Funny thing about people who adored you—they knew your cues.

They didn't need to say much, but oh, when they were positioning to attack you, and I mean verbally decimate your soul, all they needed was one word.

Or a line. Or a few of them. You get what I mean.

"You're about to hit the big three-o and still ain't got yourself a man. What the hell are you waiting for?"

"When you gonna find a beau who's worth his weight in grits?"

Ugh. She didn't need to tell me I was old and single. In fact, no one did. I could feel the life force between my legs drying up.

I tried to focus on the pretty little place that gave me so much joy.

Big windows let in buttery-yellow sunshine, and every nook and corner had a cozy reading space.

There were rows and rows of books, neatly arranged by subject and author and utterly orgasmic for my OCD-fueled mind. Hey, I was a girl who loved her lists and her shelves.

You wanted fun? You had to have a method to it.

I let out a satisfied sigh as a ray of light fell most becomingly over the dark wooden shelves. They looked lush as a lover's embrace, a comfortable in-between of secrets and safety.

My job was to make sure this place remained as calm as it looked.

Easier said than done when I was always around kids.

I couldn't help chuckling as I heard a "'squee'" from their section. Some newbies had to have found a new adventure. That's why we turn to books anyway, right?

We couldn't physically be everywhere all at once. But in the library, you could train your mind to take you wherever you wanted to go.

You could even get married to the fanciest Prince Charming. Not that it would ease my mama's heart.

Life was good in Oakmont, though, all things considered. As they said around here, "If you don't like the weather, just wait five minutes."

And I didn't mind sticking around longer. Better than going home to nothing. I could call Sadie or one of the girls.

I just didn't want another pity party today. Hell, I'd get enough of it in a week when I actually hit the big three-o.

Bam!

I jumped up from my desk to investigate the source of the loud crash. On crossing two rows, I found a group of kids who'd built a fort out of picture books.

They were all hooting and hollering, running around as if they were facing down an army of monsters.

I could hear one of them, a scrappy little boy with a missing tooth, shouting, "Y'all ain't gonna beat us! We got the strongest fort in all of Oakmont!"

Another little girl, a bandana wrapped around her head like a pirate, squealed in her tiny voice, "We'll see about that! We're gonna knock that fort down and take all your treasure!"

The boy with the missing tooth turned to me with a big smile and said, "Hey, Junie. Wanna join our army and help us beat the bad guys?"

I bit back a laugh and replied, "Well, I don't know if I have what it takes to be a soldier, but I sure can cheer you on!"

The kids all laughed and kept on battling, and I stood there a little while, basking in the warmth of their innocence.

They'd gone and made a whole little world inside the library. Anything was possible, and the only limit was their imagination.

Suddenly, my eye fell on a dark-haired boy standing some rows away and eyeing the tyrant group with sad, dog-like adoration.

I walked over to him and knelt down. "Hey there, what's your name? Are you new here?"

He shot me a furtive look before nodding. "Yep. I'm Billy. I came to get an action book."

I looked him up and down, and my gut instinct kicked in.

"How'd you like something with more adventure and magic? We're doing a reading of *The Hobbit* soon. Wanna stick around for that?"

He blushed. "Ah . . . I don't think I can."

"Why not?"

He shuffled his feet and looked down at the floor. "I . . . my dad says magic is for little sissy girls, and I need to be a man."

Ah. Of course his dad said that.

I pursed my lips together and thought for a second before replying.

"Well, little Billy, what do you want to read?"

His face was immediately lit by hope. He looked like a sunny day. You know, the kind where trees sway gently in the breeze and leaves rustle softly in the wind. You look overhead and see a brilliant shade of blue, with just a few straggly clouds drifting lazily. It's everything you hope for, especially if it's hurricane season and you don't know what the next moment holds.

"I'd love to read magic books," Billy mumbled, "but I know my dad won't be happy about that."

"Where's your dad right now?"

"He's at work. He said my nanny will come pick me up after one."

"What if we make ourselves a little secret? You stick around for *The Hobbit* readin', and I'll treat you to a good ol' fashioned fairy tale 'bout a Wishing Chair that can take you anywhere you want to go.

Why don't you give it a try and see how it makes you feel? Don't let your dad be the one callin' the shots all the time, now."

The hope that burst across that little face made my heart churn. Man, I was sure his dad loved him, but fathers could be assholes sometimes.

But then again, at least his one stuck around. Mine wasn't even there to see me get born.

"You won't tell on me?"

I made a three-finger salute. "Scout's honor."

After Billy pottered away to join the other kids, I made my way to the history section. I was doing a bit of reading about the Ku Klux Klan, and it caught my interest.

This fascination had begun the very night I finished my tenth re-read of *Gone With The Wind.* Say what you would, but I'd never get enough of O'Hara and her damned gumption.

I was neck-deep in the Civil War era when I felt a gentle tap on my shoulder. Turning, I smiled. "Hey, Harold. Here for some history?"

"No, I just came to meet you. And I saw you getting that young'un into trouble!"

Harold Montgomery, sixty-something, missing two teeth (one he'd retouched in gold), and as eccentric as a pink-haired lady driving a blue Cadillac.

He'd become my friend over the last six months. I'd met him when he was scouring through the Civil War section, looking for titles on ancestry.

We got on like a house on fire, so to speak. It was actually funny, the things we had in common.

I squared my shoulders defensively. "Ain't no one telling a kid that they can't have their fairy tales. The world will mess 'em up soon enough. Let 'em be young while they can."

Harold chuckled. "Young lady, I have no complaints. In fact, I think you did the right thing. The father deserves a sentence for trying to deprive his son!"

I relaxed. "Maybe I could go all Avenger on him."

He walked with me to the counter. "What are you doing tonight?"

Nothing. I was just gonna go home and sit on the back patio in a pair of pajamas with my mama's quilted throw over me. I'd probably bury my face in a tub of bourbon pecan ice cream straight from the tub with extra bourbon and maybe a drizzle of dark chocolate.

A perfect dinner for a single lady on the verge of discovering her first gray hairs.

In all fairness, this dinner would pass muster with my mama.

She approved of a lot about me, even some parts that could make others run the instant I opened my mouth.

Harold probably surmised the extent of my evening adventures from the dreamy look on my face.

"I can see you're getting distracted, so I'll be quick. I'm hosting a dinner at my mansion. I want you there."

My eyes bulged. No way.

Nestled amid old oaks and magnolias in the very heart of Oakmont's historic district, the Montgomery mansion had become the stuff of local legend.

The house itself was a masterpiece of Antebellum architecture with its grand columns and sweeping porches, but it was the rumors that made me uneasy.

It was common hearsay that Harold's ancestors were all members of the Klan, and they'd even used the house as a meeting place during the Civil War.

Some even whispered that the hidden rooms and secret tunnels beneath the mansion housed the Klan's loot.

But despite what I'd heard, I believed my heart more.

Harold was a gentle soul, always ready with a smile and a kind word for his neighbors.

Sadie used to tell me it'd take him a lifetime to undo the reputation of his ancestors, but you had to give a man props for trying.

He continued surveying my face like I was some fascinating archaeological artifact. Or a gecko.

"So, what's it gonna be?"

I smiled. "Will you have bourbon pecan ice cream for dessert?"

Why did he look so relieved, like he *needed* me to be there?

His Southern drawl came through immediately, although he'd spent almost his entire life out of the country and in London.

Harold wasn't one for convention—it seemed to hurt his soul.

But in moments like these, he was as Southern as the rest of us.

"Bless your heart for sayin' yes. I reckon this shindig is gonna open doors for you. It's gonna be like a lit matchstick, sparkin' up a whole new flame in your life."

Well, bless his heart too. What in tarnation did that mean?

2

Juniper

I unlocked the door to my lonely, single life.

Okay, I totally did not mean to sound that bitter. At least I had my own little space in Oakmont's central precinct.

Magnolia Street was home to my quaint apartment, filled with charming brick buildings and old-world trees.

I stepped in through the front door and immediately found myself surrounded by the warm glow of the setting sun. It cast a soft halo of light across my living room.

The neighborhood cat, Bumbles, was already snoozing out on the balcony, his furry body stretched out on the cushion I'd left for him.

This was the fourth night he'd stayed with me. I knew the neighbors were gonna say I'd kept him high on catnip.

From my window, I could see a pair of graceful egrets flying toward a nearby marsh.

A group of chatty cardinals hopped along the branches of my old friend, the oak I'd named, well, Mr. Oakwood Hardy.

Yes, not all was bitter about this place. It was small, and there were days I wished I could open the door and shout, "What's for dinner?" but . . . it was okay.

I was okay.

Sighing, I made myself more sweet tea and settled down on the sofa with a new list. The sound of a distant train whistle floated through the open window.

My phone drawled out a lazy tune. I looked at the name on the screen and groaned.

"Hey, Mama."

"June bug! How about you come on back to the nest and let Mama feed ya? I'm fixin' to fry up some chicken."

My mouth watered at the words. No one could make fried chicken like my mama. Juicy and tender, it exemplified Sunday meals with her.

She did mashed potatoes and gravy, collard greens and corn-bread . . . the whole nine yards.

I loved to soak up the gravy and potatoes in the bread and do a perfect bite with a bit of everything.

But again, after I moved out, my mama's invitations to dinner became more and more of a call to an unavoidable war.

She'd feed me and bombard me with questions I had no clear answers to.

Some of them weren't all that bad—like what kids I'd met at the library or what Sadie's husband was doing.

The moment she moved to Sadie's husband, she'd redirect to ask me when I'd catch my own.

Like this was an unavoidable bout of a new strain of COVID that I just had to have.

I sighed and shook my head, almost picturing her crestfallen face.

"Mama, I'd love to, but I can't tonight."

"Oh?"

It was plain as day that her curiosity had been piqued by my words, as I could hear the telltale lilt in her voice.

Lord have mercy. I reckoned I could've phrased that a mite bit better.

No doubt she'd be fixing to inquire about my plans and whether there were any fine gentlemen involved in them.

"You headed out with a good-lookin' fella tonight?"

Talk about hitting the nail straight on my own fuckin' head.

"No, Mama. No date. I just got an invite to this fancy dinner."

"Where?"

I hesitated for a second. My mama, like all the old-timers in this city, did not trust men with a tarnished reputation—even if this reputation had nothing to do with them, per se.

They could be golden, but if there was one black sheep in the family, it meant they had a little devil in them.

Plus, my mama hated Harold Montgomery.

I honestly had no idea why. It began the day he met me in the library and insisted on dropping me home. In his Aston Martin DB11.

At the time, I was still living with Mama. I'd only moved to this place about twenty days ago, mostly because I wanted to be able to walk to work. And I felt like I was getting too old to share space with someone I loved but who also drove me nuts.

Mama took one look at him and told me never to see him again.

I didn't push it then, and I didn't want to push it now. But I was never good at one thing when it came to her. I didn't lie to her. I couldn't.

Not when that's what she'd known the entirety of her life before I came along. That's all she had from the one other person she loved—the one who got away.

"Harold Montgomery's party, Mama."

She sounded like she'd choked on a peach.

"Hell no, Junie! You're not going to that man's house! You know what they say about that place and the secrets? You know his ancestors used to torture others to get money and loot their jewels, right? Why do you want to associate yourself with that?"

Why did I, actually? Apart from the obvious curiosity I had about the house, there was just something so affable about Harold.

He was old and weathered and sweet. He talked to me like he really cared and wanted to be part of my life, even if it was just a sliver.

That meant something.

"Mama." I spoke sotto voce. "Harold's tried to undo all that his entire life. Maybe we could just give him a chance."

"Child, I ain't givin' no man like that the time of day, and neither should you. Don't you remember what I done told you about your daddy? You gotta be strong, just like your Mama. You hear me?"

Okay. Not the way I'd hoped this would go. Against my better judgment, a swell of bitterness rose inside me.

"Mama, I don't want to have this conversation. Not when I've asked you about Dad so many times and got nothing back."

"Honey, you know good and well he was nothin' but pure evil. The second he found out I was carryin' you, he up and left without a second thought."

And you've never let me forget it.

"I'm sorry I'm such an inconvenience." I spoke sharply. "But I'm old enough to make my own decisions. I understand you may not agree with them, but I hope you'll care enough to respect them, anyway."

"Junie, now you listen to me—"

I hung up.

Oh, I'd never hear the end of this. But I'd deal with her temper and tears tomorrow. I knew she meant well.

But even I got tired of being made to feel like I was responsible for her never getting married.

All I ever knew about my dad was that he was super rich, and his folks told him he could either be livin' in the boonies with my mom or he'd have to leave her and return to his roots.

No points for guessing what he chose.

I wanted to make peace with it. But that was damn hard when the topic kept cropping up like an unrelenting tide of heat poking like nails on my skin.

My phone rang again. I just flipped that switch to silent and high-tailed it outta there.

I reckoned I needed to blow off some steam, so I went to dump a bucket of ice-cold water over my head.

By the time I got out, it was already sundown. The buttery glow of the last rays of amber sunlight had melted into soft pinks and purples against a deep blue sky.

My invite said I needed to be at the party by nine, so I took some time to gussy up.

Hell, I'd be a Southern belle ready to stir up some trouble at that party.

I slipped into a ruby red cocktail dress, feeling like a hot tamale in a sea of ice cubes.

The entire next hour saw me hurling a tirade of cuss words as I tried my best to coax my curls into shape. I managed to tease my hair up high and let it fall in loose, beachy waves around my shoulders.

I could have sworn Dolly Parton would be proud of that hairdo.

The figure smiling back from the mirror was all curves, gentle, swaying, and redolent of summer scents. And I loved it.

I loved every stretch mark woven like lightning on my skin, each freckle and meander and wrinkle.

It had taken me years to come to this place where I was learning to fall in love with myself. I'd spent two decades on the other side.

Then, two heartbreaks and a side of controversy later, I realized I could spend all my life at war with myself, but it would never make living any easier.

And I didn't want to remember myself that way. When I turned gray and crocheted my way into retirement, I wanted good memories.

This was me making those happen.

I finished by adding just the right amount of sparkle to make my eyes pop and my lips pout. With that, I strode into the living room and immediately regretted my decision.

You ever been around an introvert?

You know, that special breed of people who get excited to make plans and then immediately run out of social battery the second the plans are about to begin?

Yup, that was me.

Too late to back out. My Uber had already arrived.

I stepped out of my apartment, suddenly feeling like a toad in a dress. Thankfully, my Uber driver, Hank, was an angel.

"Howdy, Ms. Davis. I'll be your Uber driver for the evening. You look pretty as a peach in that red dress!"

I chuckled. "Thank you kindly, Hank. You sure do have a way with words."

As the ride began, I lost myself in the easy ramblings of Hank's thick drawl and the sights I saw on the way.

Old oak trees blurred into a bouquet of brown, green, and yellow draped in a soft evening wind and Spanish moss.

Every brick building here had something that tied it to the remnants of life from the Civil War era.

I leaned back and sighed. "I don't think I'll ever be able to live anywhere else but the South."

Hank cleared his throat. "Well, speakin' of living here. A few years ago, I was driving this very car when all of a sudden, I hit a pothole so deep it swallowed my tire. I was stuck there on the side of the road, wondering what to do. That's when a bunch of good ol' boys in a pickup truck pulled up beside me and asked if I needed help. And you know what they did? They pulled out a rope, tied it around the car, and yanked me outta that pothole like it was nothin'!"

"Only in the South, right?"

Hank grinned. "You got that right, Miss Juniper. We may have our share of potholes, but we sure do know how to help each other out."

Before I knew it, the easy ride brought me to the drop-off leading up to the main door of the Montgomery mansion.

The pathway was lined with lights and an abundance of heady flowers. I followed a trail of guests to the door.

A tall, silver-haired figure stood at the threshold.

He looked like a direct import from England. Like he'd been flown in after a long-standing decade of serving the Queen herself.

"Name, please?"

"Ha!"

Why did I say that? Why was I so awkward? I wished the marble floors would just swallow me whole.

"I mean . . ." I fumbled, trying not to let his hawk-like eyes pierce through me. "I'm Juniper. Juniper Davis."

He took a minute to go over the names on the list he held in his hands. A very agonizing minute.

Maybe this was some joke Harold had played on me?

I nearly turned and pulled a Cinderella before he spoke again, his tone cold as day-old turkey right outta the freezer.

"Welcome to the Riviera party, Ms. Davis. You may go through to the salon."

"Thanks, you too."

Before I could give him the chance to throw me out for the stupidest comeback ever, I ran into the salon.

I was immediately bombarded by an onslaught of people in clothes worth more than my year's salary.

On any other day, I'd curse myself for being a social anomaly, but right now, I was absolutely blown away by the opulence of the interior.

The entire salon could have swallowed my apartment, with ceilings so high they could go on forever. Tall windows, rich, warm walls, and ornate moldings were everywhere.

I meandered through the room, but not before I overheard a conversation between two guests.

"My dear, it comes as no surprise that Mr. Montgomery has spared no expense for this evening's affair."

"I hear he's preparing to make a rather momentous announcement. No doubt, an attempt to conceal the origins of his vast wealth."

"Truly, the Montgomery family has a dubious reputation in certain circles. There are whispers of thievery and deceit."

"I have heard tales of a scandalous affair involving Mr. Montgomery and a woman of questionable reputation in his younger days."

"It is quite clear that he is a man with many secrets."

They turned around and saw me, and one of them—a big ol' fella in a fancy vest, his eye accentuated by a ridiculous monocle, scowled.

I took off running quicker than a spooked hen.

Trying to shake off the heaviness of the air, I approached a group of people near the bar.

"Hey there," I said, raising my voice and giving in to the sudden burst of social energy. "What's everyone drinking?"

One of the men in the group turned to me and grinned. "Whiskey, of course. We're in the south, honey. What else would we be drinking?"

I chuckled and shook my head. "I shoulda known better. Make mine a double."

A few drinks later, my bladder had a mind of its own. I rushed out of the salon and found myself in a maze of a corridor. Where the hell was the washroom?

I was about to give up when one of the doors burst open and Harold stormed out, his face red, angry, and unlike anything I'd ever seen before.

Something made me hide behind the wall opposite the room.

A young man followed him his hands bunched into fists.

"You're gonna regret this. You hear me?"

I realized I knew his face. And it was one of the few things I wanted to forget most in the world.

End of preview. *Get the entire story here.*

ABOUT THE AUTHOR

Ajme Williams writes emotional, angsty contemporary romance. All her books can be enjoyed as full length, standalone romances and are FREE to read in Kindle Unlimited .

Books do not have to be read in order.

Heart of Hope Series
Our Last Chance | An Irish Affair | So Wrong | Imperfect Love | Eight Long Years | Friends to Lovers | The One and Only | Best Friend's Brother | Maybe It's Fate | Gone Too Far | Christmas with Brother's Best Friend | Fighting for US | Against All Odds | Hoping to Score | Thankful for Us | The Vegas Bluff | 365 Days | Meant to Be | Mile High Baby | Silver Fox's Secret Baby

The Why Choose Haremland (Reverse Harem Series - this series)
Protecting Their Princess | Protecting Her Secret | Unwrapping their Christmas Present | Cupid Strikes... 3 Times | Their Easter Bunny | SEAL Daddies Next Door | Naughty Lessons

High Stakes

Bet On It | A Friendly Wager | Triple or Nothing | Press Your Luck

Billionaire Secrets
Twin Secrets | Just A Sham | Let's Start Over | The Baby Contract | Too Complicated

Dominant Bosses
His Rules | His Desires | His Needs | His Punishments | His Secret

Strong Brothers
Say Yes to Love | Giving In to Love | Wrong to Love You | Hate to Love You

Fake Marriage Series
Accidental Love | Accidental Baby | Accidental Affair | Accidental Meeting

Irresistible Billionaires
Admit You Miss Me | Admit You Love Me | Admit You Want Me | Admit You Need Me

Check out Ajme's full Amazon catalogue here.

Join her VIP NL here.

WANT MORE AJME WILLIAMS?

Join my no spam mailing list here.

You'll only be sent emails about my new releases, extended epilogues, deleted scenes and occasional FREE books.

Printed in Great Britain
by Amazon

27699039R00165